UNFORGIVEN

Books by Shelley Shepard Gray

A SEASON IN PINECRAFT
Her Heart's Desire
Her Only Wish
Her Secret Hope

UNFORGIVEN

SHELLEY
SHEPARD GRAY

Revell

a division of Baker Publishing Group
Grand Rapids, Michigan

Published by Revell
a division of Baker Publishing Group
Grand Rapids, Michigan
RevellBooks.com

Printed in the United States of America

Library of Congress Cataloging-in-Publication Control Number: 2024004164
ISBN 9780800745790 (paper)
ISBN 9780800745899 (casebound)
ISBN 9781493445561 (ebook)

Scripture quotations are from the Holy Bible, New International Version®, NIV®. Copyright © 1973, 1978, 1984, 2011 by Biblica, Inc.® Used by permission of Zondervan. All rights reserved worldwide. www.zondervan.com. The "NIV" and "New International Version" are trademarks registered in the United States Patent and Trademark Office by Biblica, Inc.®

Scripture quotations are from the *Holy Bible*, New Living Translation. Copyright © 1996, 2004, 2015 by Tyndale House Foundation. Used by permission of Tyndale House Publishers, Carol Stream, Illinois 60188. All rights reserved.

This book is a work of fiction. Names, characters, places, and incidents are the product of the author's imagination or are used fictitiously. Any resemblance to actual events, locales, or persons, living or dead, is coincidental.

The author is represented by The Seymour Agency.

Baker Publishing Group publications use paper produced from sustainable forestry practices and postconsumer waste whenever possible.

24 25 26 27 28 29 30   7 6 5 4 3 2 1

For everyone who still believes
in second chances.

Though your sins are like scarlet,
I will make them as white as snow.

Isaiah 1:18 NLT

Never look down on someone
unless you're helping them up.

Amish proverb

1

OCTOBER, CRITTENDEN COUNTY, KY

He'd come back. Taking care to hide behind the curtain partially covering her living room window, Tabitha watched Seth Zimmerman walk down her front porch steps after knocking on the door. He'd waited for her to answer, of course. Maybe thirty seconds? Maybe longer?

The amount of time he waited didn't really matter anyway. Tabitha didn't open her door for anyone. Well, no one except for her sister Mary once a month. She hadn't greeted anyone else for a long time.

After another couple of minutes passed, Seth walked to his truck, peeled off his tan canvas jacket, and set it on the hood. Then he fished out an ax from his truck's bed and walked to the woodpile and started chopping.

It wasn't the first time he'd done any of this. Almost two years earlier, Seth had dropped off a pile of logs. He'd knocked on the door, no doubt to tell her about it. When she hadn't answered, he'd written a short note explaining why he was there.

When she'd read his note, Tabitha had felt so guilty. Common courtesy said that she should thank him for his kindness. Open the door and face him.

At the very least.

But the knot of tension in her chest—and the mess of nerves zipping through her body—had prevented her from doing even that much. She'd learned a lot about fear in the last ten years. Enough to realize that being cautious wasn't necessarily a bad thing.

Sometimes it even saved one's life.

Even though she knew Seth was no Leon and she likely had nothing to fear, Tabitha still hadn't budged. Instead, she continued to stand behind the heavy curtain and watch Seth chop wood. Like some kind of twisted stalker.

Or maybe because she was a lonely woman and the sight of Seth Zimmerman chopping wood was surely something to see. All brawn and muscle, his body moved in perfect synchronicity as he chopped those logs. Three months ago, the weather had been hot and his cotton T-shirt had become damp, clinging to his chest and arms like a second skin.

After chopping several of the logs into small, manageable pieces, he'd placed them in a stack near the front porch. And then drove off.

Now, here he was again. This time, the October day was cool. And though he'd taken off his jacket, his body still moved in an easy, fluid motion. Every time he lifted that heavy ax and then brought it down with a satisfying *thunk*, her insides jumped a bit.

Her former student had grown into a fine-looking man.

Boy, she hoped he'd found himself a sweet girl to court. Seth deserved that. Even back when she'd been his teacher, she'd known there was an innate goodness to him. He'd proved it to her in a dozen ways the year she'd taught him. He'd assisted other students, helped her clean up the classroom from time to time. Once, he'd intervened when one of the oldest boys had gotten mad and knocked over a chair. And here he was again, doing her yet another favor that she couldn't repay.

Tabitha knew she should somehow find a way to tell him that it wasn't necessary for him to come out to her house and do chores. Her mother would've chided her for taking advantage of his kindness. But even after all this time, Tabitha hadn't. All she seemed to be able to do was stare at him from the shadows of her home.

What a sight he was too. His face, carefully shaven, was lightly tanned. The muscles in his arms, now uncovered, clenched with every swing. Again and again he swung. He handled the ax like it weighed next to nothing. He hadn't even broken a sweat.

She was embarrassed she noticed.

But maybe not surprised. Seth had been visiting her once a week for months and months now. The first time he'd appeared, he'd knocked on her door. She'd peeked out, saw his six-foot form, short blond hair, and chiseled features, and knew exactly who he was. Her former Amish community's only ex-con.

She'd been so frightened of him, she'd hurried to the back of her house and hidden in the bedroom's closet. There she'd sat, practically hyperventilating. Reminding herself over and over that her door was locked and he was nothing like her ex-husband. She couldn't imagine him raising a hand to her for some imagined slight.

An hour later, after working hard to get her breathing under control, she'd ventured back out. When she confirmed he was gone, she'd opened the door. And found a paper sack with some apples, fruit, cheese, and fresh bread along with a note.

> *Tabitha, I don't blame you for not wanting to answer the door. All I wanted to do was chop some of your wood and drop this food off. A lady out in Marion gave me too much. You take care now. Seth.*

That had been the first of many visits. Sometimes he'd chopped wood. Sometimes he only stopped over to drop off a carton of food. Once, he'd trimmed her hedges. Maybe about every fifth time, he knocked on the door, waited for a response that never came, then wrote a note.

She'd saved them all.

Seth Zimmerman might have gone to prison for killing Peter Miller, but he wasn't a bad man. The rumors were that Peter had attacked Bethanne Hostetler and Seth had stopped it. No one but Seth and God knew for sure what happened next. All that had been proven was that the two men had fought, Peter had fallen and hit his head on a rock.

Since she knew just how much could happen when no one was watching, Tabitha reckoned almost anything could've transpired. Truth had a way of getting twisted and turned when it touched the bright light of day.

Returning to the present, she rested her head against the window's frame and watched Seth some more. After yet another thwack of the ax, he put it down and stretched his arms. Then he turned and looked her way. Stark, steel-blue eyes met hers.

And took her breath away.

Tabitha gulped.

There was no kidding herself now. Seth knew that she'd been watching him. Probably felt her eyes on him every time he'd come out. He knew she watched him but didn't have the nerve to even say hello.

He probably thought she was the same woman he used to know. His teacher who had been barely three years older than him. The woman he used to tease about mice and bugs while she pretended to be too mature to tease him back.

Thinking of all the kindnesses he'd done, all the gifts and food he'd given her, Tabitha went to the kitchen and filled one of her baskets with homemade bread and a jar of the strawberry jam she'd put up at the beginning of summer.

She braced herself, then walked to the door. It was time to go outside and thank him in person. At last.

Yes, she knew a lot about fear now, and her heart and head weren't in as good a shape as they used to be. But that didn't mean she didn't know right from wrong. Besides, even if something bad did happen between her and Seth Zimmerman, Tabitha knew she could take it.

She'd learned that there was an awful lot that she could take.

2

After depositing his ax in the back seat of his truck, Seth eyed the pile of wood he'd just chopped. Would it be enough for Tabitha? He wasn't sure. Last night's temperatures had hovered close to forty degrees, and the weather reports said that a cold front was on the way.

He hated the idea of her being cold.

Actually, he hated the thought of Tabitha suffering at all. She was such a tiny thing and had already been through too much. Leon Yoder had been a mean son of a gun. Just about everyone had given him a wide berth, Seth included. And everyone had been shocked when their new schoolteacher consented to marry him. She'd been only seventeen.

Back then, Seth was one of her students. He'd been four-teen, anxious to pass his graduation tests and get out of school. But he'd also had an awful crush on his teacher. She was so sweet and so pretty with her long brown hair tucked neatly under a crisp white kapp. He'd spent hours wondering what her hair looked like around her shoulders. He knew he wasn't the only boy thinking about things like that, either. Why, the whole class had fallen in love with her. It had been a very dark day when Miss Tabitha announced that she was getting married and that her fiancé didn't want her working anymore.

Eight months later, when Seth had spied her at the market, Tabitha looked like a different woman. Her plump cheeks had thinned, her perfect skin had grown pale, and most of the light in her brown eyes had faded. And a little more than a year after that, she'd worn a haunted expression as Leon announced that his wife was with child. Tabitha had stood so stiff by his side that Seth reckoned a strong wind could break her in two.

When his mother tried to hug her, Tabitha had flinched at being touched. Mamm had acted as if nothing was amiss, but Seth had known better. He'd been sure that Tabitha was hiding bruises under the long sleeves of her dress.

Back in those days, Seth had been full of righteous indignation. He'd hated that Leon was mistreating Tabitha and he'd yearned to put a stop to it. But no one had wanted to hear about it. His father had told him not to gossip and his mother had acted shocked that he would mention such a thing. She hadn't looked him in the eye when she'd lectured him, though. Like she was going through the motions. Simply saying the words that should be said. Even when neither of them believed for certain that they were true.

A few months after that, right about the time Seth had come upon Peter Miller assaulting Bethanne Hostetler, accidentally killed him, and then landed in prison, Tabitha lost her baby. His sister, Melonie, had told him all about it. Well, she'd written letter after letter to him while he was in prison. In each one, she'd detailed all the gossip around their former teacher's circumstances. And then Leon had beaten up Tabitha so badly that she'd had to go to the hospital. There, she'd lost a whole lot of blood and her baby too.

Next thing everyone knew, Tabitha had pressed charges and Sheriff Johnson arrested Leon. And then, maybe just a day or two later, Tabitha Yoder was gone and no one saw hide nor hair of her for almost an entire year. Rumor had it that she'd gotten herself a lawyer and divorced Leon.

Melonie wrote that everyone had an opinion about that. Some folks had acted shocked that she would do such a thing. Divorce was forbidden. Melonie had shared that though their mother didn't participate in the gossip, even she had been surprised by Tabitha's actions.

Tabitha hadn't been shunned for filing charges against Leon. No one could find it in their heart to cast out a woman who'd been hurt so much in marriage. However, her decision to hire a lawyer and get a divorce had forced Tabitha to leave their faith. His sister had told him that more than a couple of folks thought Tabitha should've simply remained separated from Leon. After all, if he had apologized and had been arrested and even had to serve six months behind bars, shouldn't she give him another chance?

She had not.

Sitting in a cold cell behind bars, Seth had been so proud of her that he'd written her a note and posted it. She'd never responded, though. He hadn't been surprised. He was a convict, and she'd been a victim of violence. Of course she wouldn't want to have anything to do with him.

Still, her silence hurt. Seth knew in his heart that he was not cut from the same cloth as Leon. He would never hurt a woman, and especially not a woman he cared deeply about. Then again, words didn't mean all that much. Not anymore.

Shaking off the memories, Seth focused on the present. He needed to take care of Tabitha and then get on his way. He was working a construction job on the other side of Marion, and he'd told the foreman he'd put in five or six hours' work in the afternoon. Figuring it was time to go, he picked up several pieces of wood and carried them to her front door.

Just in time for her to open it.

Seth didn't know who was more shocked to realize that after all this time they were only a foot apart.

"Tabitha."

Her brown eyes widened. "Jah. Um . . . Good day, Seth."

She was talking as if they'd been chatting each time he'd come over. Well, he supposed he could play this game too. "Good day to you." Realizing that he still held the wood in his arms, he walked over to where he usually stacked it. "It's getting colder. I thought you might need more wood today."

"It's so kind of you to do that." She watched him neatly stack the logs, then added, "I mean, I'm grateful for all the things you've done for me, Seth. I don't know why you are, but it's appreciated."

"I have time." He didn't see the need to mention the obvious—that no one looked out for her anymore. Sometimes he wondered if anyone ever really had.

"Someone told me that you work at a construction company."

He nodded. "Porter. I do the carpentry and trim work. I'm heading there now."

Looking flustered, she stared down at her hands. "Oh, wait a moment, would you? I forgot the item I was going to bring out for you."

Tabitha didn't wait for his response, just darted back inside the house. Though he still had to fetch the rest of the wood, Seth remained where he was. She was as skittish as a newborn fawn. No way was he going to do anything to make her think he left.

Two minutes later, she opened the door again and stepped out onto the porch. In her free hand was a beautiful red woven basket with a dishcloth covering the contents. "Here. This is for you."

He took it from her and held it with both hands. "Tell me about this."

She blinked. "Well, inside is a loaf of fresh bread and a jar of strawberry jam." Looking unsure again, she added, "I hope you like both?"

"Homemade bread and jam? Of course I do. Don't you remember how my little sister, Melonie, was always teasing me about my breakfast of jam and toast?"

Something in her eyes faded. "Sometimes I forget that I was once your teacher."

"I can't seem to forget it." He smiled. "You were a good teacher."

Tabitha looked even more uncomfortable. "I don't know about that."

Hearing the self-deprecating way she spoke about herself hurt him. Almost as much as realizing that she didn't like being reminded of their long acquaintance. Feeling more uneasy, he studied her face. "Do you not want me to mention it?"

"Of course not. It's just . . . well, those days seem like a lifetime ago."

"I reckon that's because my classroom days did happen a lifetime ago. I was young then."

"I was too."

He hated that he'd brought those bad memories to the surface again. "So, tell me about this jam and bread. Did you make them both?"

"I did. The bread yesterday and the jam back in June."

Looking at the basket again, she winced. "It's really not much, is it? I mean, not compared to everything you've done for me," she continued in a rush. "I should've thanked you before too. I'm—"

"It's fine," he blurted. No way was he going to let her apologize for being wary around him. She looked so alone, so in need of kindness, Seth wished he could pull her into his arms and tell her that everything was eventually going to be okay. That he would make sure her life got better, someway or somehow.

But of course, holding a fine woman like her was only going to happen in his dreams.

Instead, he inclined his head. "Your gift is appreciated. I'll enjoy both. Let me give you back your basket, though. It's too fine to pass on."

"No, the basket is for you as well. I have lots of baskets." She bit her bottom lip. "Too many."

Encouraged that they were still conversing, he kept his voice soft. "Is that right? Where did you get them?"

"Nowhere. I mean, I make baskets."

He couldn't have been more surprised. "And the red?"

"It's red from berries. I stained the wood."

She knew how to color wood from berries. She knew how to weave beautiful, finely woven baskets—and fill them with homemade bread and jam. Any one of those things was something to be proud of. Altogether? It was rather awe-inspiring. At least to a man like him.

"You are full of surprises today, Tabitha Yoder." He didn't expect her to comment on that. Seth supposed he'd muttered the phrase to himself mainly because he felt it needed to be said. Yet again he thought about what a shame it was that such an amazing woman was hiding in the shadows.

She met his gaze. Her brown eyes pinned him down. Making him feel that for a split second they had a connection. For a second, Seth was sure she was about to smile. But then she turned and went back inside. The door shut with a heavy *thunk*, and the click of a deadbolt followed. She was in her safe place again.

But she'd come outside today and spoken to him. They'd had a conversation.

Unable to help himself, Seth grinned as he turned around to take her basket to his truck. Yeah, Tabitha was unsure and skittish, and chatting with her took the patience of a saint. But he didn't care. As far as he was concerned, their conversation had been perfect. After all this time, she'd trusted him enough to step outside her door. She'd blessed him with that trust.

As he returned to the woodpile to finish stacking the wood, he decided that maybe he wouldn't wait so long to stop by again.

Maybe he wouldn't wait very long at all.

3

I think that's the last of it, Tab," Mary said as her eldest son, Jack, deposited a ten-pound bag of flour on Tabitha's freshly mopped kitchen floor. It landed with a thud and a small cloud of white dust. Seconds later, her cabinets glowed with a powdery sheen.

Tabitha pretended not to notice. She didn't care about having to dust again anyway. Her sister and nephews' visit was always the highlight of her month. Mary's husband, Roy, only allowed his wife and children to see Tabitha every couple of weeks.

"Danke, Mary. And thank you, Jack, Anson, John, and Petey," she added with a sunny smile. "You strong boys made my day much easier. And brighter."

Little Petey wrapped his arms around her legs. "I miss you, Aunt Tab."

Kneeling, she gave the five-year-old a proper hug. Mary's youngest smelled like soap and dirt and dog, as always. Despite his mother's best efforts to keep him clean, Petey couldn't help himself from getting dirty. Mud and mess seemed to call hourly.

It was exhausting for her sister, but Tabitha secretly hoped Petey wouldn't change anytime soon. She enjoyed knowing that there were still little boys who hugged dogs, played in the dirt, and forgot to do chores. The rest of one's life was so hard. As far as she was concerned, children needed to savor those carefree years as much as they could.

"I miss you too."

Anson and John moved closer.

"May I have a hug from you two as well, boys?"

"Sure, Aunt Tabby," John said.

As she hugged each of them, her eyes stung. Mary and Roy's four boys had her heart. "You two are getting so big. There was a time when neither of you could've carried in the groceries that you did today."

"I'm almost as big as Jack," Anson declared.

His twelve-year-old brother scoffed. "Not hardly."

Just as Anson puffed up his chest, Mary rested a hand on his shoulder. "We are not going to start one-upping each other in your aunt's haus."

"All right," Anson said, though it was evident he would much rather press his point.

Tabitha glanced at John. As usual, the quietest of her boys simply stared at her—and at the groceries and dry goods in the four tote bags resting next to the giant bag of flour on the kitchen floor. "Do you need any more help, Aunt Tab?"

"Nee." If there was something she had in spades, it was time to clean and organize.

John looked skeptical. "Are you sure?"

"I am sure." Knowing that saying goodbye would be harder the longer she drew it out, she handed each boy a paper sack filled with fresh pumpkin bars and oatmeal cookies. "Here you go. Something to eat on the way home."

"Thank you, Aunt Tabby," they chorused.

While the boys were putting their shoes on, Tabitha handed Mary an envelope of cash to pay for the groceries Mary bought. Mary also took a dozen baskets at a time. She and her husband took them to a broker, who in turn sold them in big cities like St. Louis and Louisville. The baskets brought a pretty price and enabled Tabitha to pay for her food and crafting materials. Mary had also agreed to keep a portion.

Mary took the envelope but didn't immediately put it in her dress pocket. Looking guilty, she whispered, "Are you sure you don't need this more?"

"I am sure." Mary and Roy had four little boys to feed and clothe, after all. All she had was herself.

"Aunt Tab?"

"Yes, Jack?"

"Are you ever going to come over to our haus?"

"I don't know." Apparently, Mary and Roy didn't tell the boys that the limits on their interaction came from them and not her.

Roy was a good man, but he was also a self-righteous one. She'd always gotten the impression that he thought she should've tried harder to make Leon happy. Roy also had never hidden his disapproval of Tabitha's divorce.

It didn't matter anyway. As much as she enjoyed her nephews' hugs and chatter, she still had a difficult time venturing off her property.

"You don't have to be afraid," John said in an earnest voice. "I could stay by your side."

Ack, but the boy surely had her heart.

She hated these goodbyes as much as she loved her nephews. "I appreciate that. Maybe one day, jah?" She kept her voice light as she fended off the dark feeling that once again threatened to plummet her spirits.

Two lines formed between Jack's brows. "But—"

"That's enough, Jack," Mary said. "We've already talked about this, remember?"

He looked down at his feet. "Yes'm."

"Gut." She reached out and hugged Tabitha tight. "We all love you. Don't forget."

"Never. I'll see you next month."

Mary's expression tightened, but she nodded. "Next month." After clearing her throat, she said, "Let's go, boys."

Anson led the way to the door. One by one they filed out and hopped into the buggy. Tabitha stayed on the porch and watched as Mary allowed Jack to hold the leads for the horse. Then, after another chorus of goodbyes, her guests departed. Seconds later, they were out of sight and only the memory of their voices remained.

Tabitha sat down on the porch step, looking out at the expanse of land surrounding her farmhouse. The wood creaked under her weight.

It was such a rickety thing. Just like the rest of the house, she supposed. The house had been Leon's grandparents' home before they'd passed, and his parents had "gifted" it to them. Leon had been pleased, she less so. The house was on three acres, near a creek that often flooded, and in disrepair. Leon had never been one for carpentry and was far too proud to ask for help, so none of the broken floorboards, drawers, or shutters had been fixed. It was drafty in the winter and damp during the spring. Summer brought in stifling heat and bugs. Sometimes her pride got in the way and she'd wish she had a better, prettier place to welcome guests.

Not that anyone would visit anyway. Her divorce had cre-

ated a barrier between her and the rest of the community
that seemed to have gotten thicker and taller with each passing month.

After losing her child and then divorcing Leon, she'd had
a hard time believing her lawyer's promises that she could
keep the house. It wasn't as if she'd had any money of her
own when she'd come into the marriage.

Mia Rothaker had felt otherwise. After seeing the pictures that the police had taken of Tabitha at the hospital
and reading the doctor's report, Mia had promised to do
everything in her power to make sure Tabitha felt safe. And
somehow the judge agreed. Even Leon's parents hadn't pro-
tested Tabitha being awarded the property. Mary had told
her that someone from their community had been in the
hospital when Tabitha had been brought in. The news about
the amount of blood she'd lost had spread like wildfire.

In any case, though Tabitha wasn't exactly whole anymore, she wasn't as broken as she used to be. And she did
have a home. It was one of the Lord's mysteries how the very
place that had been the site of the worst moments in her life
had somehow become her refuge.

The snap of a twig followed by the rustle of leaves brought
her to her feet. As much as she didn't want to believe Leon
would return, it was a possibility. Heaven knew he'd taunted
her many times that no judge's decree would ever be enough
to keep him out of her life.

Her breath hitched as her lungs tightened. Her brow, even
though her hair was neatly pulled back from her face with
a band, felt damp.

"You're okay," she whispered to herself. "You're okay.
You're—" She stopped in midreassurance. Seth Zimmerman
appeared out of the opening in the woods nearby.

This time just four days after he'd come before.

She couldn't help but stare. Today he had on a baseball cap, a dark gray hoodie, thick-looking army green pants, and tan boots. Every bit of his clothing suited him and fit like a glove.

But worse than that, she hated that she was feeling a little charge of awareness. It was like her brain couldn't seem to think about anything else but him whenever he was in her vicinity.

"Tabitha, hey!"

Remaining seated, she watched him stride forward.

She had no idea why Seth had come by again—or what to do, since it was too late to hide from sight. Before she could run, Tabitha found herself raising her hand in greeting. "Hiya, Seth."

"Hallelujah. You've decided to speak to me yet again." His tone was teasing and his smile kind.

When her insides jumped a little in anticipation, Tabitha knew she was in trouble. Seth Zimmerman really did make her feel too much.

4

Tabitha had paled and looked unsteady on her feet. Seth feared she was about to pass out in the middle of her front porch. If she did, that would be his fault. His stupid joke had scared her silly.

Gritting his teeth, Seth called himself ten kinds a fool. Of course she was rattled. The woman barely walked out her door when someone else was on her property. He knew better than to approach so quietly—or to call out nonsense in the hopes of catching a smile. She was not going to be smiling with him anytime soon.

Part of him wanted to turn right back around and not grace her land for another twenty-eight days. But that wasn't possible. Not when she'd stepped outside to speak to him and had been so kind as to give him that basket of bread and jam. He was no psychologist, but Seth was pretty sure that if he retreated now, it might take him another year to get her to trust him again.

He didn't want to wait that long. Not ever again.

That meant there was only one choice, and that was to be up-front and honest. If she didn't want him to come around again, he wanted to hear her say the words. Plus, he had a notion that a frank conversation would be real good for both of them. She would feel like she had a choice about who was on her property, and he'd know if she didn't want him around. If she told him to his face to keep away, he would. He had no doubt about that.

"I hope you don't mind that I stopped by here so soon," he said when he was about three feet from the porch. "But if you do, tell me now and I'll leave."

Her eyes widened, but she said nothing.

"I mean it. I won't get mad. Not at all."

She remained silent.

Okay, then. It looked like he would be able to stay for a spell. Hoping to put her mind at ease, he kept talking. "Listen, I could make up a story about how I just happened to be around, so I thought I'd stop by, but we'd both know that was a lie. The truth is that I wanted to see you again."

Unable to force her to meet his gaze any longer, he turned his head away. Looked out at the yellow-brown overgrown grass in the field just beyond her. "Now, don't get too worried about that, though. I like looking out for people and checking on folks who I think might need a hand."

"Like me."

She'd spoken. Relief poured through him, though he tried to look oblivious to that fact as he gazed up at her. "Jah."

Her throat worked. Even from his distance, he could see that she was mentally coaxing herself to get up the nerve to talk to him. As painful as it was to watch, he didn't dare push her along. Instead, he shoved his hands in the pockets of his jacket. If she was willing to speak to him, he was willing to listen.

"Why?" Her voice sounded husky, almost rough.

It would be so easy to say something meaningless, but he wouldn't feel good about that. "Because there's something about you that appeals to me."

"How so?" She loosened the grip she had on the railing.

"Well, beyond the fact that you're the reason I know how to calculate percentages, I figure you and me are a lot alike."

"You honestly see some similarities?"

They were both outcasts. That was obvious. But how did one tell someone that? Staring at the dormant grass again, Seth nodded his head toward the distance. "I guess you and me are a lot like that field over there. Right now, it looks like that old pasture might need a helping hand. The overgrown grass needs to be cut, and underneath, the soil needs to be worked. But, by chance, if someone takes a closer look at it, they're going to see something else."

"What's that?"

He turned back to her. "Promise."

She cocked her head to one side. "I'm not following you."

He pointed. "That grass out there, come April or May, is going to be just fine. It'll be green and healthy and thick. If a city guy drove by and took the time to notice it, he might even say it looks real pretty."

"So you're saying that the two of us are just in a bit of a depression."

He laughed. "I reckon so."

"Hmm." She looked a little offended.

He held up his hands. "Come now. Don't get all riled up about being compared to dead grass."

"I am not riled, Seth Zimmerman."

Ah. There it was. Tabitha almost sounded like the school-teacher he used to know. The seventeen-year-old beauty he'd had a crush on. The girl who'd been so fond of light blue dresses and rarely wore black stockings. The young woman he'd been tongue-tied around because he was fourteen and she only saw him as a child who didn't study enough or spell all that well.

"If you need a better reason for me being drawn to you, it's because you're quiet."

Tabitha inhaled. For a split second, he was pretty sure she'd been tempted to smile.

"Some might say that I'm a bit too quiet," she murmured.

"I reckon they would. I'm partial to it, however." When she stared at him, seeming to silently wait for him to tell her more, Seth added, "It was real noisy in prison. During the day, during the night, it didn't matter. Doors clanged, men yelled. Cried. It was difficult to get used to."

He stood still, waiting for her to ask him to leave now that he'd reminded her of where he'd been. Of what he'd done.

She didn't look taken aback by the reminder. Instead, she studied him more closely. Seth fought against fidgeting and let her look her fill. Then, to his surprise, she added, "Would you like something to drink?"

"Jah." He wasn't particularly thirsty, but no way was he gonna ever pass up anything she offered.

Tabitha froze for a second but then got her bearings. Lifting her chin, she said, "I have cold cider and water. Oh! I've got cider on the stove with some spices too. Do you like hot apple cider?"

He doubted he did but wasn't going to tell her that. "I don't know."

"You don't?"

He shook his head, doing his best to keep the smile teasing his lips from seeing the light of day. "I don't believe anyone's ever served me hot spiced cider." His younger self would have run from such a thing.

"It's probably time someone did, then." Tabitha turned and went inside. When he didn't follow, she cleared her throat as she held the door open. "Are you coming?"

"You sure you don't mind me inside your haus?"

"I'm sure." She looked so determined. So brave.

Reminding himself to let her call the shots, he climbed the steps and crossed the porch. Alone in the living room, he closed the door and looked around. The floorboards were uneven, the walls scuffed, and even the stones around the fireplace were in disrepair. It was obvious that her ex-husband had never invested much time working on the house and that it was far too much for her to handle. The house didn't just need a helping hand. Nothing less than an army of workers and a pile of money would make it shine.

But amid the dents and scratches was the scent of warm bread and a woman's presence. And, he supposed, the aroma of spiced apple cider.

"I'm in here," she said.

He walked through the living room to a small seating area and finally into a surprisingly spacious kitchen. Like the rest of the house, it looked worse for wear. The laminate on the counters was peeling up in places, the stove was old, and the refrigerator made a low humming noise.

However, it was also spotlessly clean. And surprisingly pretty. She'd put some wildflowers in a jar on the counter. Two quilts rested on the living room sofa. There was even a bright yellow tablecloth covering the table.

When their eyes met, she grimaced. She'd been watching him take it all in. "I know it's not much."

She was right. It wasn't. But once upon a time the house

had been special and it could be again. Just like Tabitha. "It suits you."

She flinched. "Maybe it does."

Seth swallowed, embarrassed that his words had come out the wrong way. But who was to say what was the right way? It wasn't like he had a lot of practice saying anything of worth to women. "I didn't mean any disrespect, Tabitha."

"No?"

"No." Sure, he could say more to try to defend himself, but what was the point? What remained true was the simple fact that she had been through hell at the hands of the one man on earth who'd vowed to care for her until his last breath. Instead, he'd betrayed that trust in the worst way possible.

To make matters worse, what little trust and faith she'd possessed had been trampled on by many of the people in their community's tight circle. Too many folks had sided with a book of rules and their long-held traditions instead of what their eyes and ears told them was true.

In the stiff silence between them, Tabitha looked around, seeming to study the space with fresh eyes. "I suppose this old house does suit me. It's broken but still standing."

"I meant that it looks comfortable and pretty," he said quickly.

Her eyes flared before she tamped that down. "I'm neither, Seth."

"You are to me. I find you relaxing to be around."

Her lips parted. Her tongue darted out, moistened her bottom lip.

He pretended not to notice.

Carefully she poured two mugs of cider. "Well, um, here you go. Hot cider." Looking a little unsure, she added, "Do you want to sit at the table?"

He'd just noticed the filled canvas bags on the floor as well as a giant bag of flour. "What is all this?"

"Groceries. My sister and her boys stop by once a month. They left a few moments before you arrived."

"Want me to help you put them away?"

"Nee. It will give me something to do later." She carried the mugs to the table.

"All right, then." He followed and sat down across from her.

"Oh! I forgot." In a flash she was on her feet again, fluttering around the kitchen like a scared bird.

Tabitha pulled a plate out of a cabinet, opened a pie safe, and sliced a piece of apple pie. Despite how he was fairly sure he didn't like spiced cider, he sipped his drink, needing something to do as he attempted to come to terms with her generosity. It was hot and a bit too sweet but not awful.

"You didn't have to do this," he murmured when she set the plate and a fork in front of him.

"You've been bringing me meat and produce for months. You've split most of my wood. I don't think a slice of pie is too much to give in return."

True. "Perhaps not."

He closed his eyes and silently gave thanks. It was their way. And even though he was no longer Amish, he still found comfort in giving thanks to the Lord for His gifts.

When he opened his eyes again, he found her watching him from across the table. "Do you still pray before meals too?"

"Sometimes."

"It's hard to give up, ain't so?"

"I have no need to stop." Her voice lowered. "I understand why I had to leave the order. Marriage is a sacred vow before the Lord and the community. I know some couples whose marriages fail choose to separate and live apart, but that didn't feel right to me. I felt as if I had no choice. I didn't want any ties to Leon."

"I understand." He tentatively took another sip.

"Do you? Some women came here soon after I told the bishop about my divorce lawyer."

"What did they say?"

She looked down at her untouched drink. "About what you'd imagine. They reminded me of my marriage vows."

"I was in prison, but I still heard about how badly you were beaten. It wasn't the first time, was it?"

Those eyes, so soft and vulnerable, met his again. "It wasn't even the worst," she whispered. "But I still lost my baby."

"You did what you had to do, Tabitha. Even if folks here in Crittenden County don't understand, I do. I think God does too."

Tabitha curved her hands around her mug but still didn't take a sip. "I hope He does. I made my peace with His will some time ago. I decided that no matter what, I'll have to face my Maker one day, but until then I have to live on this earth. I couldn't live like that anymore."

Seth had never imagined he was a kind person. Certainly not sensitive. He had no experience hugging children or holding a woman in his arms while she cried. But at that moment, he wanted to hold her hand. That was it. Simply hold her hand in between his two work-roughened ones. Give her a bit of contact. Give her a reminder that she wasn't alone in this world. Nee, remind her that she wasn't going to have to wait until death to find comfort.

"You haven't tried the pie."

He couldn't help but grin at that. "And you haven't tried the cider."

Her eyes brightened as she brought the earthenware cup to her lips and sipped while he took a bite.

Just as he'd imagined, it was delicious. The crust was flaky and light while the filling was cold and tart and sweet. Cinnamon teased his tongue.

She was watching him.

"It's very good. Better than that, actually."

"Thank you."

"You're very welcome."

She smiled slowly. It was tentative yet genuine.

Seth realized he needed nothing else in the world at that moment. Except, perhaps, to stay another moment longer.

5

Elias Weaver was waiting for him when Seth returned home. His horse and buggy were parked off to the side.

"I was beginning to think you were dodging me," he called out when Seth was about halfway up his driveway.

"Why's that?"

"Your truck is sitting here and the engine was cold. I thought you were around but didn't care to talk."

The truth was that Seth wasn't in any great hurry to speak to Elias at the moment. Even though Elias was one of his oldest friends and had even taken the time to write to him a couple of times when he'd been in jail, Seth sometimes found him to be nosy. Elias might say his questions stemmed from interest and concern, but Seth had always gotten the feeling that the man simply enjoyed gleaning information.

Though that could be helpful, it could also come back to bite him. The last thing he wanted was for Elias to get into his business with Tabitha. That was private and no business of anyone else's.

Besides, Seth needed some more time to replay Tabitha's words in his head. All the way back home, some of her words and phrases had come back to him, playing over and over like they'd been recorded. During their conversation, he'd been so focused on not spooking her, he hadn't allowed himself to react to the things she'd said. He was anxious to do that . . . but couldn't with Elias over.

Of course, that wasn't fair to his buddy.

Hoping that Elias would sense that he wasn't in the mood to chat, Seth stopped a few feet from him. "I didn't need my truck for where I had to go."

"Which was . . . where, exactly?"

"Why are you here, Elias?"

Elias looked taken aback. And maybe a little bit hurt. "Do I have to have a reason for coming over?"

"No, but you usually do." He folded his arms across his chest and waited.

Elias hated silence. After a few seconds passed, he sighed. "I came here to ask for a favor." His eyes kept darting to one side.

Time hadn't been all that good to Elias. His middle had gotten thick, and more than a couple wrinkles had appeared on his face. He'd also had a number of financial setbacks. Like when he was a child, he was full of impulsiveness—and now regrets. Though he and Seth were almost the same age, Elias carried a smattering of fine lines around his eyes. Seth always thought that was an ironic twist. How could a man look worse than his best friend who'd been in prison?

Regardless of all his flaws, Elias was a proud man. So proud that Seth had always figured he'd rather stride through a raging river than ask for a helping hand to get into a boat. Of course, that was why his friend's words caught him off guard.

Immediately he ran through scenarios that would necessitate Elias being there. The best—and worst—possibility had to do with Melonie. Seth's younger sister always had his heart, but she was stuck between a rock and a hard place. She wanted to spend time with Seth but also needed to mind their parents. They'd reluctantly allowed Melonie to see him from time to time but otherwise kept their distance.

"Is everything okay with Melonie?"

And just like that, Elias's proud countenance slipped into soft sympathy. "Jah." Squeezing Seth's shoulder, he added, "Your sister is gut, buddy."

A couple of years ago, Elias had mentioned to Seth that he'd like to court her one day. Seth had shut that down, saying that he was sure his sister would never think of him as anything but an older brother. Elias had been disappointed but had eventually agreed.

It turned out that he'd done a real fine job of filling that spot for Seth when he'd been in prison. Elias had looked after her, spoke with her after church services, and even stopped by to see Melonie and their parents from time to time. Melonie had often written him about Elias's visits, easing Seth's mind. Later, when Seth returned to Crittenden County and realized that his parents weren't going to welcome him with open arms, Elias had continued to be supportive to both him and his sister.

Seth appreciated everything his buddy did for him and his family. He truly did. But he would be lying if he said that he wasn't jealous of his longtime friend. In some ways, Elias had taken Seth's spot in the Zimmerman family. In his weakest moments, Seth tried to imagine what his life would have been like if he'd never stepped in to defend Bethanne.

As much as even thinking about Melonie hurt, Elias's news eased his insides. "I hope our mother is keeping an eye on her. A train could be coming and half the time I think

Melonie would still walk across those tracks." Of course, from what Seth had gathered, their father was always working and their mother had taken to bed with a constant stream of headaches. Melonie could do all sorts of things without either of them knowing.

"I don't think she's that oblivious. At least, not anymore. So there's no need to worry about her." He cleared his throat. "This has to do with me."

Concern for his friend made Seth study him closer. If Elias was hurting, he was doing a good job of hiding it. "Let's go on inside."

"Danke."

Looking at the horse, Seth added, "Want to unhitch Lightning?"

"We might as well, I reckon."

When he stepped toward the horse, Seth stopped him. "I got it." He carefully unhitched the lines from the horse and moved him over to a grassy area where another hitching post stood. After attaching the lines to it, he strode to the barn, found an old bucket, and used the spigot outside to fill it with water before carrying it to Lightning's side.

Elias watched it all, an expression of bemusement playing on his features. "You can still tend to a horse better than most anyone around."

Seth felt like rolling his eyes. Even his good friends didn't seem able to look beyond his jeans, T-shirt, sleeve of tattoos, and short English haircut. It was as if his changed appearance had changed his heart and his mind. What he would've been happy to tell Elias—and anyone else who took the trouble to ask—was that he was still very much the same man he'd always been. He still did love working with horses. He'd even considered being a blacksmith or working in a livery, but that dream ended when he realized that no Amish person would give him their business.

Though Seth didn't regret the things he'd done that landed him in prison, he did regret that he was never going to be able to remove it from anyone's memory. He wasn't a completely different person because a man died in a fight with him and he'd served time, but the experiences had altered him. He thought he was stronger because of his hardships. Unfortunately, even his parents weren't willing to associate with him anymore.

Running a hand down Lightning's flank, he said, "I might not be Amish anymore, but my brain still works."

"Thank the good Lord for that," Elias muttered and followed Seth inside.

Like always, his modest house's interior brought Seth a sense of comfort. The floors were a dark-stained hickory, the walls a vanilla white. His kitchen had stainless-steel appliances and his living room a large couch covered in fawn-colored suede. The decor was sparse for an English home, fancy for an Amish one, and luxurious by his own standard.

It was also clean and tidy—a consequence of his upbringing, his years incarcerated, and a natural inclination toward order. The house was warm, thanks to the gas fireplace he'd installed last year. Outside, the October weather was crisp. Because the sky was overcast, the inside was shadowy. Until he turned on the lights.

Elias whistled softly. "Last time I came over, we sat out on the porch. When did you connect the electricity?"

"A while back. I figured there was no reason to stay in the dark since I decided not to be baptized in the Amish faith."

"I reckon I would've done the same thing."

Seth led the way into the kitchen. "Would you care for a glass of water? Soda? Coffee?"

"You got coffee made?"

"I don't, but it's no trouble." He headed to the coffee maker.

"Wait. You got a Coke?"

He grinned. Elias looked so hopeful it was almost comical. "I do."

"I'll have that, then."

Seth detoured to the fridge, then opened the door and pulled out two cans of soda. He wasn't particularly thirsty but knew Elias would have something to say if Seth didn't join him.

After handing him one of the cans, Seth sat down on the rocking chair next to the fireplace. The rocker had been his grandfather's. He hardly used it, preferring the comfort of the couch, but there was something in Elias's eyes that put Seth a little on guard. Like he was about to hear something that he was going to need to have all his wits about him for. The hard discomfort of his dawdi's chair would serve that purpose.

"What's the favor, Elias?"

"I want you to talk to Lott."

Lott—Bethanne's younger brother.

Seth had never expected the Hostetlers to thank him for what he'd done. To his surprise, both of Bethanne's parents had come to the prison to thank him in person. And Bethanne had sent him a long letter. In it, she'd not only thanked him for fighting off Peter Miller but also apologized for her decision to leave a gathering with Peter. She was sure what had happened was all her fault, that she should've known better than to go out walking with Peter in the dark.

Seth knew she was wrong. The fault didn't lie with her but

with Peter. And Seth was pretty certain he was at fault too. If he hadn't gotten so angry when he spied Bethanne trying to fend off Peter, he might not have pushed him so hard.

Seth had never written Bethanne back, mainly because he knew word would get around that she'd received a letter from the penitentiary. He figured she had enough to bear without being reminded about Peter's attack or having to answer questions about why Seth Zimmerman was writing to her—or both.

Course, he might have jumped the gun. The Hostetler family could have decided that their duty to thank Seth was fulfilled and not wanted to receive letters from a convict. It had felt right to keep his distance from the family since his release. Everyone knew that Bethanne was still having a difficult time moving on. His presence wouldn't help.

And then there was Lott. The kid had a cocky air about him that grated on Seth's nerves. Stories abounded that he was pushing the boundaries a bit. Okay, more than a bit. Seth would've hoped that the guy would have more respect for his parents than that.

But most of all, he didn't think he was anyone's role model. He might not regret helping Bethanne, but he did regret fighting with Peter. He'd let his anger get the best of him. As far as he was concerned, there were many other men in town who would be better suited to offer Lott advice. Starting with Elias himself.

"What do you say, Seth?"

There was only one thing to say. "Nee."

"Nee?"

"Nee, as in no way do I want to speak to Lott Hostetler." Imitating Elias's raised eyebrow, he added, "Is that clear enough for you?"

"It is not. That's about as clear as mud."

Irritated that his friend had brought back a flood of difficult memories, Seth added, "I'm not the right person to speak to Lott. I'm too tied to one of the worst moments in his family's life."

"I disagree. He needs to speak with someone who's had to deal with the consequences of his actions."

Seth stood up, popped open his can of soda, and took a long gulp. "You knew I'd say no. I can't believe you came over anyway."

Elias held up both hands. "I'm not going to deny that I knew this request would be hard for you."

"But you showed up here and asked anyway."

"Whatever. What I'm trying to say is that it took a lot for me to ask this, Seth. You know it." His gray eyes, so unusual, were filled with pain. "Hear me out."

"Fine."

"It's like this. Lott has been a little too wild during his rumspringa. He's been drinking and even fighting from time to time."

"I heard the same things. It's none of my business, though."

"I think differently. He's angry, Seth."

"So?"

"Stop arguing and listen. Seth, I think he's angry because of Bethanne. Because Peter Miller's parents are still wearing black and mourning their son, and Peter's younger brother Joe is walking around whispering that he knows the whole story about what really happened."

Seth shook his head. "Joe doesn't know what he's talking about. Bethanne was sixteen at the time, I was eighteen. Joe was a lot younger."

"I think he was fourteen."

"It doesn't matter how old he was. All I do know is that he wasn't at that gathering. No one that young was there."

"Calm down. Of course Joe wasn't there. But not everyone wants to hear the truth when a made-up story is a lot more interesting, Seth."

Seth clenched his jaw so hard, a dull pain radiated along the back of his neck. "What am I supposed to say to Lott? That he shouldn't be angry that Joe is telling stories? That he shouldn't defend his sister? I'm not going to tell him that." His mind kept clicking. "Or are you looking for someone to tell him to turn the other cheek?"

Elias's expression tightened. "I didn't say any of that."

"You should be glad you didn't, because I'm not going to tell Lott any of it."

"I'm not suggesting that either." Folding his arms across his chest, he sighed.

Seth felt bad for acting like a jerk. But he had enough on his plate without Elias or Lott Hostetler dredging up the past. "Just tell me, then."

Elias leaned forward, placing his elbows on his knees. "John and Martha feel like Lott is at a crossroads. He's been acting out, he's angry. They're hoping you might be able to connect with him in a way that no one has seemed to be able to. Maybe tell Lott more about what happened the night Peter died."

"He knows what happened. If he wants to know more, he should ask his sister."

"Yeah, that ain't gonna happen."

"Because?"

"Because Bethanne refuses to speak of it."

Seth paused. "Are you sure?"

"Of course I'm sure. I wouldn't lie about that."

He was surprised to hear that. Bethanne's note to him in prison had been long and filled with her feelings about both Peter and Seth's conviction. So, had her parents and brother not given her a chance to tell her side of the story? Or had Bethanne been the one to keep them in the dark for a reason all her own?

Realizing her reasons didn't matter and that he was going to have to visit with Lott, if for no other reason than he owed Elias so much, Seth released a ragged sigh. "Fine."

"You'll do it? You'll speak to Lott?"

He nodded. "I don't see what purpose it will serve, though."

"If you can help Lott cool his heels and find a way to ignore Joe and accept some peace, it will help him and you."

He understood that Lott needed to find some peace, but he had no idea why Elias thought he needed to find some peace. "Why are you worried about me?"

Elias sighed. "Because Lott wants to court Melonie."

"Wait. My baby sister?"

"Seth, Melonie is seventeen and no baby."

"She's too young for a caller." And she deserved someone better than Lott Hostetler.

"You know that ain't true."

"Okay, how about this? Lott is way too full of himself. If he's acting hotheaded about Joe Miller, then he still has some growing up to do. Plus, he's gone out of his way to avoid me."

"I think he's afraid of you."

"Because I'm a killer?" he asked sarcastically.

"No one who was around when all that happened thinks you're some cold-blooded killer. I think he believes that prison hardened you a bit. And he knows you dote on Melonie."

Surviving prison had made him harder, that was true. And he did dote on Mel. Studying Elias, he said, "I can't believe you're involved in all of this."

"I think the Lord knew it was a good idea because everyone needs to forgive each other and move on." He waved a hand. "Bethanne needs to stop hiding and move forward. Lott Hostetler needs to start settling down. And the Millers—especially Joe—need to make peace with Peter's actions and move on." Elias lowered his voice. "Seth, you need to not only forgive yourself for losing your temper when you were trying to help Bethanne but accept that you are still a good man. A worthy man." His eyes twinkled. "Finally, you need to let your sister make up her own mind about Lott."

Man, he wished Elias hadn't shown up at his door. "Elias, not a bit of that is easy."

"I didn't say it would be. But there isn't anything you can do about it either. Time marches on, with or without you. And Lott had already called on Melonie once when Joe Miller started shooting his mouth off about you and Peter and Bethanne."

The whole thing was convoluted and filled with upcoming conversations he'd never wanted to have. But it seemed the Lord had other plans. "I don't have a choice, do I?" Sooner or later he was going to have to speak to Lott.

"Everyone has choices, Seth," Elias drawled, sounding like the wise mentor he so absolutely wasn't. "What you and I and the Lord know, however, is that not every choice is either easy . . . or the right one."

Seth closed his eyes. Even though Elias was right, he really wasn't happy about how much of the past was about to be churned up. "I really wish you hadn't come by."

Elias grinned. "Does this mean you're going to talk to Lott?"

Seth nodded. As much as he wished he wasn't, he was invested now. Besides, even if he never saw Bethanne again, he wanted to be close to Melonie. It would be foolish to pretend that his actions and imprisonment didn't affect his sister. They did. There was no way he would ever not do everything he could to help her. She had a hard enough time holding up her head when the whole community somehow thought his actions tainted her reputation.

"Jah. I'll talk to him."

His old friend grinned. "Gut. I told him you'd stop by one evening this week."

Elias had totally played him. "I hate you so much right now." Sure, Seth was joking, but at the moment the sentiment felt real.

"No, you don't." Elias's smile proved he hadn't taken offense. "You could never hate me."

"And you know this how?"

"Because I could never hate you, Seth Zimmerman. You're one of the best men I've ever met."

Seth mumbled something about having to go to the bathroom as he strode down the hall. It was either that or let Elias see the tears that were threatening to fall.

He couldn't have that.

6

Lott Hostetler was in trouble again. Unfortunately, this was nothing new. Of late, everything in his life seemed to set him off, and that was a far sight too much. Worse, no matter how hard he prayed or cautioned himself, he couldn't seem to control his actions. Or listen to his parents' advice.

Now, to his dismay, he was being forced to talk to none other than Seth Zimmerman. Not only was Seth former Amish but he'd served time in prison. The man was an ex-con. Sure, he'd gotten there by trying to help Lott's sister, but that almost made everything seem worse. People said that Seth's hard punch had knocked Peter down to the ground. It wasn't the punch that killed him. It was the rock that Peter had landed on. It kind of sounded like an accident, but the judge still made him serve time for it.

Ever since that night, Bethanne had been quiet and timid. She kept to herself even though the bishop had spent a lot of time trying to convince Bethy that neither Peter's death nor Seth's incarceration was her fault. She thought otherwise. So, things were bad at his house. He did things he shouldn't while his sister didn't do anything. The last thing he needed was to chat with Seth Zimmerman about life. Wasn't it time for all of them to leave the past in the past?

As far as Lott was concerned, his life would be a whole lot easier if Seth had never returned to Crittenden County. Maybe if he'd gone somewhere else when he'd gotten released, everyone could pretend that the man didn't exist. Especially since Lott was hung up on Seth's sister.

Even thinking about Melonie made him feel out of control. Blond like her older brother and with the same blue eyes, Melonie was pretty and sweet and good. Too good for Lott to be half in love with her too.

But no matter how hard Lott tried to stay away, he couldn't help himself. He couldn't stay away from her any more than he could wish for time to go backward. It was what it was.

The low purr of an engine brought him back to the present. When he spied Seth's silver truck pull into their driveway, resentment hit him hard. Boy, he hated Elias Weaver right now. Elias had finagled this meeting, and Lott's parents were practically buzzing, they were so sure that Seth Zimmerman's words would put Lott back on the straight and narrow.

He knew that wasn't going to happen.

As Lott watched from the living room window, Seth climbed out of the truck's cab and sauntered toward the house. Here this guy was, practically pushing the fact that he'd left the order in his face. No, in *all* of their faces. The only reason Lott hadn't taken off an hour ago was because he had nowhere else to go. His parents had been watching him like a hawk.

Lott ground his teeth.

His father, who had been sitting with him, must have noticed. "Lott, I hope you'll have a real conversation with Seth.

Try to listen to what he has to say. It was good of him to come over here. You should take his advice and consider it well."

"I canna believe you want me to talk to him. We don't have anything in common."

"I disagree," Daed murmured.

As he stepped onto the porch, Seth pulled off his sunglasses and put them in a pocket of his barn jacket. It had been a while since Lott had seen the man up so close. He was big—at least six feet—and muscular too. But it was those eyes of his that made Lott's mouth go dry. Whereas Melonie's eyes were filled with wonder and grace, Seth's were hard and calculating. No one was going to be able to get away with much around Seth Zimmerman.

He knocked on the door. Two short raps.

"Daed, what about Mamm?" Lott asked. "Aren't you worried about her being in the same house as him?" He knew he was grasping at straws, but he needed some kind of an excuse to get out of the conversation.

"Of course not. She's fond of Seth. She and I both are."

His parents were so naive. "Daed—"

His father got to his feet, his voice icy. "Lott, I don't tell you this often enough, but I want you to listen to me now. Don't ignore me and don't be disrespectful to Seth either. He's doing you a favor coming over here."

Lott doubted Seth had anything else going on in his life, but he was smart enough not to talk back to his father. "I'll listen." At least, he would look like he was listening. He didn't care what his parents said. Seth might be fooling some folks with his do-gooder attitude, but Lott knew better.

His father stared at him for a long moment before clasping him on the shoulder. "Gut." He went to the door, opened it, and greeted Seth, and the two shook hands. "It's good to see you. It's been far too long." Then the door closed as his father joined Seth on the porch.

His father hadn't called for him, so Lott figured he could stay where he was. It might have been cowardly, but that gave him some time to get a better look at the man.

He thought back. Until now, the closest he'd been to Seth in the last year was when they were on opposite sides of the farmers' market. Seth had been buying up a ton of fruits and vegetables. Way more than for just one person. He'd surmised that Seth must have been buying food for one of his ex-con friends.

Well, that had been what a couple of the guys Lott had been with said. Gossiping about Seth was a favorite pastime. Actually, they all talked about him a lot when there wasn't anyone around to overhear them. That's when they guessed about what being in prison was like. They'd wondered if any of the other men discovered that Seth had been Amish—and if he'd had to fight a lot or if he'd been hurt or what he'd done to survive. They'd all agreed that he must have changed somehow. One didn't walk out of a penitentiary without scars.

At least, Lott didn't think so.

Now, here he was, still seated in his living room, waiting to be summoned. To Lott's surprise, they didn't come inside right away. Instead, they chatted for a few minutes. Lott watched Seth's posture ease and a hint of a smile play across his features. It was almost like his father and Seth were friends.

How could that be? As far as he knew, neither of his parents ever mentioned Seth Zimmerman. Did they meet with him in secret? Or did they just not speak about Seth to Lott, just like they never mentioned what happened to Bethanne? That possibility floored Lott. Sometimes, his parents' silence had bothered him so much, he'd wondered if they'd forgotten that Bethanne had been attacked.

But of course they hadn't.

Getting to his feet, Lott continued to watch the two of them talk. Wondered how long he was going to have to wait. And then practically swallowed his tongue when Seth turned and looked directly at him through the window. Even from the distance, Seth's eyes still looked hard and cold. They also seemed to see too much.

A chill ran through Lott, but he did his best not to act like anything was amiss. He attempted to look bored as he stared right back at Seth. Then tried not to shy away when Seth didn't avert his gaze.

Natural curiosity won over as Lott's eyes drifted over the man's features. Seth had a nose that had obviously been broken once and never set right, sharp cheekbones, a light tan, and no beard. He was wearing jeans and Red Wings, and his black long-sleeved knit shirt was tucked in, showing that Seth's body was strong and fit.

No, that was putting it mildly. Seth was not only a good four inches taller than Lott, he was also probably seventy or eighty pounds heavier. And not because he had fat on him. No, everything about the man looked muscular and hard. Like he wouldn't need to think twice about grabbing someone if he had a mind to do it.

Lott's mouth went dry. Had Seth always been that way? Or had all that time in prison done it?

Realizing that Seth was still watching him, Lott swallowed hard. Man, he wished he hadn't stayed in the house instead of joining his father. Now he had to sit here and wait. Instead of feeling like he was in the right, Lott felt small. Like a foolish child pretending to be someone he wasn't.

Maybe someone he'd never been.

As if his father had suddenly realized that Lott wasn't standing with them, he called him outside.

Lott joined them on the porch.

Seth inclined his head but didn't say anything.

"Lott, you know Seth, jah?"

"Yeah."

His father frowned at his poor manners. "Lott—"

"It's all right," Seth said. "We know each other but not all that well. Apart from work, we don't have a reason to speak to each other."

He was right. They didn't. Unless one counted the fact that Seth had saved his older sister from getting raped. Lott felt his cheeks heat.

"I'm sure Martha has put out a spread for you. Come on in."

Seth seemed taken aback. "There was no need to go to any trouble, John."

"You might not think so, but Martha and I feel differently." Treating Lott to a look that said everything about behaving himself, Daed opened the door and gestured for Seth to proceed both him and Lott.

Seth paused at the door. "Your floor looks shiny. Martha must have just washed it."

"Likely so. She's been looking forward to your visit."

"Should I take my shoes off?"

"If they're muddy, yes. Otherwise, there's no need."

Their guest looked down at his feet like he had to double-check his shoes' condition, then he followed Daed into the parlor.

Lott closed the door behind them. He couldn't remember the last time he'd ever noticed when his mother had mopped.

"Go straight into the parlor, Son."

This was getting worse and worse. The only time Mamm ever allowed them in the parlor was when either Preacher Zachariah or Bishop Wood came calling.

Lott followed Seth in, being careful to keep his distance.

"Welcome to our home, Seth." Wearing a dark gray dress with a white apron and her white kapp, Mamm approached. "I'm sorry that we haven't had you over until now."

"No apology needed, ma'am. I understood."

Sympathy filled his mother's gaze, but she nodded. "Help yourself to some sandwiches or cookies. Would you care for water or kaffi? The kaffi is fresh."

"Coffee sounds mighty gut. Danke."

"Lott?"

"Jah?"

Her eyebrows raised. "What do you want to drink?"

"Kaffi?"

"All right. Sit down and I'll bring it to you."

Lott glanced at his father. "What about Daed?"

"I'm not staying," his father said. "Get yourself something to eat and sit down."

Lott wasn't hungry, but he did as he was told. Seth also didn't seem too enthused, but he helped himself to a plate of sandwiches and a handful of cookies.

Just as tension began to rise between the two of them again, his mother returned. "Here you go, Seth," she said as she handed him a steaming cup. "And here you go, Lott."

"Danke, Martha," Seth said.

"It's no trouble." Smiling at his plate, she said, "Do you have a sweet tooth?"

Seth chuckled. "I reckon I do. I don't have much of an occasion to buy sweets."

"I'll make sure to send some home with you."

"That's very kind of ya. Danke."

And then, before he was ready, Lott was alone with Seth. By this time, Seth had already eaten three of the four sandwich squares and two of the cookies. He was studying Lott like he was trying to figure him out.

"Why are you looking at me like that?"

"I'm wondering what's got you in such a state. Is it me? Is it my past? Or is it something else? Are you this grumpy all the time?"

"Grumpy?"

"I respect your parents enough to keep my mouth G-rated. I'm thinking of something a little more pointed."

"My parents can't hear you. Say whatever you want."

"Is that what you're doing?" He waved a hand. "Are you saying everything you're thinking?"

"Nee." Lott felt a line of perspiration trickle down the center of his back. He was starting to feel like he was in over his head. "I'm not a kid, you know."

"I know." He ate another cookie. "Where's Bethanne?"

"She's likely upstairs in her room. She likes to keep to herself."

Seth seemed to think on that for a moment. Then he fastened a cold gaze on him. "I heard you've been trying to spend time with my sister."

Seth's voice was soft. Almost like a whisper. The question was mild. If he hadn't been so stressed, Lott might not have even heard the touch of judgment in his tone.

But he had.

His guard went up as he felt the full weight of the other man's gaze settle on him. Seth was obviously taking his measure and finding him wanting. Lott's mouth turned dry. He should have known this was coming. Melonie was so kind and proper, it was easy to forget that Seth was her brother. "I've paid a call on her." He cleared his throat. "Once."

"Only once?" His eyes narrowed.

"I've been visiting with her for a while but have paid only one formal call."

Seth's lips thinned. "Do you like her?"

That was a loaded question if he'd ever heard one. So he lied. "I don't know."

One eyebrow rose. "You've been seeing my little sister without even being sure if you like her or not?"

Lott was digging himself deeper into a hole. A hole that he hadn't even seen coming. "I don't know."

Seth leaned forward, his expression hard. "I sure hope you aren't playing games with her."

"I'm not."

"You'd better not." After staring at him a minute longer, Seth rubbed the back of his neck.

"Lott, Elias asked me to come talk to you. Do you know why?"

"Nope."

Seth looked down a moment, then back at him. "Boy, I respect your parents and have a soft spot for your sister. I also am beholden enough to Elias Weaver to come over here and spend time with you. But that said, I'm losing patience with your attitude."

"There's no reason for me to be saying anything, because I have no idea why you're here." Unless it was to warn him off from Melonie.

"Let me be real clear, then. Elias told me about your temper. I asked around and heard about some of the other stuff you've been doing." He lowered his voice. "You've been drinking and carousing and making one bad choice after the next."

"It's allowed. I'm in rumspringa."

Seth sneered. "Give that excuse to someone who cares. The road you're going down is a rough one. You can't go through life imagining you'll have no consequences. You need to stop acting as if you're invincible."

"I'm not doing that."

"People say differently. Listen, no one is above the law. Even when you think that everyone will save you or that they'll intervene because you're a sheltered Amish boy, you learn real fast that ain't the case."

"I'm not going to kill anyone, Seth." At Seth's dark look, Lott felt his face heat up.

"I hope not. You don't want to live with that knowledge for the rest of your life, and you sure don't want to feel the guilt and pain that I have."

"I won't."

"I hope that's true."

Lott was shaken by Seth's words, but he tried not to show it. Right now he didn't have much pride left. He felt like he had hardly anything to stand on. If Lott allowed himself to be vulnerable, Seth might realize just what a mess he actually was.

Looking at him intently, Seth stood up. "I'm out of here. But before I go, I'm gonna leave you with this. When you're sitting here in this nice room where everything is clean and quiet and safe, it's easy to drift into a false sense of security. By and large, the folks here in Crittenden County are good. They give their neighbors space. Try to be polite. Sometimes, they might even give you the benefit of the doubt."

Lowering his voice, he continued. "Maybe so much, you

start to believe you have the right to do whatever you want and be forgiven. Like maybe your sins aren't all that bad. You might even convince yourself that twenty-four months ain't a real long time to be behind bars." His jaw hardened as he averted his eyes. "But it is. Three days feels like a long time. And even those first three hours feel too long."

It was taking everything Lott had to not tremble. "Is all this talk because you don't want me around Melonie?"

"It's one of the reasons. My sister might not want to listen to me and she might never want to believe a thing I say. But she's precious to me, and I don't want her to get hurt." His eyes turned to ice. "If I begin to think that you're doing anything less than respecting her the way she deserves, I'm going to step in. And then I'll do whatever I can to make sure that she's free of you."

Lott swallowed. "That sounds like a threat."

"You're wrong, boy. It's not a threat, it's a promise. You'd best not forget that."

• • • •

Later, long after Seth Zimmerman left, Lott's parents grilled him about their conversation. Then Bethanne came downstairs, they had supper, and Lott did his chores in the barn. After that, he lay in bed and thought about Melonie and her parents and how they didn't like having much to do with Seth. He remembered the man's voice and the pain in his eyes. Finally, he thought about his own family. The way his mother greeted Seth. The fact that Elias had asked Seth to come over.

A dark feeling grabbed ahold of Lott and pulled hard. As much as he didn't want to believe it, he was afraid that some of what Seth had warned him about did have merit. Maybe he had taken a wrong turn. Maybe he had been thinking about and attempting to do some things that he shouldn't. And maybe Seth had been right that some of what he'd been doing did have consequences.

He wasn't anxious to discover what those were.

7

After a bout of nightmares, Tabitha had woken up to the season's first frost. It was a cloudy, dreary day and the wind was blowing. October was already hinting that their winter was going to be a long one.

The wool shawl she wrapped around her shoulders felt like tissue paper as she hurried to the barn to milk the cow and feed the chickens. She worked as efficiently as she could so they could go back to sleep. Bessie the cow seemed particularly pleased when Tabitha closed the barn door again.

Back in the house, she washed the eggs and put the milk into a Mason jar in the refrigerator to allow the cream to rise. She'd skim the top and separate the cream later and then eventually make yogurt and butter.

When everything was clean and neat again, she finally poured her first cup of coffee of the day. The fire she'd lit in the fireplace before she'd gone to the barn provided a welcome warmth to the living room, and after retrieving another blanket from the closet, she wrapped it over her legs and took a sip of the warm drink.

It was impossible to not take a moment to give thanks

for her blessings, as she did each morning. She had so many things to be grateful for these days—the house, her animals, the money her crafts brought in that enabled her to live without too many financial worries. But most of all, she gave thanks for peace.

There had been so many mornings when Leon had woken up in a mood and taken it out on her before the sun had completely risen. He'd been so cruel, and that cruelty had transformed her life. She'd become a person she hadn't known she could be, someone who was timid and nervous and desperate.

Tabitha was sure that if Mia Rothaker hadn't visited her in the hospital and assured her that she could leave Leon and still be safe, she would've never left him. Leon's rages had gotten worse and worse. She would've been dead now.

As it was, she would carry the scars from his last beating for the rest of her life.

As dark thoughts filled her again, Tabitha had to admit that she would've done anything to find her freedom. Even things that she knew were wrong. She should be ashamed about that, but she couldn't quite bring herself to be. When fear ran rampant in a person's life, it overtook most everything else.

Her lawyer had assured her that such a thing was natural. Mia had sat Tabitha down with a counselor friend of hers and talked her through something called Maslow's Hierarchy of Needs. According to that, one's body and brain sought food and water and safety before many other things. Even before something as basic as shelter. And that desire to live free of pain was so strong that a person could develop the strength and the will to fight or flee or even do things one wouldn't have thought possible in "normal" circumstances.

Tabitha had listened to the counselor's words with a combination of confusion and hope. All that had been laced with a hefty addition of renewed faith. She'd prayed for so long for Leon to get better. Or for her to be safe and to shield her baby from harm. When she'd lost the baby, her faith had wavered . . . but then she had gotten stronger and left Leon.

When she'd been released from the hospital, she'd been taken to a safe house in the middle of the night. Jeanie and Marv, the folks who had run the house, had been godsends. They'd let her heal and rest for several weeks. Little by little, she'd begun to feel more like herself.

The worst day of her life had enabled her to have many more days of life. That didn't mean she lived without worry. But it did mean that she could wake up without the gnawing sense of dread that had been a constant presence during her marriage.

Perhaps that was why she might be wary around Seth but she didn't automatically assume that he was a horrible person. All sorts of things could make someone do something unexpected.

Even something most people found unforgivable.

A scratching at her front door brought her to her feet. Carefully she went to the door and peeked out through the peephole. No one was there. But then the noise came again, and she hurried to a window and looked out.

That's when she saw the dog. A skinny thing with matted blond fur and brown eyes. And soaked from the morning's storm.

After grabbing a towel from the closet, Tabitha pulled open the door. The animal flinched in response but didn't move. He shivered, looking at her but too afraid to approach, and she felt a fresh burst of pity flow through her.

"I know," she whispered. "I know how you're feeling. I really do."

The dog stared up at her, silently beseeching.

She knelt in the doorway. "It's cold and wet out here," she whispered. "I've got a clean dry towel for you to use and a warm fire too. Come on in."

The hund cowered, but the new glint in his eyes looked everything like hope.

Tabitha got to her feet and stepped back. "Come on, then. I'll give you some milk too. And maybe an egg? Surely you're hungry."

The dog tilted his head to one side and seemed to weigh his options just as a gust of wet wind reached them. It whistled as it shook tree limbs, reminding Tabitha that violent weather was always possible.

She needed to close the door. "It's time to trust me, dog. I know you want to. Otherwise, why would you have come calling?"

Maybe it was her words or maybe the dog was simply enough of a realist to realize that being warm and dry was better than being cold and wet. Whatever the reason, he finally stepped through the doorway.

"You made the right decision," she murmured. "I know you don't trust me, but you don't have to. All you have to do is rest for a spell. Go on now, lie down on this towel in front of the fireplace. We'll take things one step at a time."

Five minutes later, the dog was asleep in front of the fireplace and Tabitha was sitting in her chair once again. Gazing at him, she wondered if he would stay for a while. Hopefully he would, but if he changed his mind, she wouldn't try to stop him.

She'd learned better than to do that.

• • • •

By seven that night, Tabitha had come to the conclusion that she now had a dog. He seemed inclined to stay. She supposed she couldn't blame him. A lingering chill hung in the air now that it was mid-October, but it was warm and cozy in front of the fireplace.

Then there was the fact that she had not only fed him but treated him kindly. Tabitha knew from experience that kindness mattered a lot. After taking him outside to go to the bathroom, she'd waited on the porch to see what he would do. He quickly did his business and returned to her side, where he sat patiently with a look of hope in his big brown eyes.

She'd had a feeling that if she'd told him to leave, the dog would've gone. He didn't expect much. Which was all she'd needed to know to cement her decision. "What am I going to call you, dog?" she'd asked as she opened the door and led him inside.

His only response had been a head tilt, as if to signify that choosing a new name was an important undertaking.

"I've never had a dog," Tabitha had said as they returned to the living room. "My mother liked cats. And Leon? Well, Leon didn't like a lot of things."

The dog stretched out on the rug, then curled into a ball. He even went so far as to curl his tail around his snout.

Tabitha watched as the firelight flickered against his blond fur, turning it almost a copper color. And then she remembered Seth Zimmerman's little speech about how she and he were like the field to her west. How there was more to that dead-looking grass than met the eye. Just like the two of them.

No, just like the three of them. She was fairly certain that this dog, just like her and Seth, was full of something good on the inside. If only one took the time to look.

No, if only someone took a chance on him.

Chance.

"What do you think, dog? Are you partial to Chance?"

The dog wagged his tail.

Tabitha knew little about dogs but figured they wagged their tails for all sorts of reasons. Even if it was just to say hello. But since she didn't know much about pet ownership, she reckoned that she was allowed to make some mistakes. "I think we should give Chance a chance. What do you think?" She smiled at the play on words.

The dog lumbered to his feet and walked closer.

She smiled. "Chance it is."

8

Seth hadn't visited Melonie in five months. That was no accident. He didn't belong in his childhood home, especially since he wasn't a child and the large, white house was no longer his home. He also did his best to avoid their parents—not that he needed to do that. His mamm and daed avoided him just fine on their own. He reckoned the four of them had a tricky relationship, and that was putting it mildly.

Soon after he'd been sentenced to prison, Preacher Zachariah had paid him a visit. After making sure that Seth was all right, he had brought up the topic of Seth's future. Seth had never been baptized in the Amish faith. Because of that, he wouldn't have to worry about being shunned, but the preacher had encouraged him to pray about his future. Seth had done that and had believed it would be some time before anyone in their tight-knit community would accept him. Violence was frowned upon, and the fact that he'd fought Peter would always be remembered.

Then there was the fact that he was going to be living among the English for an extended time and be subjected to other people's rules and customs. It might be too hard to return to the simple way of life. Seth had listened to the preacher's awkward conversation in silence. He hadn't disagreed with anything the man had said, though inwardly his heart was breaking. That's when Preacher Zachariah mentioned that forgiveness was always possible and that time healed a great many things. Perhaps one day Seth would be accepted in the Amish community and would want to be baptized.

Seth had sat alone in his cell for hours afterward, thinking about his community and rules and Jesus and Bethanne. He'd prayed for forgiveness and he'd prayed for clarity. But even though he knew he'd made a lot of mistakes in his life, he didn't believe that helping Bethanne had been one of them. Her cries for help couldn't have been ignored.

All that was why he still wasn't on great terms with his parents. Though they didn't refuse to acknowledge or see him from time to time, they didn't treat him like they used to. Seth didn't blame them. Whether he was Amish or English, he would never be able to change the fact that he was an ex-con.

That said, he'd had a need to see Melonie and he wanted to do the visit right. Plus, he was hoping that one of their parents would give him an inkling about how they felt about Lott's interest in her. If they were supportive of his interest and seemed to be vigilant in their monitoring of them, Seth would step back and stay out of Melonie's courtship. But if neither of them seemed to be watching Lott like a hawk and asking questions, then he would get involved.

As expected, his father allowed him inside but didn't actively welcome his presence. Though Mamm and Daed had made a point of letting him know that they forgave his transgressions and believed his time in prison had been more than enough penance to the Lord, they were wary around him.

Seth understood. He was different than the boy they'd raised. He was harder and far less trusting. Surviving life in prison had required that he learn a bunch of skills that weren't suitable in an Amish community.

He was a changed man, marked by everything that had happened. Even though he knew the bishop would forgive him and eventually allow him to be baptized, Seth knew it wasn't the right fit for him any longer. He was too worldly. He'd long ago come to terms with that.

His parents had not.

"This is a surprise, Seth," Mamm said after she hugged him hello. Worry etched her eyes as she scanned his face. "Is something wrong?"

"Nee. I'm fine. I came over to see Melonie."

"Ah." She exchanged a glance with his father. "That's probably a gut idea, I think."

It almost sounded as if they welcomed him being there. "Why do you say that?"

"Melonie is fine," Daed said. "However, she is . . . she is headstrong." His expression conveyed everything his benign words didn't.

Against his will, Seth felt the same twinge he used to feel back when he still lived in this house. He'd wanted to be happy. Ached to feel comfortable. But that comfort and ease had been hard to find. "Is she all right?" he asked.

"I believe so," his mother said. "She might tell you differently, though."

Seth was torn between chuckling and peppering them with questions. He knew better than to show too much emotion, however. His father had always believed that his formerly un-reserved tendencies would get him into trouble. Seth figured he'd probably been right about that.

"So, is Melonie around? May I speak with her?"

His mother inclined her head. "She's in the basement pinning laundry to the line. She should be done soon."

He made a move toward the back of the house. "I'll go downstairs, then."

"You don't want to wait until she comes back up?" Daed asked. "You'll see her soon enough. She's not going anywhere."

Seth felt a familiar tightening in his chest. His parents had expectations about chores and jobs and the way they should be done. Sometimes they seemed to forget that everything in one's life shouldn't be about duty. "There's no reason to wait," he said. "I still remember where the basement is. I can give her a hand."

"No reason to do that. She knows what to do," Mamm said. "Don't you let her step away without finishing."

"I won't."

As always, the small window at the top of the passageway did little to illuminate the space. Memories hit him hard. Growing up, he'd run up and down those wooden stairs, his bare feet sure and steady. Now he reached for the banister and found himself wishing for a flashlight. It seemed he'd gotten used to light.

At least the small, stark basement was brighter. Faint light filtered through the four windows that lined the top of the basement's space. Added to that was a floor lamp powered by a small propane unit. It cast a pretty golden glow around the space, making the room look better than the way he remembered it.

Or maybe it was simply the sight of Melonie that made everything look better than it was. Even wearing a pale green dress and pinning clothes on the line, she was a sight to behold.

It was no wonder Lott wanted to be around her.

He took care to step hard on the final stairstep so she wouldn't be startled. "Hiya, Melonie," he said in a soft tone.

She jumped. When she turned to look at him, her grip on the article of clothing loosened. It dropped to the floor in a damp heap. "Seth."

He strode across the floor and picked up the piece. It was blue cotton. One of their father's shirts. He shook it out. "Sorry about that. I tried not to startle you."

"I thought I heard footsteps, but I assumed they were from Mamm or Daed walking around in the kitchen. Why are you down here?"

Not wanting to immediately dive into his concerns about Lott, he shrugged. "I was nearby."

Melonie raised an eyebrow. "I know that isn't the reason."

"Okay, how about this? Maybe I had a notion to see if I could still pin laundry on the clothesline."

"Have you ever pinned up laundry in your life? I don't recall you doing it even once."

"I might have done it a time or two."

"You might have. Or . . . not." She took the shirt from his hands, shook it out again, and then deftly pinned it on the line their father had strung along the length of the basement.

He bent down, picked up a wet bath towel, grabbed two pins from the wicker basket, and then neatly pinned it on the line before grabbing another item. "It's not too cold out. Why aren't you hanging all this outside?"

Melonie's brow wrinkled. She seemed torn between accepting his help and feeling honor bound to remind him that he was a guest. After visibly weighing the pros and cons, she simply grabbed another article, this time a pair of women's underwear, and pinned it on the line. "Mamm prefers the clothes down here. She says it's easier on her back."

"Interesting."

She laughed softly. "Obviously you've never carried an armful of wet towels and sheets up those stairs."

"You're right. I haven't." He reached for a pillowcase.

Melonie picked up a dress and smoothed the damp fabric before moving down the line. "Who does your laundry now? Do you send it out?"

"No. I do my own."

"Truly? Where do you pin—oh, wait. You have a clothes dryer."

He winked at her. "I do."

"That must be nice."

"If you ever want to, you can bring some laundry over to my house. It wouldn't be a problem."

She looked shocked. "Mamm would never allow that."

"Maybe she wouldn't need to know about it."

"Seth, don't tease."

He chuckled. "Come on, Mel. It's a load of laundry. Nothing scandalous."

"It depends on your definition of scandalous."

"True, that."

They continued pinning the last of the laundry. Then he stood to one side as Melonie returned the small basket of clothespins to the proper spot and straightened the rest of the area. Only then did she ask the question that had no doubt been burning in her mind for the last fifteen minutes.

"Seth, why did you really come over today?"

"I wanted to talk to you about Lott Hostetler."

She sighed. "Do we have to?"

"I'm not going to make you do anything you don't want to do, but I'd appreciate it if you'd give me some of your time."

"And listen to a lecture?"

"No." When her eyes widened at his sharp tone, he said, "I'm not Daed, Mel. I'm not going to order you around, and even if I did, I wouldn't expect you to do what I want. But I do care about you."

"And you care so much that you need to talk to me about Lott."

"Yes."

Staring at him intently, she came to a decision. "All right. Fine. But not here in the basement."

"Where would you like to go? Want to go for a drive with me? We could go get an ice cream or a coffee."

"Mamm and Daed wouldn't like me going off with you. But maybe we could just go sit in your truck?"

Any other time, he would've teased her. The notion of simply sitting in a parked truck was a little laughable. But he could see her point. There was no reason for Melonie to make things worse between her and their parents. It was a blessing that they still allowed him inside the house from time to time. "That's a good idea. Come on, then."

Ten minutes later, Seth was wishing that he'd thought things through a bit more before speaking with his sister. She had taken umbrage and was now wearing a mutinous expression and had her arms folded over her chest. It was tempting to simply help her out of his vehicle and be on his way, but he didn't do it. He wanted to do the right thing by her, and that meant talking about hard things.

"Melonie, you've got to know that I'm right about Lott. A relationship with him isn't going to make your life easier."

"It already isn't easy."

Her frank statement took him by surprise, but he reckoned she wasn't wrong. "I suppose it isn't."

"You suppose?" Her eyes flashed. "You left me and went to prison, Seth."

"Not by choice! Believe me, I would rather have been anywhere else."

"It was your choice to fight Peter."

"What would you rather have had me do? Pretend he wasn't about to force Bethanne to the ground?" Only because she was innocent did he leave out exactly what would have happened to Bethanne.

She inhaled sharply. "Of course not."

"Then what?"

"I don't know," she said in a small voice.

"Melonie, you know his death was an accident. But surely you also realize that if I hadn't been there, Bethanne could've been really hurt."

"I know that. I just wish Peter hadn't died and you hadn't gone to prison."

She wasn't the only one. "I do too. But I'll tell you something. I had a lot of time to think about my actions when I was sitting in a jail cell. I was wrong to fight, but I wasn't wrong to get involved. I don't regret a thing." He turned so he could face her fully. "I'm not saying that Lott is bad for you, Melonie, but he has some growing up to do. He's a bit wild right now."

"You don't know him. There's a lot of good things about Lott."

"You sound so sure."

"I am." She tugged his sleeve. "Please try to get to know him. Now that he's at Porter Construction Company, you'll have a chance, yes?"

"Yes." Though as a brand-new apprentice, Lott wasn't likely to cross his path often.

"Please?"

Looking into his sister's eyes—carbon copies of his own—Seth felt his heart melt. He couldn't deny that she had a point. Plus, it was her life and she had every right to make her own choices and even her own mistakes. "All right."

She smiled brightly. "Danke, Bruder."

"You're welcome." He hopped out of his side, walked to hers, and opened the passenger door. Then he swung her out, thinking that she was just a little thing. Adorable. He really hoped Lott didn't break her heart. Pressing a kiss to her brow, he said, "I'll try to see you soon."

"I'll visit you too. I love you, Seth."

"I love you back. Be good."

Instead of replying, she giggled and walked toward the house.

The girl was maddening. For the first time ever, he understood why their parents had given him so many chores. It had been an attempt to keep him out of trouble.

Unfortunately, trouble had still found him.

He hoped the same thing wouldn't happen to Melonie.

9

Melonie Zimmerman was disappointed in herself. It wasn't a good feeling and she wasn't proud about it either. Especially since this sense of regret was kind of a new thing. Until fairly recently, she'd tried hard to be as close to perfect as she could get. It had been a foolish goal, of course. No one was perfect.

But now she realized that she'd also been very misguided.

Maybe that was a gradual development, or maybe the good Lord had decided to let her know that it was time she became a better person. Whatever the reason, she knew she needed to start doing things differently, even if changing meant that everyone else was going to be caught off guard. And, perhaps, be disappointed.

The fact was, she'd never done enough to try to get her parents to think more highly of Seth. She could blame it on her age, or that she'd been happy to be the "good" child. She loved her mother and father, but they had expectations. Sometimes unrealistic ones. When Seth was in prison, it had been so easy to let him take the brunt of their parents' disappointment. For a while, it had even been a relief.

But now that she'd looked at her actions, she decided that taking the path of least resistance wasn't good. So she determined to make a change. She was going to put on her boots, walk out the front door, and upset a great many people. Maybe she should care about that, she didn't know.

All she did care about was that it was time to put her brother first. Past time, as far as she was concerned. She wasn't going to stop herself no matter the consequences.

She was also going to put her future first . . . and that meant her relationship with Lott Hostetler. He was important to her. She knew their relationship was something special. She needed to have enough faith in herself and in Lott to push aside everyone's misgivings about him and let Lott know that she was on his side.

Yes. She really needed to do all of that.

"Melonie, have you left for the market yet?" Mamm called out.

Startled, she looked around her. She was standing in the parlor, staring out the window. Daydreaming about being brave one day.

"Melonie, did you hear me?"

"Jah, Mamm!"

"Well, then, answer me, child."

"All right. I haven't left for the market yet." Obviously. "I'm about to, though." She glanced at the coatrack next to the door. Did she need a shawl? Or maybe she should go to her room and pull on her favorite navy blue cardigan?

"Why haven't you gone? Do you need money?"

Ack. Her mother's tone was sour now. Bordering on irritated. "Nee. I have some money."

"Oh?" Her mother walked down the hall, glanced in through the doorway of the parlor. "Why are you in here?"

"I like this room. I decided I'm tired of only sitting here when we have company. And don't tell me I shouldn't be in here." Inwardly, she winced. She could practically hear her conscience remind her that she'd just decided to be a better person.

Her mother folded her arms across her chest. "I wasn't going to chastise you for being in the parlor. I wanted to know where you got your grocery money from."

"Oh."

Mamm tapped her foot. "Melonie, where did you get it?"

Her parents liked to pretend that Seth didn't leave money in an envelope under their welcome mat once a month. She used to help them do that, but now she almost got an awful sort of rush knowing that it made her mother uncomfortable by bringing it up. Once again, shame coursed through her. She really did need to be better.

"Seth brought money when he came over yesterday." And yes, she could've told her mother how much he'd brought, but some twisted part of her wanted to make Mamm ask. Just like she wanted to ask Mamm if one day she was going to acknowledge that the cash had come from her other child—and that she should thank him.

"I see." She gripped the casing around the doorway. "How was your conversation with him? Did it go well?"

"It did." It went as well as it could, considering he had been trying to dissuade her from seeing Lott. "Did you and Daed spend much time with him this time?"

Her mother inhaled. "Melonie, I think you should watch your tongue."

"I would, if I understood why you are so distant from your son."

"You know why. We love Seth, but he's not Amish and

77

likely never will be. You know. It's hard to find the right balance for our new relationship."

That statement said everything, Melonie reckoned. Her parents were giving the community a say in how they treated their son. "I'm surprised you find it difficult. You and Daed seem to accept his money without a problem."

Her mother's expression pinched. "That is enough, Melonie."

"Mamm, you know I love you and Daed, but I love Seth too. He is such a good man and he cares about all of us. I want you to accept that."

"I love him too. But a lot of our relationships are out of our control, Daughter. He was never baptized and has strayed too far from our beliefs."

"He is still my brother and your son. I think you should be more accepting of him and his choices."

Mamm's face paled. "It's not as easy as you make it sound, Melonie."

"Mother, you don't really believe that practically ignoring Seth is right, do you?"

"It doesn't matter what I think. It's our way."

Melonie heard the tremble in her voice. Even though her mother was saying the words, she clearly didn't believe them. And although it was tempting to argue with Mamm about that, she didn't. She needed to concentrate on herself first. "Fine." She bent down, straightened the lace on her boot, and then picked up her shawl and headed toward the door. "I'm leaving. I'll be back in a while."

"It might rain. Hurry now, and come home as soon as you do the shopping."

It was half past three. They wouldn't eat until six or half

past the hour. Not until her chores were done for the day. "I'm going to stop by the library or to see Jo."

"One or the other?"

"Jah, or both. Jo might want to go to the library with me." The lies were coming far too quickly.

"But the rain—"

"Won't make me melt. I'll be fine, Mamm." As long as she left the haus and got some space, she would. She needed to get out or before long she wouldn't want to come back.

As if her mother could read her mind, she stood up a little bit straighter. "I'll see you in a while, then. Don't tarry too long."

"I won't." She could practically feel the word *LIAR* being etched on her forehead.

Wrapping the shawl around her shoulders, Melonie escaped at last.

Each step brought her closer to freedom. Maybe not literally, but in her mind. They lived in a small haus on the edge of the Amish community. It was one of the closest to Marion, which was helpful for her father, since he worked for the Jensens. The Englishers were good people, if not very smart when it came to either farming or raising horses. However, they insisted on trying to do a bit of both—which was why they'd hired her father soon after Seth was sentenced to prison and her mother had hung her head in shame.

God had known what he was doing, though, because the job suited her father like a well-worn glove. To everyone's surprise, Wayne Zimmerman had a wealth of patience for Carter and Emory Jensen. He liked their horses, and liked how Carter enjoyed learning from him but lost interest after a few hours, so her daed got to spend the rest of his days either tending to the large garden or exercising the horses and whatever livestock Carter had at the moment.

Melonie knew Daed liked coming home afterward with cash in his pocket and no worries about how to pay the bills for the five horses, three lambs, and all the equipment for the garden. Though they still counted on Seth to pay for things like food.

Pushing away all the thoughts about money and how it came to be in her possession, she darted across a vacant field, sidestepping a pile of old tires nestled in weeds, turned right near an abandoned single-wide trailer, and then at last came to an abandoned barn.

To be fair, calling it a barn was a bit of a stretch. It was about the size of a car, surrounded by weeds, and had a number of boards missing from the siding.

It was the perfect place to meet in secret.

"I'm here," she called out.

Everything remained still.

Her heart beat faster as she listened for a sign that she wasn't alone.

"Finally," Lott whispered.

Her heart felt like it had just stopped. "You scared me!" He must have been hiding in the thicket of bushes just beyond them.

"Sorry, but the temptation is hard to ignore. You're always afraid that someone else will be here."

"It's to be expected. We canna be the only people who come here."

"I think we are, though. I thought you'd never get here. And why are you laughing?"

As always, his dark blond hair was covered by a dark gray

knit hat. His eyes were almost the same color and as piercing as ever. He was wearing a dark shirt and pants too.

All the girls in their school had long ago decided that he was the most handsome and most dangerous-looking boy they knew. Melonie wasn't sure if that was the case anymore. After all, her brother, with his scars and tattoos, looked far more scary. But Lott was a close second. Especially since he sometimes acted as if he didn't have a thing to lose.

"I'm laughing because you wanted to make sure it was me, even though you say no other boy comes calling."

"You never know."

Stepping closer, Lott looked her over from head to toe. His gaze, so slow and thorough, felt like a caress. It made her feel self-conscious but so many other things too. Mature and pretty. Worthy and special. All wrapped up in a neatly tied bow of guilt. Neither her parents nor Seth were going to like that she was meeting him in secret.

She could handle her parents' disappointment. After all, they always seemed to be disappointed in her for one reason or another. But upsetting Seth was another thing entirely. She didn't want to hurt him in any way. He did so much for them. It wasn't right that she didn't seem to mind disappointing him.

"Hey, what's wrong? You're frowning."

"Nothing. I was just thinking about something."

He leaned down and kissed her cheek. "Don't think about it, then," he whispered in her ear. "We only have a few minutes together."

"You don't want me to think about anything else but you?" she teased. Inside, she was melting, though.

"That's right. I want you all to myself. Even your thoughts." He grinned.

She knew he was joking. How could he not be? But there was a part of her that felt a little bit apprehensive. Was it normal for a man to be so in love with her that he wanted all of her to be focused on him? Even her thoughts?

Deciding to think about that later, she lowered herself onto an old barrel. "Tell me about your day. How was work?"

He sat down beside her and shrugged. "It was all right."

"You don't like it?"

"I like it fine."

"Lott. Talk to me."

"I don't know." He stared straight ahead as if visualizing his workplace. "Since I'm a brand-new apprentice, I have to do everything no one else wants to do."

"Like what?"

"Errands. Pick up trash. Sweep floors." He rolled his eyes. "I do the same things every day. It's so boring."

"What do you wish you were doing?"

"I want to do real woodworking like your brother does. Or have a cool job like your father's."

"Work for rich and clueless Englishers?" She knew the Jensens were more than that, but there were times when that description fit them best.

"Carter and Emory are rich, but they're good people. I think it's gut that they know to hire your daed to take care of their things." Lott studied her expression. "What does your father think? Does he not like that job?"

"He likes it a lot. I'm sorry. I didn't mean to put the Jensens down. Daed has told me more than once that he wished more gentleman farmers cared enough about their land and stock to hire someone who knew what they were doing to take care of them. Plus, they care about our family and always ask about us. They've given my father nice bonuses too."

Considering all she'd just shared, she added, "And now I reckon that I've made them sound like saints." She slumped a bit.

Lott sighed. "Melonie, I'm the one who should apologize to you. I'm in a bad mood because I want to be happier. I want to have a job I love. I want to be making enough money to propose and marry you and live on our own. I want things to be different. Your daed glared at me the entire time I was at your haus."

"Things will get better." She sure didn't know how, though. Seth had told her more than once that it wasn't possible to change the past and that the best thing to do was to come to terms with it and move on. Not everyone believed that, however.

"I hope things do get better." He looked at her intently. Then, after kissing her lightly on the lips, he turned away. "I'm going to go."

"Already?" They'd hardly gotten settled.

Lott looked regretful but determined. "I need to go home and shower. Plus, what did you say you were doing?"

"That I was going to the market."

"You'd better do that, then. Your mother's going to wonder what happened to you if you don't return soon."

Lott wasn't wrong. "Yeah. I guess I'd better get on my way too."

Just like they were spies in a novel, they always took care to leave separately.

Melonie half-heartedly stood up. But just as she did, a rustle came from the thick woods behind them. The hair on her arms stood up as she craned her neck to try to see where the noise had come from. "Did you hear that?" she whispered.

"Nee. It's fine, Mel. I'll watch you go. No one is there."

She watched the shrubs and bushes near her as she walked. Looking for movement. Listening for any twigs breaking.

But nothing happened.

Obviously she'd let her imagination get the best of her again. She just really needed to be careful and not get caught. She was trespassing on someone else's property and meeting Lott Hostetler, who was far from her parents' dream suitor.

She knew better, but she was between a rock and a hard place. They had no choice but to sneak around.

At least, that's what she told herself. The sad thing was that she didn't believe that lie any more than anyone else would.

10

ethanne was sitting on the front porch when Lott got home from work. Like always, his sister had a book in her hands. He'd long ago come to terms with the fact that she found comfort in a bunch of printed pages. To her, they were close to being friends.

Often when he would walk by, she barely seemed to notice if he was near. Their mother said that was rude. Lott didn't know if it was or not. Bethanne was coping the best she could. He figured coping was better than not.

Right at that moment, he was glad she was preoccupied with something. He had a lot on his mind and needed a break. All he wanted to do was take a hot shower, put on clean clothes, and sit for a spell before supper. He had to get his head wrapped around what was going on with him and Melonie.

His mind on those few moments of bliss, he started up the front porch's stairs, intending to walk right by Bethanne.

Instead, she closed her book. "Hey," she said.

It caught him off guard. Curious about what she could

want, he stopped on the second step leading up to the porch. "Hiya, Bethy. Um, how's your book?"

She shrugged. "Good enough, I guess. How are you?"

He wasn't good. That's how he was. He was sneaking around seeing Melonie and trying his best not to get in a fight with Joe Miller. But it wasn't like he could tell his sister that. She was delicate, and no one in their family ever did anything to upset her.

"I don't know," he said at last. Of course, on its heels was the knowledge that he should've lied and said he was good. If he'd done that, he could be climbing the stairs to his bedroom and she wouldn't be frowning.

"Oh no. What's wrong?"

Everything was wrong.

Why she was asking, he didn't know. Ever since the incident with Peter, the focus in their haus had shifted. Now everyone worried about Bethanne all the time. Lott didn't mind that. He never had. In the course of one evening, she'd been attacked, witnessed a man's death, and even watched her hero get taken away in handcuffs. That was enough to shake anyone up for a good long while.

But there were times when he didn't want to be singularly focused on his sister's needs. This was one of them. "Nothing's wrong," he said. "I mean, nothing that you need to worry about."

"How come?"

"Because it don't concern you." He climbed the rest of the steps. Gazed at their haus's shiny black front door. It beckoned him like a portal in a novel. If he could get through, he would be able to relax. But then the setting sun hit her reflection on the window just to the side of the door. It caught it just right, and he saw her flinch.

"I see," she said.

But that kind of wasn't true. She didn't see a thing. All she was seeing was him acting awful. Their parents would have his hide, but worse than that, he was ashamed of himself.

"I'm sorry," he said as he turned back around. "I shouldn't have spoken to you like that."

"Why? Because I'm so messed up?"

Lott was pretty sure he was gaping at her. "I didn't say that, Bethy."

Instead of looking even more flustered or retreating back into the pages of her novel, she continued to gaze at him pointedly. "Were you thinking it, though?"

"Nee." With longing, Lott glanced at the front door once again. Now he felt guilty, exhausted, and angry. It wasn't a good combination. Honestly, his mood was so sour, he wondered if it would be better if he kept walking across the porch, opened the door, and went inside. All without speaking to his sister the rest of the evening. If he avoided her, things would be better.

But what would happen then? Would she tell their parents? And if she did, how much trouble would he get in? Or would she keep her silence, ironically making things worse? How guilty would he feel then?

"Lott, I know I'm putting you on the spot, but please don't go." Bethanne rubbed her temples like she was fighting off a headache. When she looked at him again, her expression was pained but intent. "Look at me, barely giving you a choice. Now I'm the one who needs to apologize. I'm sorry for making you uncomfortable, but I'm trying to speak my mind more. But sometimes the things I think are so dark, they don't come out of my mouth in a good way."

"The same thing happens to me sometimes," he said.

"Really?" Hope shone in her eyes.

"Yeah."

"I'm kind of glad I'm not the only one." Her eyes widened as she covered her mouth with one hand. "Boy, I don't think I'm supposed to admit that."

He stepped closer. "Who says you're not? Is that what the counselor says?" She still visited with a counselor once a month.

"Nee. I guess I learned that from Mamm and Daed." She lowered her voice. "Or maybe not."

"If you learned to keep your mouth shut from them, I did too. We've been brought up to work hard and not complain."

She swallowed. "I suppose so." Looking at the empty chair next to her, she said, "Would you please sit here with me for another couple of minutes? I know you're anxious to go inside, but I've been waiting for you."

"Of course I'll stay." Everything she was saying took him by surprise. It was freaking him out. She might be his older sister, but he felt like the stronger one. After taking the seat, he leaned forward. "Bethanne, what's wrong? Tell me the whole truth."

"All right." She took a bracing breath, then blurted, "I need to find a way to see Seth Zimmerman. You're working with him at Porter Construction, right?"

"I'm working there. And Seth is too. But I'm just an apprentice and right now they're giving me stupid jobs. I have to clean and sweep a lot."

"Are you able to see Seth or not?"

"I see him from time to time, but we don't talk all that much."

"Why not? Is it because he's too busy?"

"Jah. And because Porter, my boss, said that he didn't

hire me to bother everyone. Porter Construction is a really good company, you know. They've got lots of projects they're working on, and each of those clients want things done well and completed as quickly as possible."

"Could you maybe go in a couple of minutes early or stay a couple minutes late and ask if I could see him?"

She made everything sound so easy. "Where are you planning to have this meeting? Mamm and Daed might want to know about this—they'll notice if he shows up at the haus."

"I don't want them getting in the middle of it. I thought I would go to his haus."

She couldn't be— "You can't do that."

She scowled. "You don't really think he's dangerous, do you?"

"Not really. But going to an ex-con's haus by yourself will damage your reputation." He felt like pulling his hair out. What had happened to Bethanne over the last couple of years? It was like she'd forgotten how everything functioned in the real world.

"Oh, please."

"Bethanne, you are an unmarried woman. You aren't supposed to go to any man's haus without a chaperone. It's going to cause talk."

"Oh, for Pete's sake. Do you really think I'm worried about my reputation?"

"You should be." Though, he was starting to realize that he was sounding ridiculous.

After glancing over her shoulder, she lowered her voice. "You know that a lot of people think that Seth started fighting Peter after he'd already raped me."

"No one thinks that."

"Sure they do. Everyone is sure that I'm ruined. That's why no man has come calling since it happened."

He shook his head. "You don't know that's—"

"I know, Lott."

She sounded so sarcastic, and he was starting to regret not going through their front door. "Is this another one of those times when you're wishing that you'd kept your mouth shut?"

She chuckled. "Nee, but I have a feeling this is one of those days when you wish you didn't have to talk to me."

"You're right about that." They both knew he was kidding.

"Please help me, Lott."

"Why do you need to see Seth?" he asked.

"Because I want to apologize to him."

"You already did apologize in your letter."

"He never wrote me back. I don't think it was a good enough apology."

"Bethy, that's sweet, but you don't owe anyone anything."

"That's not true. I owe Seth a conversation, you and our parents a break, and me a fresh start. It's past time."

He studied her. Something had changed. Maybe it was that she suddenly had hope, maybe it was just that she'd had enough of reliving the one night that changed everyone's life. She'd made her point. "Fine."

Her eyes brightened. "Really? You'll help me?"

"I'll ask Seth if you can see him." Thinking through it, he added, "Maybe he'll be okay with seeing you if both me and Melonie are there." He relaxed, imagining that scenario. Melonie would make things go smoothly. She had that way about her.

"I don't want Melonie to be there. Or you." She waved

a hand. "I mean, you can go with me, but I'm not going to want you to be in the same room. You'll have to wait for us someplace else."

"I'm already involved. So's Melonie." Feeling impatient, he added, "Why are you being so difficult?"

"I'm not, but I want some space when I speak to Seth."

"Listen, we also need to be there because none of us live in a vacuum, Bethy. I wasn't in the woods when Peter assaulted you, and Melonie wasn't at the party that Seth left, but we might as well have been there. Everything that happened affected us all." It had changed his life. All of their lives. He wished she would realize that.

He also wished he hadn't brought it up.

The expression on her face told him that she had been affected by his little speech. It had made her feel guilty too. Even though she had nothing to feel guilty about.

But seconds later, Bethanne pulled herself together. "All right. Fine," she said around an exhale. "When will you see Seth again?"

"Tomorrow."

"And you'll speak to him then?"

"I'll try."

"Danke."

He nodded as he went inside.

Their whole conversation had thrown him for a loop. He hoped it also wasn't going to cause a lot of trouble for everyone involved.

But how could it not?

11

Somehow, over the last three weeks, Tabitha had been opening up to Seth. It happened little by little, a mishmash of a dozen things that he'd done to set her at ease. What surprised her the most was that she didn't even realize that she was trusting him more. Maybe it wasn't even possible to pinpoint exactly what had happened. All she could put her finger on was the number of small ways that their interactions had changed.

When he came over these days, Seth no longer had to knock quietly before taking a step back so he wouldn't be too close when she peeked through the peephole or carefully opened the door. He also didn't seem to spend the first thirty seconds in her company gauging her mood so he wouldn't scare her or make her worry if she didn't seem in a particularly strong frame of mind.

Now, Tabitha simply opened her door the moment she spied him on her driveway. It was both exhilarating and slightly jarring too. She was doing things she hadn't thought possible even a few months ago.

Seth seemed grateful for her progress. She was pretty sure he overthought his actions and words whenever he was around her. He seemed to be very conscious of the fact that she was older than him and used to be his teacher. She hadn't cared about that at all. He might be younger by a few years, but Seth surpassed her in many other ways. He was strong and dependable. She hoped she would one day be like that too.

She'd also started smiling at him more and chatting too. Some might even categorize their exchanges as real conversations. Oh, not that they ever talked about anything too private. She wasn't ready for that. But they did talk about things beyond the weather now. Beyond whatever Seth had brought to her house or whatever chore he was set to get done for her. Sometimes, when she was feeling pretty brave, she even initiated the conversation. Seth seemed to like it the most when she did that.

Whenever she brought up a new topic, he'd almost smile. She really liked those almost-smiles. Because of that, they'd started discussing all sorts of things. Favorite foods. Favorite seasons of the year. And, of course, her new dog. Tabitha loved talking about Chance. She knew she was being silly, going on about how adorable and smart he was, but she couldn't help herself.

Considering she'd spent most of the last five years as a recluse, Tabitha couldn't believe that she'd talked so much to anyone. Sometimes she even had a hard time conversing with Mary, and she was her sister. But there was something about Seth that called to Tabitha and made her want to be different. Whether it was his kindness, the way he did so much for her without asking for a thing in return, or because he was having to live a very different life than he'd once imagined, she didn't know. All she was sure about was that she almost felt comfortable around Seth Zimmerman. That was enough.

No—that was a milestone.

She knew the Lord was working through both of them. He was giving them proof that there was still hope to make their lives different. That whatever unintended path they were on didn't have to be an awful one. All they had to do was trust Him for their next steps.

Today when he visited, though, Seth looked preoccupied. He'd answered her questions about the weather and his health easily enough, but he wasn't exactly concentrating on his answers. Even Chance's exuberance when he arrived didn't remove the shadows from his eyes. After dutifully petting the dog for a few moments, Seth pulled back into himself. Everything about him seemed strained.

She started to worry that he'd come over only out of duty. "You know, you don't have to stay if you have other things you need to do," she said as she gestured to the two chairs in her living room. Though the temperature wasn't too low, there was a new chill in the air. The cold air seemed to settle into her bones if she sat outside for too long.

"I don't."

"Oh. Well, all right." Glad she'd just made a fresh pot of coffee, she carried over two cups. As she placed them on the table, she glanced his way again. Seth usually had a confident, cool air about him, but it was absent today. "I just wanted you to know that I was fine."

After taking a sip of the warm brew, he set the cup on her coffee table. "I wouldn't be here if I didn't want to be," he said in a sharp tone.

She drew back. "Of course. I'm sorry to press."

He winced. "I'm the one who's sorry, Tabitha. Even

though I usually don't let things bother me, my parents have sure gotten under my skin."

She knew Wayne and Anna Zimmerman. She'd been their children's teacher, though the family belonged to a different church district than she'd attended.

Though she hadn't seen Wayne and Anna for some time, she did know they were good people. They also were private folks who believed in rules and tradition. Seth's actions—and his incarceration—had to have been devastating for them.

She was tempted to say something trite, something to show that she was sorry about whatever had happened with him and his parents, but nothing came to mind. Instead, she sipped her coffee.

Running a hand through his hair, he squinted at the horizon beyond the window. The sky was covered in clouds, and a faint sheen hung in the air, like frozen mist was stuck there and had nowhere to go. "I just wish things were different, you know?"

She knew. "Do you want to talk about it? And before you start telling me that you don't want to burden me with your problems, let me remind you that listening to a friend isn't a burden. It's a privilege."

His lips twitched. "That sounds like something a bishop would say."

"I guess. But maybe it sounds like the truth too?"

Against her will, she tensed. Then noticed that her insides were shaking a bit. Leon had done such a good job of making sure she didn't voice an opinion about anything, she still felt like she was about to feel his displeasure.

Seth's expression softened. "Listen to you, Tabitha. You've sure come a long way in a short amount of time. Now you aren't only talking to me, you're throwing out words of wisdom."

She supposed he was right. Doubt set in. "If I'm being pushy, then ignore me. I don't want to overstep."

"You aren't," Seth said quickly. "Forgive the teasing. I don't think it's possible for you to overstep, at least not as far as I'm concerned."

"All I want is for you to feel better."

"You are helping with that and more. You have a way of making all my worries fade away," he said.

Really? "How so?"

"I first started coming over here as a way to forget all my problems." Resting his palms behind his head, he kicked out a leg. "You know, I thought if I helped you for a couple of hours a week, I would find some peace inside myself."

Thinking back to all the things he'd done—the way he'd shoveled her entire driveway when they'd had an unexpected burst of October snow, dropped off fresh meat and groceries, weeded her garden in the heat, and chopped wood during the fall—Tabitha shook her head. "If you needed peace in your life, I think you could have gone a different route. You've done way too many of my chores to feel a sense of peace." Smiling at him, she added, "More likely, all you got was a backache and a lighter wallet."

"I was glad to give you a helping hand. I promise, I'm not lying. Helping you makes me feel good."

"I think that sense of peace works both ways. Helping you might make me feel good too. And since chopping wood at your house isn't an option, we'll have to settle for talking."

"Hmm."

"So, what's going on?" she asked.

Bending over toward Chance, he scratched behind the dog's ears. He shrugged. "I think my parents should be looking after my sister better."

"How old is Melonie now?"

"She's seventeen." He raised his eyebrows.

"So she isn't a child at all."

Seth frowned. "I didn't say that. I think she's close enough to being one, don't you?"

"Maybe you don't want to see her as almost an adult because she's your younger sister. Most Amish seventeen-year-olds are responsible." She shot him a meaningful glance. "They've got jobs and apprenticeships. Some women even become schoolteachers."

An awareness flared in his eyes before he tamped it down. "I know that."

Unable to stop herself, she continued. "Some women are married at seventeen, Seth. Others are being courted." When he scowled, she gentled her tone. "I know you don't want to hear it, but that's the way of our world."

"I don't have to like it. I think she's too young."

"I know."

He grunted. Almost impatiently. "Don't you wish you had waited to marry?"

"I wish I had done a lot of things differently with Leon, but I can't honestly say that things would have turned out better for me if I had been older when I married him. I really did feel like I could handle anything back then."

"That was a bad example. Sorry."

"Don't be sorry. It was a good question, and I didn't mind answering it. Now, how about I ask you a question. What's happened with Melonie that has you so spun up?"

He exhaled. "I just wish I was closer to her. I wish she

felt like she could confide in me. But every time I ask her something too personal, she shuts me down." He groaned.

"I hate to say it, but she might not be shutting you out because she doesn't trust you. I think you might be just encountering a seventeen-year-old girl."

"Seventeen-year-old girl? You're acting like that's a thing."

"Since I was once one, I'd say it is. You see, they like their privacy. Melonie might not be leaving you in the dark because of your past, Seth. It might just have to do with the fact that you're older and her brother."

He looked thoughtful. "That makes sense."

"I hope so. If that's the case, it should ease your mind. It's not personal."

"What should I do, then?"

"Listen. Continue to ask questions but maybe not get so upset when she doesn't give you answers right away."

He sighed. "And that, Tab, is why I really should learn to keep my mouth shut around you. You're full of practical advice."

"Nothing wrong with that."

"How about if I offer you some?"

Uneasiness filled her. "About?"

"About the way you still haven't ventured out much past the farm. Remember how we've talked about you being around people more often?"

She remembered, but even the idea scared her. "You know I can't. Most people don't want anything to do with me."

"Your circumstances aren't like mine. I might not have been shunned, but I did some things that many find unforgivable."

"I did too."

"A lot of people don't blame you for divorcing Leon." He tempered his voice. "I think they'd help you if you'd let them.

I know some of the people who were once your friends would want to be again. That would be a good thing."

Here was her chance. She could either half-heartedly promise to think about his words like she usually did or she could be more honest. "I'm still afraid."

"Of what?"

A new barrage of hurt feelings slammed into her heart. "You know." She could barely even say those two words.

Seth shook his head slowly. "Sorry, I don't. I don't know what happened to you. I mean, I know that husband of yours hurt you."

She flinched. She didn't want to wear her hurts on her sleeve, but he had to realize that saying Leon hurt her was like saying Seth had been in jail for a while. Both might be true, but neither descriptor did the actuality justice.

"Why are you acting like I said something wrong?"

"You didn't."

"Can't you be honest with me? You know I'm not going to judge you." Obviously frustrated, he ran a hand through his hair again. He'd taken off his coat and was wearing only a thick flannel shirt over a white undershirt. When he moved his arm, his flannel sleeve rode up, exposing part of his wrist. His left wrist, which—along with the rest of his arm—was covered in colorful tattoos.

She stared at the bright ink.

His lips pursed. "Do they bother you?"

"The tattoos? No. I was staring at them because they're so colorful."

Looking down at his arm, he said, "I reckon they are. The ones I got in prison were black. When I got out and decided to add more, I chose to add color. It's, uh, a good reminder of the fact that I'm free to do what I want now."

Free to do what I want. Wouldn't that be something?

"I wish I was brave enough to get a tattoo too."

He smirked. "Are you joking with me, Tab?"

"Kind of. I like the idea of being able to do what I want, though. It would make me brave."

"You're living on your own. You survived getting beaten bad enough to land in the hospital. You were brave enough to work with a lawyer and the cops and free yourself from that guy. If you can do all of that, you're braver than most folks."

"Thank you."

"So, what are you afraid of? If not an abusive ex-husband, what?"

"Part of it is that Leon made me afraid to leave the house."

"And the other part?"

She hesitated, then blurted, "I'm afraid of facing everyone."

"No one is going to hurt you, Tab."

"Maybe not with their hands."

"Most won't even try to hurt you with words. But you'll never know if you don't give people a chance to prove you wrong."

"Maybe I'm judging them some too," she whispered.

"So you blame everyone for . . . what?"

"For pretending that my brokenness was none of their business. Everyone acted as if they couldn't see what was happening to me, but they did."

Awareness came to his eyes. "And no one helped."

"No one helped and I couldn't leave. I had nothing. Until I almost died."

"I'm sorry."

She laughed bitterly. "For what? You weren't around."

"I was at first."

"Yes, but you were also just a kid." When she saw a muscle

in his jaw twitch in umbrage, she almost smiled. "I haven't forgotten that you're three years younger than me. Have you?"

"No. It doesn't matter now, though."

"I reckon not. Besides, friendship with people of all ages is a good thing."

He looked like he was about to say something but held his tongue.

Tabitha knew she shouldn't have sounded so real or so bitter. "I'm sorry," she said. Just as her phone rang.

She'd never been so happy to hear a telephone ring. "I better get that." She got up and rushed into the kitchen.

. . . .

In the open doorway, Seth watched Tabitha pick up the cell phone from the table and hold it to her ear. He couldn't help but smile at her tentativeness. Clearly, she didn't talk on the phone very often. Maybe next to never.

"Hello?" she said, her voice carrying down the hall. "Yes. I'm Tabitha Yoder."

Realizing that he should give her more privacy, Seth backed up. But just as he was about to turn around, Tabitha froze, then with a stricken expression, pressed a hand to the wall. He changed course and strode forward.

No longer caring about her privacy, he rushed to her side. "Tab," he whispered.

Tabitha's eyes lifted to his. Her face was pale, and she had the phone in a death grip.

Seth had the urge to remove it from her hand and talk to whoever was on the other end himself. Then he'd tell her what she needed to know. He was eager to do anything to make her life easier. No, shield her as much as he could.

Shield her and maybe take her into his arms.

But of course that wouldn't be right. So he didn't touch her, though he remained where he was. He turned away slightly so not to stare at her. A small attempt to respect her privacy while still reminding her that she wasn't alone.

Tabitha didn't move away from him. Not an inch.

The call continued. Every minute or so she would whisper "okay." After the third or fourth utterance, her voice sounded thick with emotion.

Unable to stop himself, he turned back to her. Their eyes met, and Tabitha's expression was so filled with pain that he knew he had to touch her. He finally gave in to temptation and reached for the hand she had braced against the wall. She flinched but then curved her fingers around his.

While she continued to listen, looking more stricken with each passing minute, he pulled over one of her kitchen chairs and made her sit down. Then he brought over another, sat down, and took her hand again. Even though he would have rather been holding her in his arms, he was thankful she accepted him this much.

At last she exhaled, a ragged release of breath that sounded rattly and exhausted. Chance padded over and lay down near her feet.

"Jah. I mean, thank you, Mia," Tabitha said at long last. "Goodbye."

She seemed to be in shock. When Seth took the phone from her and pressed the icon to end the call, she didn't seem to notice.

"Tabitha?"

"Hmm?"

"Do you still need your phone?"

No answer. Almost as if she hadn't heard him.

"Tab, is there anyone you'd like to call right now? You know, anyone you'd like to have by your side?" He wasn't going to let himself believe he was the one she needed.

His questions seemed to finally wake her up. "Hmm? Oh, nee. There's no one."

Still concerned, Seth returned to the living room and came back with her coffee cup, then refilled it and placed it in her hands. "Here, Tab. Want a sip? It's hot."

"Danke." She dutifully sipped before handing it back to him.

After another minute passed, Seth knelt in front of her and took her hands. "Tabitha, who was on the phone? What happened?"

"That was Mia."

"Who is she?"

"My lawyer."

"What did she want?" A handful of reasons for her lawyer to be calling entered his mind. Not a one of them was good.

Tabitha stared down at their joined hands. "She . . . she called to say that Leon had been picked up for aggravated assault near Bowling Green but was released because the victim was unreliable." She pursed her lips.

"What does this have to do with you?"

"Oh. They believe he could be in Crittenden County now. And, ah, even though I have a restraining order against him, no one believes that will do much good."

Seth was usually pretty good at reading between the lines, but he felt like he was missing something. Maybe a lot of somethings. "Do much good against what?"

"When he was arrested for beating me and killing our baby, Leon promised that I'd regret pressing charges," she explained. "When the divorce was finalized and I was awarded this house, he was very upset. He threatened me."

"How?"

"He said he was going to kill me." She swallowed hard. "Leon said the next time he saw me, he would beat me so bad that I'd never survive."

Seth felt as if the bottom had just dropped out of his life.

12

How long had it been since she'd felt so helpless? Two years? Three?

Yesterday?

Tabitha wasn't completely sure. Nor was she even sure why she was asking herself such things. The amount of time that had passed didn't matter. All she knew for certain was that her head was buzzing, her mind was racing, and she felt more vulnerable than when she'd woken up that morning.

That said a lot.

"I . . . I . . ."

Seth was on his feet, looking panicked. "I don't know how to help you, Tabitha. Do you want a glass of water or maybe some hot chocolate?" He paused, obviously wracking his brain. "Do you want me to call the sheriff for you? I could ask him to stop by."

For some reason, his panic seemed to set her mind at ease. She couldn't help but smile at his barrage of questions. "Hot chocolate?"

Looking embarrassed, he ran his fingers through his hair. "I know. You've got a cup of coffee sitting there right in front of you. I mentioned hot chocolate because that's what used to help my sister when she was small. Then I, uh, recalled that she's not a child anymore and neither are you."

"No, I'm not. I haven't been a child for a long time." What she was really thinking about was that no one had been so anxious to soothe her for a long time. But how did one mention that?

Pulling herself out of her fog, Tabitha stood up. "Thank you for offering to call the sheriff, but there's no need. Mia already called him."

The concern in Seth's eyes didn't ease. "Is he going to do anything?"

"I don't know. Mia sounded calm but not especially hopeful."

"Really?"

"She thinks Sheriff Johnson will probably stop by, but it might just be a courtesy call."

Seth frowned. "Why only that?"

She shrugged, hoping she looked more self-assured than she felt. "There's not much he can do, right? It's not like the sheriff or one of his deputies can guard me 24/7. I'm on my own."

"I hate that you're okay with that." After looking at her more closely, his voice softened. "Wait a minute. You aren't okay, are you?"

"I don't know. Maybe. Maybe not?" Her mind was buzzing so much, she wasn't sure of anything. "I'm still trying to come to terms with the news. I think I was happy to pretend that I'd never see Leon again. It's been so long since he was released from jail."

"Where has he been?"

She waved a hand. "I don't know all the details—only

what Mia has told me. But after serving three years, he had to live in a halfway house for almost a year. Then, I believe, he had to stay near his parole officer and attend some anger management classes."

Seth's expression remained neutral. "And then?"

"And then, um . . . well, I believe he was allowed more freedom because he had a job and had done all the things he'd been asked to do." She looked at Seth curiously. "Isn't that what happens?"

"Jah. More or less."

"Well, then." She swallowed. "Anyway, supposedly Leon stayed on the straight and narrow for a time but then, ah . . ."

"He went back to intimidating and abusing women."

"Yes." She supposed she should say more but didn't feel up to it. Even after all this time, Leon's cruelty toward her still felt fresh.

"You really think he's going to come here?"

She hoped not, but . . . "Mia seems to think it's a possibility."

"She might not know. She's only guessing, right?"

"She believed in me when no one else did, Seth. I trust her instincts."

"I hope one day you'll trust mine too." His voice gentled. "But I can't help you if I don't know what you need."

Seth's words were kind and his tone tender. If she was still a young girl and hadn't watched so many of her dreams shatter, Tabitha might've even believed him. But she knew what the real world was like, and it wasn't always rosy or fair.

Choosing her words with care, she said, "I've learned over time that hoping for things that are next to impossible doesn't do me any good. I'll be all right." Or . . . she wouldn't. All she could do was hope that Leon would have forgotten his vow or that he was so reluctant to get picked up again that he was going to honor the restraining order in place.

"Hey, you're not alone," he murmured.

"I know." She meant it too. His words were kind. But what did they even mean? She and Seth were not close friends. They sure weren't anything close to being a couple. She didn't even know if he cared about her in a romantic way. It wasn't like they had ever discussed their feelings for each other.

Seth didn't seem relieved by her easy acceptance, however. "I mean it, Tabitha. I'm not going to take off and start pretending that everything is the same as it ever was when it's not."

"I know it isn't."

"Then you agree with me?" His expression eased, like he was delighted to have gotten his way.

"I don't know what you're expecting me to agree to." Figuring she had nothing to lose, she studied his face. "Seth, I'm sorry, but I don't understand why you even care."

"Tabitha, come on."

"I'm serious." When he continued to look at her incredulously, she went on, pulling back on all her insecurities and shields. "There's nothing between us. Nothing beyond the fact that I used to be your teacher."

"You know there is more between us, Tabitha," he said in a tone that finally settled her mind and caught her complete attention. "I couldn't care less that you used to be my teacher. That has nothing to do with my offer."

She wanted to believe him. She really did. But everything she was thinking about seemed so fanciful and outlandish. "You still aren't telling me why."

He looked like he had to think about that for a few seconds. Formulate a suitable reply. "Isn't our friendship enough?"

"No. I refuse to believe that you go around offering to help women in need around Crittenden County in your spare time."

"Good. Because I don't."

She raised an eyebrow. "Then . . ."

He groaned under his breath. "You're going to make me say it, aren't you?"

She didn't know what he was withholding from her, but she nodded. "I'm sorry, Seth. I don't want to make you mad at me, but I canna read your mind."

"I care about you." The four words were stark and seemed to be pulled from somewhere deep inside of him. Reluctantly.

Tabitha inhaled sharply.

"Nee. Don't look nervous. Don't look afraid of me. Or of what I want. I would never hurt you. I would never."

"I know that. But, Seth, are you saying that—"

"Yes." Even though she was near tears and he looked helpless and frustrated, there was something about the way he'd said it that made them both smile. "Tabitha Yoder, here's what you've needed to hear but I never wanted to say. I've had a crush on you since I sat in that fool Amish school and you walked in the first day. I thought I'd never seen a prettier woman in my life. And then when you started talking, you were so sweet. Kind. Everyone in that school thought you were special." His voice deepened. "But I used to think other things, even though I knew I shouldn't. I thought you would be perfect for me even though I was your student and you were older than me."

He looked down at his feet. "But then you married Leon and I fought with Peter Miller and ended up in prison. And now . . . now I know I'm nothing to you. I probably have no chance. But I wish I did. I want a chance with you. I'm willing to wait as long as you need me to. I'm willing to wait for weeks, months, years . . ." He held out a hand. "However long it takes for you to feel the same way. If there's even a chance for you to feel the same way."

He sucked in a breath. "But if there isn't, if you know that you deserve someone better than me, I understand. I do. But I'm still determined to help you because you matter." His eyes flashed hurt and conviction and something else she was afraid to identify. "Even if we go back to me dropping off food and chopping wood while you avoid me, the basic truth about you won't change."

"Basic truth?" She raised an eyebrow, showing him that she thought he was going a little bit over the top.

He didn't take the bait, though. "Yeah, basic truth. If you need me to be even more clear, here it is: You. Matter. To. Me," he continued, punching every word. "No matter what happens in our future, that will never change."

She hadn't known such speeches were possible. Or, if they were, that such speeches would ever be given to her. The tears that she'd been trying so hard to keep at bay released of their own accord.

Seth looked crushed. "Tabitha. I'm sorry."

"Nee." She couldn't say more because her throat was so choked up, she wasn't sure if she was going to be able to swallow, never mind speak.

"Do you want me to leave?"

She shook her head. She didn't know what she wanted except for him to stay where he was. "Stay." When he stilled, she knew she needed to give him more. Even if it embarrassed her, she needed to do this. And so she walked the three steps it took to get by his side and hugged him.

She was glad she couldn't see his face. Glad that he wasn't

saying a word. All she needed was what he gave her. He folded his arms around her, guiding her closer until her head rested on his chest. Then he exhaled, easing his stance so they moved imperceptibly together. Practically perfectly meshed.

She wrapped her arms around his waist and held on to him. Unable to help herself, all her senses came alive. She felt the solid pectoral muscles. The soft scratch of cotton against her cheek. And inhaled his scent. He was a mixture of peppermint and lime, pure Seth and soap. It was perfect, soothing her senses.

But over it all was his heat and the way he made her feel. Like she was someone worth caring about.

You matter. You matter to me. The words roared in her head. Teasing her with their meaning and tempting her to believe it too. She had no words—until she realized that she actually did have something to give to Seth. "You matter to me too," she whispered.

"Ah, Tabitha. There it is."

She released her breath. Because Seth was right. Her feelings were finally out in the open. For better or worse.

Seeming like he didn't need her to say another word, at least not for a few moments, Seth pressed his lips to the top of her head. She felt that touch all the way to her toes.

It might have been wrong, but she was never so glad that she was no longer Amish. Him pressing his lips on her kapp wouldn't have been the same.

Not even close.

13

Seth had walked almost a mile toward his house before he needed to sit down and pull himself together. He'd left Tabitha completely alone and essentially isolated.

He hadn't wanted to do that, but she'd given him no choice. His hands were tied. He hadn't wanted to abide by her wishes because he thought she was wrong. On the other hand, he also didn't want to be yet another person who ignored them. So he'd done what she asked. He'd begun to earn her trust, and that was almost as important to him as her safety.

But now, halfway between her house and his, Seth was regretting that decision. Tabitha's ex-husband could show up and do pretty much anything he wanted to her without a single person being the wiser. Until it was too late. Just like he'd done when she'd been his wife.

That didn't sit well with Seth. He'd learned a lot from the other inmates in prison. Some things they'd told him, about stealing cars or drug use, he could have done without. But there were other things the guys mentioned in passing that had stuck with him.

And that had been about security systems and cameras. He'd been in minimum security, so there was a good possibility that other men's and women's viewpoints differed, but just about every one of those men had shared that they would've never broken into a house that was obviously secured and had cameras. There were simply too many homes that didn't have anything.

The same stories had circulated about cars the guys had stolen. To his surprise, Seth had learned that lots of guys never broke into a vehicle. All they did was try the door handles until one was unlocked. Some of the cars even had keys under the mat. In the guys' minds, if a driver left a car unlocked with the keys inside it in a public parking lot, it was practically an invitation for someone to take it off their hands.

Tabitha needed a security system. Not to safeguard her valuables but to safeguard *her*. She was by far the most valuable thing on her property. The only problem was that he had no idea how to get her cameras and monitoring or who would install it. He might work in construction, but no one at Porter Construction was going to look at him real kindly if he started asking questions about installing cameras in a woman's home.

He was still stewing on that when he arrived at his house—and saw Melonie sitting on his front steps. That had never happened before.

"Mel? You okay?"

She beamed at him. "I'm so glad you're finally home. I've been waiting forever. Where did you go? You don't have any grocery bags with you."

He couldn't resist teasing her. "You think the only place I go is the grocery store?"

She looked embarrassed. "Obviously, you go to work, but I knew you weren't there."

"How come?"

"I walked down to the phone shanty and called Porter's."

"I see." He sat down next to her on the steps.

Melonie continued as if they played this game all the time. "I told myself if you didn't show up within the next hour, I was going to visit Elias."

"Elias?"

"Well, yeah. I was starting to worry about you and I figured he would help me no matter what. Where were you, anyway?"

"I could tell ya, but that would mean we'd be talking about me and not the fact that you're sitting here at my house by yourself. What's wrong?"

A myriad of expressions crossed her features before she lifted her chin. "Why would you ask me that?"

"Because you don't come over here to just say hello. You barely come over at all."

She pulled in her bottom lip and bit down. "I'm sorry. I should've been checking on you more often."

"Nothing to be sorry about. There's a lot of reasons not to be here." He leaned back, trying to be more at ease than he was. But it was hard. He'd just spent the last ninety minutes doing that very same thing. He was spent. "Talk to me, Melonie," he murmured.

"Things are really messed up at home."

"I was just there. Mamm and Daed seemed the same to me. What's going on?"

"You know. Lott Hostetler."

"What's happening now? I thought he'd started coming to the house."

"He has come by again, but Mamm and Daed barely tolerate him."

"They'll figure it out." Seth figured Lott and Melanie were going to have to figure things out too.

"Maybe. Maybe not. Even when I told them that Lott's stopped going out and causing trouble, they don't seem to feel any different." She frowned. "Maybe they're just determined not to like him dating me."

If that was the case, Seth didn't blame them. But he also knew that it didn't matter what he or their parents thought. Melonie's feelings were what was important. "Let's start with what really matters. What do you think of him?"

"Sometimes I feel like I'm about to fall in love with him . . . but other times I wonder if I only like him because he's coming around."

He had no advice to give, other than no man was ever going to be worthy of his sister. He was pretty sure she wouldn't take too kindly to him spouting that, though. "I'm sure you've had lots of boys interested in you, Mel."

"Not all that much."

"How come?" He wouldn't have pushed, but something else had to be going on. Her hands were fisted.

"You," she said at last.

"What about me?"

"You're no longer Amish. And then there's how you look." She raised her eyebrows like it might be news to him that his arms were covered in ink.

"Your beaus aren't fans of tattoos?"

She rolled her eyes. "I think it's because you look scary." She lowered her voice. "And because of what you did to Peter Miller."

Now Melonie showing up at his house made sense. She

wanted him out of her life. He was messing up her chances for a good future. That knowledge rocked him, but he held firm and tried to act like she hadn't just cut him deeply. "Ah."

"I'm sorry for bringing that up, Seth."

He studied her face. Melonie did look embarrassed. "Nothing to be sorry about." A good apology did mean something from time to time, but there was no reason for her to apologize for reminding him about his past. It wasn't like he ever forgot it anyway. "There's nothing I can do about Peter, though. We can't change the past."

"I know." She sounded miserable.

Seth didn't believe in defending himself. If he could live his life over, he would've done things differently. When he'd realized Peter had been assaulting Bethanne, he still would have stopped him, but he would've also called out for help. Maybe that would've changed things. Even better, he would've concentrated more on helping Bethanne once she'd gotten away from Peter. He should've looked after her instead of continuing to fight with Peter. That probably wouldn't have been possible, but he tried to believe it was.

Still, no matter how many times he'd prayed for it to happen, he'd never been able to go back in time. The Lord knew what He was doing too, because living with his regrets had made Seth stronger. And maybe better. This was going to break his heart, but ruining Melonie's chances for a happy life would break it even more. "All right. I'll try to keep some distance from you."

Melonie got to her feet. "Seth, nee! That isn't what I came over here to talk about."

He didn't stand up. Instead, he took a long look. Really saw her. Noticed the way her dark purple dress brought out the blue in her eyes. How she lifted her chin when she was determined to prove a point. How she looked at him intently when he talked, like she wanted to soak in every word.

Melonie was precious to him. It was time to give himself a reality check. And maybe her too. "No need to get riled up, girl. I've had a lot of time to come to terms with the consequences of my actions." He frowned, realizing he sounded a whole lot like one of those do-gooder counselors back in prison. "I mean, I get what you're saying and I understand."

"You don't get anything, you . . . you big loon."

He raised his eyebrows. "Are you calling me names now, Melonie?"

"Oh, stop. You know what I mean." She frowned. "Don't you?"

No. No, he did not. All he did know was that he was starving and mentally exhausted from difficult conversations with two different women in his life. He stood up. "Mel, I need some sustenance. Come on in the house and have a sandwich with me."

"You want to eat right now?"

"Obviously." He pulled the key from his pocket and unlocked the front door. "I'm starving."

"You know, there's no need to lock your door, Seth. This is Crittenden County, not St. Louis or Louisville."

"I happen to know that bad things can happen here too. Come on."

He left the door ajar and walked into his small one-bedroom house. It was warm thanks to the gas furnace, and that pleased him. As did the overhead lights he turned on. He might not have a big need for games on his phone or the latest TV series streaming, but he did like having light whenever he wanted it.

"Your haus is so bright," she said.

117

"I know."

"I don't know how you got used to that."

"It happened in prison. The lights are never completely off there at night, and in the morning they're almost blinding." He shrugged. "I got used to it."

"You never talk about prison."

"Not to you, I don't."

"What about to Mamm or Daed?"

He almost laughed. "You know I barely speak to them, Mel. No way am I going to start chatting with them about my life as a prison inmate."

"Do you want to tell me about your life there? I'd be happy to listen."

"Thank you, but I don't think that's a good idea." After walking into his tidy but basic kitchen, he pulled out some bread, peanut butter, and a jar of Tabitha's strawberry jam. "Want a sandwich?"

"A peanut butter and jelly sandwich? Nee."

"Open that cabinet and get out some chips for me."

She reached in and grabbed a bag of potato chips. "Here you go."

"Care for milk?"

"I'm not a child anymore. I don't want a glass of milk."

"Fine." But he saw her eyes tracking the sandwich he was making.

"Um, maybe I'll have a sandwich too, after all. If you don't mind."

"I don't mind." He waved a hand toward the pair of doors down the small hallway. "Bathroom's down there if you want to wash up."

"Danke."

When she disappeared from view, he breathed a sigh of

relief. He needed a moment to try to figure out what to say to her. And to prepare himself for what she'd come to tell him.

Then he remembered the Scripture verse from Proverbs: *Trust in the* LORD *with all your heart and lean not on your own understanding.* He figured the good Lord had a point there.

"Seth, your bathroom is so pretty," Melonie said when she returned to the kitchen.

He laughed as he carried their plates to the table. "I don't think bathrooms can be called that."

"I think they can. I like all the tile."

Two of the walls in the small bathroom were covered floor to ceiling with tiles in various shades of blue. "Thanks. A guy I met in prison learned to tile there. He gave me a deal."

She got the milk out of the refrigerator and poured two glasses. "Have Mamm and Daed seen your haus?"

"You know they haven't."

"Maybe they should," she said as she sat down.

"Let us give thanks." He bowed his head and silently prayed while she did the same. Then he asked, "So what did you want to talk to me about?"

"Do you think I like Lott so much because he's here?"

"Like, he's the best choice because you don't have a lot of other men to choose from?"

"Jah."

Chewing, he thought about that. "I'm not sure."

"That's unhelpful."

"I reckon so, but it's the truth. I haven't seen the two of you together, and I don't know what's in your heart. But I feel like I should remind you that you're still young, Mel. There's no hurry, is there?"

"I don't know."

"Mel, you're only seventeen. Trust me. There's no hurry. You don't need to rush into any relationship."

"So I should take my time with Lott?"

He nodded. "Talk to him. Ask him questions. Let him ask you things and see what he thinks about your answers. Pray about it. Talk to God about what you want." Seth felt like rolling his eyes. As far as he was concerned, he was the last person in Crittenden County who should be giving relationship advice.

"What should I do about Mamm and Daed?"

This was trickier. "Our parents are good people. They love you."

"And . . ."

"And I know you want to respect their wishes, but they're not always right." Then he thought of Tabitha and how scared she was of Leon. "And . . . they can't live your life with you. Only you will do that."

Melonie stared at him for a long moment. She took another bite of her sandwich and washed it down with a sip of milk, then finally spoke. "I like that idea."

"Good."

She held his gaze. "I want to come over more, Seth. I like it here. I like you here."

He chuckled. "Do you think I'm different here?"

"Jah. You're more relaxed. More like the Seth I remember."

"Then you better come back all the time," he teased.

She smiled. "Maybe I will."

14

After several more days had passed and a whole lot of talking had taken place, Lott finally persuaded Seth Zimmerman to meet with Bethanne. Seth made some stipulations, however. The place needed to be secluded so no one in the community would see them or eavesdrop, and Seth also didn't want to meet with Bethanne alone.

Lott had been fine with that. He wanted to accompany his sister anyway, both so Bethanne would feel secure and so he would know what she and Seth were talking about. If Bethanne went without him, chances were pretty good that she'd never relay what she and Seth discussed.

At last they'd come up with a time and a date—the afternoon of October thirtieth at a popular fishing spot near Cripple Creek. The creek had grown wide and deep in this section, and over the years folks had built campfires, moved logs around, and made an almost comfortable spot to while away a few hours.

During the summer, it was common to see a couple of cars or bicycles parked on the road nearby. In fact, Lott and his friends had gone swimming there a couple of times in July.

Now that it was almost November, though, very few people were there. The three of them would be able to converse in relative privacy, and he hoped that the quiet surroundings would encourage Bethanne to comfortably—and quickly—share whatever she wanted to say to Seth. Then they could go back home and his sister wouldn't think about either Seth or Peter's attack anymore.

That was the hope, anyway.

To Lott's surprise, their parents didn't act too shocked when Bethanne told them that she'd decided to go on a walk with him that afternoon. They'd seemed pleased. Daed had even pulled Lott aside and complimented him, saying that he was glad that Lott was finally growing up.

Lott didn't know if walking with his sister was a very grown-up thing or not, but the way his father was making a big deal out of something so little did embarrass him. Had he really been acting so immature and self-centered of late? No wonder Elias Weaver had asked Seth to speak with him.

Deciding to worry about his flaws later, he met Bethanne at the front door and they set out for the meeting. His sister seemed quieter than usual.

"Are you nervous?" he asked after they'd walked about half a mile.

"A little."

"Is it about being near the woods, or is it because of the meeting?"

"A little of both, I guess." She opened her mouth as if to say more but then closed it and sighed instead.

"Are you sure you still want to talk to Seth?" he asked. "If you don't, I can walk you back and then meet Seth and tell him you changed your mind."

She shook her head. "I don't know how Seth is going to respond, but I'm not going to change my mind."

That didn't make Lott feel any better. "Bethanne."

"Nee, don't try to convince me to change my mind, Brother. I need to do this."

"But if it's hard for you . . ."

"A lot of things are hard, but hard doesn't mean bad. Ain't so?"

"I suppose not."

They walked on in silence. While Bethanne seemed to be practicing whatever she planned to say to Seth, Lott prayed.

Gott, please give me the words my sister needs to feel better and find peace. Give Seth the patience he needs to talk with Bethanne about the past. And while You're at it, could You maybe also try to keep this visit short? If it lasts too long, I might not be able to handle it.

He didn't sense any response from the Lord, but his mind did ease a bit. Hopefully, that was the Lord's doing. He really needed His help.

When they at last arrived at their designated spot, Cripple Creek was barely running. They'd had no rain to speak of for a couple of weeks and it showed. Instead of looking vibrant and full of life, the area appeared to already be in the throes of winter. It was also chilly.

"I'm glad I wore my cloak," Bethanne said as she shivered in the cold. "It's so sunny, I almost didn't."

Lott looked around. "I wish I'd brought mine. When we were hiking the cold wasn't bad, but it's settling in now."

"I reckon so." She sat down on one of the thick logs around the firepit.

Figuring there was nothing wrong with starting a fire

there—they could sit a spell after Seth went on his way—Lott started gathering wood.

"Want some help?" she asked.

"Sure."

Bethanne walked to the edge of the woods opposite him and started picking up sticks, then carried them over and added them to the pile he'd started.

Lott had just gotten a spark out of two pieces of flint when he heard twigs snap in the distance. "Sounds like he's here."

Bethanne swallowed, suddenly looking a little sick. "Jah."

"Listen, if things get too hard, all you have to do is let me know. I'll intervene and get you out of here."

"I'll be fine."

"Or if Seth says something rude—"

"He won't, Lott. You know that."

"Jah." Seth Zimmerman wasn't perfect, but he wasn't going to intentionally hurt Bethanne.

More twigs snapped in the distance, and his sister jumped but stayed silent. He did too. She had enough to worry about without him asking her yet again if she was okay. Instead, he fussed with his project, blowing on the sparks and nursing them with oxygen until they grew into a decent fire.

Seth grinned when he appeared out of the woods. "I should've known you'd be making yourself useful, Lott. This fire was a good idea."

"Danke." Lott was just about to make a joke when he looked up and realized Seth hadn't come alone. Melonie was with him. He sprung to his feet. "Hiya, Melonie."

"Hello, Lott. I hope you don't mind, but I thought I'd come along." Her voice warmed as she got closer. "I figured Bethanne might appreciate not being the only girl here."

Looking at his sister, Melonie added, "It's good to see you. It's been too long."

"It's good to see you too." Visibly bracing herself, Bethanne walked to where Seth was standing. "Thank you for meeting with me."

"You're welcome," he said softly. "It wasn't a problem. Whatever I can do to help, I will."

Bethanne's cheeks reddened. "I didn't want a meeting so I could ask for more help."

"Understood." Seth clasped his hands behind his back.

"All I wanted was a few minutes of your time."

He nodded. "You have it."

Melonie glanced from Seth to Bethanne to Lott. "Hey, Lott. Maybe you and I could stay here by the fire while my brother and your sister talk?"

"Sure." Turning to his sister, he said, "Is that what you want, Bethy?"

She fisted her hands at her sides but then released them. "Jah."

Seth stuffed his hands in his pockets. "Let's go for a walk, then."

Bethanne nodded, looking apprehensive but determined, and they started toward a worn path alongside the creek. Seth's posture was relaxed and easy, as if he was perfectly used to escorting Amish girls in the woods. In contrast, Bethanne looked far more contained and tense. Neither was speaking, but they did stay in sight.

Lott continued to watch them, part of him wanting to join them, if for no other reason than to provide a shield for Bethanne. It would be terrible if Seth inadvertently made her cry. Then he reminded himself that she didn't need his protection. She was stronger than she looked.

"Are you all right?" Melonie asked.

"Jah." He forced himself to sit down on a log. "It's funny, Bethanne keeps to herself so much, it's hard to see her out like this."

"Out? Or walking beside my brother?"

He heard the defensiveness in her tone. "I meant doing anything by herself."

"Do you know why she wanted to speak to him?"

"Nee."

"Really?"

He shrugged. "Bethanne made it clear that what she had to speak to Seth about didn't concern me. What did Seth say?"

"He was more forthcoming, but I think that's because he was as in the dark as I was."

"Did he seem upset about this meeting?"

"About talking to Bethanne? Nee. Not upset." She bit her lip, then murmured, "Maybe more like worried about what she could want?"

"I can see that, since that's how I feel as well."

She smiled as she moved toward him. "Is it bad that I'm glad to have an opportunity to see you?"

He stood. "I hope not, because I feel the same way." After making sure their siblings were out of sight, Lott reached for her hands. She placed both of hers in his, and warmth spread through him.

Maybe he hadn't needed to build a fire after all.

15

Seth rarely worried about how other people perceived him anymore. He figured living behind bars surrounded by criminals and guards did that to a person.

When he'd returned home, he'd been ostracized. Most people in the Amish community acted as if he didn't exist, and the few who did acknowledge him did so with varying degrees of warmth. He'd pretended not to notice and lived his life, certain that God still loved him and was on his side. If someone at the market or on the street found fault with him, he shrugged off their concerns.

The only exception to this was Tabitha. She was so damaged, he didn't want to ever be the cause of more pain for her. So he was tentative around her. Hesitant. But not because he was nervous. He just wanted to set her mind at ease. To be the person she needed him to be so she could come out of her shell.

However, this walk with Bethanne Hostetler proved Tabitha wasn't the only exception. In spite of the chill in the air, his palms were sweating and he felt like he wasn't getting enough oxygen. Bethanne didn't look any more comfortable than he was.

Seth didn't know her very well, so he stayed silent. She had been the one to request the meeting, and he didn't want to start talking or asking questions before she had the chance to speak her mind.

But as their walk continued and she barely looked at him, dark thoughts slid into his head. Maybe she hadn't called the meeting at all. Maybe she'd felt pressured to speak with him, though he couldn't imagine why that would be. After another two minutes passed, he couldn't take the silence any longer.

"Did you change your mind about talking, Bethanne?" he asked.

"Oh, nee. I still want to."

"Where would you like to have this discussion, then? Do you want to keep walking or stop?" He knew it didn't matter, but he needed to take some control.

She stopped. When she glanced behind them, her eyes widened. "I wanted to get far enough away that our conversation would be private, but I didn't realize we walked so far. We can stop now."

They were on a narrow stretch of the dirt path. A patch of poison oak covered the ground just a couple of inches from his feet.

He gestured to a spot several feet ahead. "How about we go to that spot up by the rock? We could sit down."

"All right. I'll follow you."

When they reached the clearing, he sat down on the ground, more than ready to hear whatever was on her mind.

Bethanne sat down on a good-sized rock. She was a graceful thing. Back before the whole Peter Miller incident, she'd been a popular girl. All the boys had their eyes on her.

"Seth, I wanted to apologize to you again for ruining your life."

This was what she'd needed to say? "You've already apologized. Plus, that first apology was unnecessary. What happened between me and Peter had nothing to do with you."

"I disagree."

"Bethanne, you know what I mean. His death was not your fault. Not even a little bit."

"I disagree." She leaned forward slightly. "Obviously, I've had a lot of time to think about what happened. I'm embarrassed about how stupid I was."

He shook his head. "You weren't stupid."

"I left the party with Peter. No girl with good morals would have done that in the first place."

"Bethanne, a lot of couples were going into the woods. You weren't the first girl to want a few moments alone with her boyfriend."

She scowled for a second. "He wasn't my boyfriend. Not officially. We'd just been flirting."

Seth wondered why she was thinking such things. Had her parents tried to shame her? Someone else? He would never consider himself a man who conveyed his thoughts and feelings easily, but he had to show her that she needed to stop feeling so guilty—or at least try to. "What I'm trying to say is that everyone knew that you were innocent. And though you were smart, you were also sixteen. Pretty much everyone went into the woods for some privacy from time to time. But just because you did, that didn't make it right for Peter to force himself on you."

"If I had stayed with everyone else, he would still be alive."

"You don't know that. The Lord is in charge of our lives."

Looking impatient, she tugged at the side of her dress's apron. "Okay, how about this? If I had stayed with everyone else, you would not have gone to prison."

"Again, we don't know what would have happened. But it doesn't matter anyway. I did go, I'm out, and I'm fine. Stop worrying."

"But you aren't the same!" she blurted out, then clapped a hand over her mouth.

He stilled, finally understanding why she was so upset. "You're right. I'm not. But that's okay."

She shook her head. "You've been kept at an arm's distance because you went to prison, Seth. Even though I think Preacher Zachariah and Bishop Wood would welcome you if you asked to be baptized, the Millers don't want to forgive you."

That was true. "I know. They still blame me for Peter's death, and a lot of people in the community don't want to believe that it was an accident. But it was."

Her dark brown eyes glistened. "I don't know how to make your life better, Seth."

"You don't need to," he said simply. "My life is fine."

She opened her mouth, but he continued before she could speak. "Bethanne, look at me. Really look at me. What do you see?"

She stared at him for several seconds before averting her eyes. "I don't know what you expect me to see."

"I want you to see that I'm a grown man. That I have a good job. That I have a home. I want you to see that I didn't fall apart." He lowered his voice. "Do you see me? Do you see that I've gotten stronger? I'm okay, Bethanne."

"But your faith—"

"Is solid," he finished. "Yeah, I did have more than a couple of times when it wavered, but I still believe in God. I still talk to Him. My faith is stronger now too."

Her eyes went wide. "You're telling the truth?"

"I am." Leaning back on his hands, he said, "God was with me when I was in prison, Bethanne. Just like He's with us now. Even though we make mistakes and struggle and falter, He doesn't give up on us. And that's why I haven't given up either. Okay?"

"Okay."

"Gut."

"I guess we didn't need this meeting after all, did we?"

"No, I think we did," he said. "We never really talked. I avoided you because I didn't want to make you upset."

"And I avoided you because I avoid pretty much everyone . . . and I didn't want to make you upset either."

He stood up. "Maybe we can change things between us, then. Maybe the next time we see each other, we can say hi and even talk for a few minutes."

"I'd like that." She got to her feet.

"I would too. Now, how about we go back to the firepit and sit with Lott and Melonie for a few minutes. There's no telling what they've been doing all this time."

"I have a pretty good idea," she quipped.

So did he. "Me too. I think we better hurry."

They shared a smile as they hurried back.

16

A week had passed since Mia had called about Leon's release. Tabitha had spent most of each day staring out her windows while all the doors and windows were locked. She'd also clutched her cell phone, ready to dial 911 if she spied Leon in the woods.

She hadn't.

Today, she'd had enough. She took a shower and then carefully arranged her hair in a neat bun at the nape of her neck. After that, she put on a pair of jeans, a pretty tan sweater that had an intricate cable design, and tan socks and thick-soled brown loafers. Her heavy navy coat and black leather purse completed her outfit.

Peering in the mirror, Tabitha knew she looked very different from the proper Amish wife she'd once tried so hard to be. It wasn't altogether a bad thing, either. Not dressing Plain still felt strange, but she couldn't deny that she didn't miss her dresses all that much. She certainly didn't miss pinning her dress together with straight pins.

Mia had taken her out shopping for a few sets of English clothes after Tabitha's divorce was finalized. Her lawyer had been ready for her to be scared and worried about looking so different, but she hadn't been. As much as Tabitha had liked being Amish, so much of that life was twisted in her brain. Now the thought of wearing the dress and kapp only brought back bad memories because Leon had often found something wrong with her. Either the dress wasn't long enough or it was too tight. Or too loose. Or she hadn't pinned the fabric in the correct way. Or there was a smudge of dirt on one of the ties to her kapp.

In the months before Leon had beaten her the last time, her clothes had become a great source of stress. When Tabitha had woken up in the hospital, that had been one of the first things she'd thought about—what Leon was going to say if he saw her looking so unkempt. She'd been so scared, the doctor had even prescribed a mild sedative so she could get some rest.

The nurses and social worker had looked at her with pity. So had the sheriff. Sheriff Johnson had been so kind to her. He'd been the one to call Mia. Tabitha later learned that he'd also been the one to suggest Mia take Tabitha's case for free. Mia hadn't hesitated to represent her either. She'd been determined to help Tabitha get on her own two feet and living independently.

The day Mia had taken Tabitha to the mall had been filled with tears, both happy and sad. She'd been so relieved that Leon could no longer refer to her as "his"—and force her to do anything he wanted ever again. But all the changes in her life had made her sad too. She'd never yearned to be anything beyond a teacher and then a wife and mother.

While that hadn't happened, she knew God had a plan to redeem what had happened.

Trying on those jeans had felt dangerous and freeing. Now

she hardly wore them. More often than not, she put on loose slacks. But sometimes she knew she needed to remind herself that she was different. Today was one of those days.

When she got to town, Tabitha took care to avoid most of the Amish who were out. She also walked with her head down and avoided making eye contact with anyone she passed.

"Tabitha, is that you?"

She knew that voice. To a lot of people, the owner was probably someone they wanted to avoid. To her, the man would always represent everything good in the world. But it was still hard for her to speak to anyone.

"You can do this," she whispered to herself. "God obviously knew you could too. That's why He put the sheriff right here in your path."

Lifting her chin, she turned to face the man who'd saved her life. As usual, his bald head drew her attention before she focused on his kind-looking brown eyes. Other people might be taken aback by the man's size or the visible scar on his lip. Not her, though. That scar reminded her that she wasn't the only person who'd experienced pain.

Tabitha drew a deep breath. "Yes. Hello, Sheriff Johnson."

Smile lines appeared around his eyes. "I hoped it was you. I couldn't be sure, though, since you look so different than the last time we talked."

"I reckon that's true." The last time she'd seen him, he'd visited her house about a week after she'd gotten home from the safe house. She'd still been nursing two broken ribs, a black eye, and several cuts and other bruises. She'd also been about ten pounds lighter and wore a faded dress that had hung on her. Now here she was in jeans and a sweater.

"You're looking very nice today. Your new look suits you."

"Thank you." She gripped a bit of the denim that covered her legs. "I'm still getting used to wearing jeans."

"I imagine so." His voice easy, he asked, "Are you doing okay?"

She shrugged, determined to be honest.

He nodded in understanding. "I spoke to Mia." He frowned. "And the folks out in Bowling Green."

Tabitha appreciated him being so direct. "That's why I came to town. I wanted to speak to you. I mean, if I may."

"Of course. Let's go to my office."

She nodded and stayed by his side as they walked the two blocks to the sheriff's department.

"I promised Kristie I'd pick up a couple of things for supper," he said when she eyed the canvas bag half filled with groceries that he carried. "Now we just have to hope I remember to take them out of the staff refrigerator when I leave."

She chuckled. "If you forgot, that would be bad."

"It sure would, because we'd end up having sandwiches instead of tacos tonight." He winked. "A cold ham sandwich just isn't the same."

"I don't think so either."

Looking pleased that they were in agreement, Sheriff Johnson opened the door to the building and gestured for her to go first.

"Hey, Sheriff," a woman called out with a thick drawl. She was around Tabitha's age and wore about a dozen woven bracelets on both wrists. "You got a couple of messages."

Tabitha tried to remember her name. Courtney? Yes, that was it.

"Can they wait? Tabitha and I are going to visit for a spell."

She looked down at the stack of notes laid out in front of her. "Sure thing. None of these looks urgent."

"Where's Junior?"

The receptionist grinned. "He's visiting with our favorite Bigfoot tracker."

"Glad to hear it."

"I know, right?" As if she was finally placing Tabitha, Courtney gentled her voice. "Hey. How are you?"

"I'm fine, thank you. And you?"

"I can't complain." Courtney stood and wiggled her fingers. "Hand over those groceries, Billy. I'll put 'em in the fridge." The phone rang and she picked it up. "Crittenden County Sheriff's Department."

After placing the bag on the corner of Courtney's desk, Sheriff Johnson opened the door to his office. "Come on in, Tabitha. If we stay, Courtney's going to decide I need to speak to someone and you'll be waiting out here till the cows come home."

She followed Sheriff Johnson in and then took a chair in front of his desk while he closed the door and got settled. "As you can see, things are just as busy as ever around here."

"Sorry, I don't want to be rude, but . . . we've got a Bigfoot tracker?"

"It's nothing to worry about. There's a lady out in Walker Woods who's sure she's seen Bigfoot. She calls in her reports a couple of times a month." He shrugged. "She's lonely, I'm afraid. Junior and I take turns paying her a call. We listen to her report while she serves us pie."

"I see."

"It's okay if you don't," he said with a laugh. "But she's harmless. Besides, everyone needs a little bit of help sometimes, right?"

"Right." Her body relaxed a bit.

"Are you ready to talk, Tabitha?"

"Yes."

"Anything in particular worrying you?"

"I'm afraid Leon's going to show up at the house." She clenched her hands, half prepared to defend herself when he shrugged off her worry.

Sheriff Johnson didn't do that at all. Instead, he looked her in the eye. "I know you're worried. I think that's to be expected. There's nothing wrong with being concerned, either. But as soon as I heard from Mia, I double-checked the status of his restraining order. It's still in effect and it's not going anywhere."

"Do you think that will keep him away?"

"I'm not going to lie to you, Tabitha. All I can say is that I hope so." He opened a drawer, pulled out a folder, and then glanced at a sheet of paper with handwritten notes scribbled across the top half of it. "I spoke with a lieutenant over in Bowling Green. He said that Leon's case is going to go before the grand jury in a week or two. A witness has come forward."

"I don't understand why he's not in jail."

"He's got some people on his side, I guess. They put up the bail. It was a good amount, Tabitha."

"How did he get so much money?" She'd always believed the root of Leon's quick temper was his financial troubles. They hadn't much to speak of when they'd been married. At least, she hadn't believed they did.

"I asked the same thing." Glancing down at his notes again, Sheriff Johnson frowned. "The lieutenant seemed just as concerned as I was. I'm not going to be shy about asking around, though, and neither are the folks in Bowling Green." He exhaled. "But you and I know things like this take time."

She nodded slowly. "I understand."

He closed his folder, seemed to come to a decision, and walked around his desk to take the chair next to her. "Tabitha, I'm going to stop by your place as often as I can, and Deputy Ernst will too. You'll see our cars driving by several times a day."

She swallowed. "All right." When he didn't speak, merely studied her, feeling frustrated, she said, "If Leon decides to come to the house and one of you is there, he's just going to wait until you leave."

"I know." He folded his hands on his lap. "Is there someplace else you can go for a spell?"

"No."

"Are you sure? Isn't your family still in the area?"

"I see my sister Mary some, but I can't impose. She has four little boys. And her husband is nice and all, but he's wary about being around me."

"Because of the divorce."

"Jah. Roy is kind of a stickler, you see."

Sheriff Johnson frowned. "I'm afraid I don't. Roy's your brother-in-law?"

"He is, but rules are important to him. I wasn't shunned, but divorce is very frowned upon. Plus, now that some time has passed, people's memories twist and turn. They start remembering things differently."

"Even Roy."

"Jah." As difficult as it was to admit it, she forced herself to be honest. "A couple of people told me that I was being disrespectful to Leon. They've painted me to be the culprit."

Sympathy pinched his expression. "I'm sorry about that."

"I am too." She swallowed. "I think some folks feel guilty about never stepping in to help me. Maybe it's easier for them to repaint the past instead of coming to terms with their own faults?"

"If that's the case, it wouldn't be the first time that's happened. Glass houses and all that."

Tabitha wasn't sure exactly what he meant but thought she got the gist of it. "All that matters to me anymore is that I know the truth and so does God." She took a deep breath and added, "And Leon. He knows what he did, Sheriff Johnson."

"I do too, Tabitha. I won't ever forget the state I found you in. Now, would you like me to find you someplace temporary? There are some agencies that provide safe houses."

She shook her head. "I don't want to leave. If I do leave and he shows up, he's liable to try to stay."

"Deputy Ernst and I would help him move out."

"I know, but it's home now. I don't want him there at all."

He looked at her for the span of a heartbeat. "I understand," he said at last. "You might not be safe, though."

"I've also become friends with Seth Zimmerman." She didn't have to ask if he knew Seth. The answer was written all over Sheriff Johnson's face. "He's not afraid of Leon."

"No, I don't imagine he is."

Tabitha wasn't sure whether she heard a note of sarcasm in his voice or not. "I've known Seth a long time."

"Are you sure he's the best person to turn to? I fear his stint in prison changed him. A man has to become hard in order to survive behind bars."

"I don't need a friend with a spotless past, Sheriff. You might not think Seth is worthy of forgiveness, but I do."

"Tabitha, I didn't say he wasn't worthy. Actually, as much as I don't like what happened to Peter, I firmly believe that his death was an accident. Seth could've probably gotten out of serving time if he'd fought harder for himself."

"Do you think he wanted to punish himself?"

"I couldn't say. But, here's the thing, Tabitha. It's always been my belief that a person can ask others for forgiveness but the hardest person to grant absolution to is oneself."

"You're saying he hasn't forgiven himself."

"I'm saying that's my opinion. I could very well be wrong." He stood up. "Now, if there's nothing else you'd like to tell me, I should go help out Courtney and start answering all those messages. You talk to Seth and I will too. If we all work together, we'll be able to keep you safe. I'll be in touch."

"Thank you, Sheriff."

He reached out and clasped her hand with both of his. "I do think that we've got a little bit of time before Leon heads this way. He's running scared, and the folks in Bowling Green are going to be keeping a close eye on him. Maybe that will give you some comfort?"

Tabitha nodded but didn't reply. Knowing that she might have to wait even longer for Leon to show up didn't make her feel too good. Not good at all.

But there seemed to be nothing else to say.

17

"I want you to accompany Lorne to the singing tonight," Mamm announced as she entered Melonie's room. "Your poor cousin is bored stiff."

Melonie had been lying on her bed with a book in her hands. She'd also been looking out the window while wondering why she was so attracted to Lott when he was the last person in the world she should have feelings for.

Lott ran hot and cold more often than water in the kitchen sink. It was really too bad he was easy to talk to. And so handsome. No man that handsome should be so bad for her state of mind.

That's why she thought she should be forgiven for blinking at her mother's sudden intrusion.

Mamm folded her arms across her chest—a sure sign that she was unhappy. "Melonie, did you hear me?"

"Jah." With reluctance, she set her book down.

Mamm tapped her toe.

Belatedly, her mother's words registered. They didn't make sense, though.

Lorne and his parents had arrived at the haus two hours

before supper the day before. By the time their first meal together was over, she and her cousin both knew they had next to nothing in common. Melonie couldn't imagine anything worse than spending an entire evening by his side.

But she couldn't tell her mother that.

After sitting up, she straightened her kapp. "Sorry, Mamm, but I wasn't planning to go to the singing."

"It's a good thing I came in here to fetch you, then. You can change your mind."

"I don't want to change my mind."

"I think you should." Her mother took a step back and closed the bedroom door. "Since you now have a reason to go."

Even a year ago, Melonie would've caved. She was older now. Older and tired of living with the consequences of constantly being agreeable. "I don't want to go."

Her mother's eyes narrowed.

Melonie looked away but held her ground. Not only did she not want to go to yet another singing, she really didn't want to go with Lorne. Her cousin barely spoke, and when he did it was mostly judgments and gossip. She would be bored stiff. "Why are you making a big deal about this? Isn't he leaving tomorrow?"

"Not anymore." Her mother smiled like a cat with a full bowl of cream. "I've convinced Fran and her family to consider staying a few more days. I think they've just about made up their minds to do that."

"Mamm, really?" Lorne's entire family was staying in the dawdi haus, which meant that her grandparents were now sleeping in Seth's old room. They weren't happy about it, and neither was she. Worse, Lorne's family had found fault with everything about the dawdi haus. Actually, they found fault with most everything . . . and that wasn't even counting how they felt about Seth.

"You need to have a better attitude about this, Melonie. It will give you and Lorne some precious time to get to know each other."

Precious time? What in the world? Every word her mother was saying felt like the buzzing of an annoying fly. "Why do you think Lorne and me need to know each other better? I barely see him once a year. I can't remember the last time you got together with your cousin Fran."

Her mother wandered to the window and peeked out. "While it's true that our families haven't always been close, that can be changed."

"Why?" As in, why would her mother want to see them more often?

"Well, we were talking. Fran and I, that is. We believe you and Lorne would be a good match."

Match? Melonie climbed off her bed. "What are you talking about?"

"You heard me." Her mother lowered her voice. "Melonie, Lorne is in the middle of a somewhat shy and awkward phase, but he's a good man. He would make you a fair and generous husband."

"I don't want someone fair and generous. I want to fall in love, Mamm."

"Falling in love is overrated. Stability is what counts."

Stability sounded like a poor excuse for unhappiness. "I disagree."

"That's because you don't know any different. When you are in an easy, stable relationship, the value will shine through. You need to give Lorne a chance."

Her mother had lost her mind. "Mother, you canna be

serious." When her mamm just stared, Melonie waved a hand. "He's my cousin!" Wasn't that illegal or something?

After glancing at the door to make sure it was closed, her mother inched forward. "Keep your voice down and stop acting so shocked. Lorne is your second cousin."

"Same difference."

"I disagree. There's nothing wrong with second cousins marrying." She propped her hands on her hips. "It happens all the time."

"No, it doesn't. And even if it did, there are a lot of things wrong with this scheme of yours. First of all, he's my cousin, so *eww*. Second, we don't know each other. We're practically strangers." Before her mother could speak, she added, "Third, what I do know of him isn't good. Lorne and I have nothing in common."

"You two could, if you gave him a chance."

"We won't, because he's boring."

"Melonie, you shouldn't say such things." Mamm sounded so disappointed in her.

She reckoned her mother was right. She should be ashamed for sounding so heartless. But what could she do? Sometimes only plain speaking got one's point across. And she really needed to get her point across. Loud and clear. "Mother, this matchmaking serves no purpose anyway because . . . because I have my eye on someone else."

A muscle in her mother's cheek jumped. "If you are referring to Lott Hostetler, we both know that you could do better."

"I'm not sure about that." At least she wasn't related to Lott.

Mamm shook her head. "Your father and I think you need someone older. Studious. More mature."

"I disagree. I . . . I think I'm in love with him."

Her mother inhaled sharply, then quickly tried to gather her bearings. "You don't know the first thing about love or relationships."

"I do."

"I don't see how. Of course you have your father and me as role models, but your brother doesn't have anyone."

"There's a whole lot more people in our community besides just our family, Mamm. Besides, Seth does have someone. He's seeing Tabitha Yoder," she blurted.

Then of course wished she could take her words right back.

Mamm looked scandalized. "Surely not."

Shame poured through Melonie like black paint. She felt dirty and stained. What was wrong with her? Why did she need to defend herself so much that she'd willingly share Seth's personal life? "Never mind. Forget I said anything."

"That woman is older than him. Plus, she's *divorced*." Her mother said *divorced* like it was a curse word.

"Mother, even I know what happened to poor Tabitha. How can you blame her for not wanting to get beaten?"

"None of us know what really happened." She pursed her lips. "Why do you think Seth is interested in her? Do you think he doesn't feel worthy of another woman's love?"

There were so many things wrong with her mother's questions, starting and ending with how an upstanding woman like Tabitha wasn't good enough for Seth. "Mother, you might not believe in divorce, but you canna say that Tabitha is a bad person."

Mamm stilled. "I didn't say she was. I just think there would be a better match for your brother."

Her brother, the ex-Amish ex-con. Before her mother

could start down another conversational path where all things Seth and poor Tabitha were dissected, Melonie decided to end the conversation, fast. Unfortunately, there was only one way to do that. "Mamm, I'll take Lorne to the singing tonight. Tell him we'll go right after supper."

Her mother's eyes lit with pleasure that she'd gotten her way. "Wear one of your new dresses, Daughter."

"Fine, but I'm going to have a cloak on, Mamm. No one will see it."

"Lorne will," she said and opened the door. "That's all that matters, ain't so?"

Melonie got up and closed it again, then threw herself on the bed. Thinking of one of the books she'd recently read, she decided her mother could've been a sought-after interrogator in another life. She was that good at gleaning information . . . and getting her way.

Melonie sighed. She couldn't believe she'd said so much instead of keeping her mouth shut. And then she'd even agreed to put on a new dress and accompany her cousin to a singing. What was wrong with her?

Just when she thought her life couldn't get more confusing, it did. "Why, *Gott*?" she murmured as she hugged her pillow tight. "What do You need me to learn?"

She had an idea His answer would be that she still needed to learn quite a bit.

• • • •

Three hours later, Melonie was walking next to Lorne down one of the winding shortcuts to the Bylers' farm. Overgrown plants and foliage brushed against their clothes, and damp leaves squished under their feet. When a squirrel chattered just to their right, she jumped.

Lorne looked just as appalled as she was about their evening's activities. With a grimace, he smacked his hand against his cheek. "I think something just bit me."

"It could be a mosquito."

"Great."

Sneaking a glance at him, Melonie tried to figure out if he actually was better looking than she'd thought. He was kind of overweight, had pale brown hair and a smattering of spots on his face, and his eyes were set close together. But worse, he always looked like he'd just smelled something bad.

She'd never liked him much, even when they were small. Even Seth, who'd always been a person to go out of his way to befriend someone in need, always ignored him.

Melonie had no idea who she could introduce him to at the singing. Not only would most of the people there be coupled up, most of the girls wouldn't be attracted to Lorne. Worse, she was pretty sure the men she knew would be bored with her cousin in five minutes. Worse yet, she'd probably have to spend most of her time making sure no one teased him too much.

"Where is this haus?" he asked. "We've already been walking fifteen minutes."

"The Bylers' place is another ten or fifteen minutes away."

"You said this was a shortcut."

"It is."

He sighed, like it was her fault they were walking in the middle of Kentucky. "What are the Bylers like? Are they good people?"

She shrugged. "I don't know. I was close friends with Hannah Byler when I was in school."

"But not anymore?"

"We're friendly but don't see each other much. Hannah is a nanny for a Mennonite family on the other side of Marion."

"I hope she isn't expected to walk there."

Melonie wasn't sure if Lorne was joking or complaining. Not that it mattered. "I believe they pick her up and take her home whenever she works. She's a nice girl."

"I hope so."

What did that mean? "We can stay as long or as short a time as you'd like."

"I'll let you know what I want to do."

"Sounds good." It was hard not to roll her eyes.

He cast another dark look her way. "You know, doing this together wasn't my idea. It was our mothers'."

"I know. I guess we'll both have to get through the rest of the visit as best we can."

"I didn't mind. At least I got to come here. I'm looking for a spouse, you know."

His phrasing set her off, but she wasn't exactly sure what didn't sit well with her. Was it the term *spouse*? Or was it that he was looking for a wife instead of hoping to fall in love? She didn't know what to say to that, so she merely stuffed her hands in her cloak and started praying that the Bylers' haus would suddenly appear over the next ridge.

"I have no interest in you. I hope you know that."

She looked up at him. "I do now." She smiled, hoping he understood that this was a good thing. Only proper manners prevented her from telling Lorne exactly what she thought of him.

His lips didn't curve even a millimeter. "My parents are too polite to mention your brother, but he has tainted your reputation."

"Are you serious?" She couldn't believe he had the nerve to talk bad about Seth.

"To be sure. He's a murderer."

"Seth is not. The man he was fighting fell and hit his head on a rock. The death was an accident."

"Obviously the police and the judge thought differently."

"You have no idea what you're talking about."

"I have a better idea than you do." He scoffed. "Do you really imagine that any man of good standing would want anything to do with you now?"

Lott did. She held on to that feeling while cautioning herself to choose her words carefully. "Lorne, I think we should turn around and go home."

"No way. If we return right now, I'm going to be forced to sit in your family's living room and play cards."

At last—or maybe unfortunately—the Bylers' haus was up ahead. In the yard were a bonfire, some tiki torches, and a good-sized gathering. At least thirty people, most everyone holding a can of soda. The Bylers had gone all out. A long table with a tablecloth on it held an array of food.

Lorne straightened up and squared his shoulders—like he was anxious to charge in and meet girls.

"You better not embarrass me," she warned.

"The only thing that will be embarrassing is having to admit to people that we're related. Hopefully no one will hold that against me." Looking her over, he said, "After all, one can't help who one is related to."

"I was just thinking that very same thing," she said, her voice full of sarcasm.

But of course Lorne didn't catch it. He was already scanning the crowd.

Her footsteps slowed as she noticed several people turn her

way but not acknowledge her. Had Lorne been right? Were people polite to her face but actually didn't want anything to do with her?

She felt her cheeks heat.

"Mel, what's wrong?"

A warm, tingly feeling swelled in her stomach. She would know that low drawl anywhere. Anticipation made her turn on her heel. "Lott! What are you doing here?"

"I could ask you the same thing. I thought you were staying home because you had family in town." His voice matched his eyes, which were gazing at her intently. Looking so soft and caring.

There was no doubt about it. She really was in love.

But when she opened her mouth to reply, she noticed that he was staring at Lorne with a very different expression. Lott wasn't happy. He wasn't happy at all.

18

ott had hardly been able to believe it when he'd looked over and saw Melonie standing with another guy. Then, when he overheard a couple of girls say that the man was Melonie's new beau, he'd been stunned.

He'd also been kind of hurt.

While he and Melonie didn't exactly have anything settled between them, they had an understanding. Or at least it sure had seemed that way to him when they'd shared those moments together while Seth and Bethanne had gone on their walk. Melonie had been as sweet as could be. He knew she would've let him kiss her if he'd tried. Though he'd been tempted, he hadn't dared, wanting her to know that he respected her and was willing to wait to take their relationship to another level. As far as he was concerned, all that meant Melonie should not be going anywhere on the arm of another man.

And most especially not the man she was standing with. Lott knew he wasn't the most handsome guy in the county, but he was sure a far sight better looking than the man at

Melonie's side. He looked like he had a permanent frown on his face.

Melonie had a ton of stuff on her plate. She needed to be around a man who made her happy. This guy looked like he didn't know the definition of happiness. What did she see in him?

Walking up to the stranger, he said, "I don't think we've met."

"Lott, this is my cousin Lorne Holst," Melonie told him.

Things were looking up. "You two are cousins?"

"Second cousins," Lorne said. "We don't know each other very well."

"Lorne is visiting from Ohio."

Melonie looked like she was trying real hard not to grimace. That almost made Lott smile. "Welcome to Crittenden County."

"Danke." Then Lorne blurted, "Could you introduce me to some women?"

Who was this guy? "Nee."

"Why not?" Lorne looked stunned.

"We don't know each other." Besides, Lott was pretty sure he already didn't like him.

Lorne raised his chin. "I'll have you know that I have a very good reputation back home."

"But no girlfriend?"

"That ain't none of your business."

"I'm just saying, if you have a girl, you shouldn't be flirting with other ones. Or with Melonie." Sure, he sounded possessive, but what was wrong with that? Someone needed to look out for Mel. Glancing her way, Lott wasn't sure if she was trying to keep from laughing or throwing herself into his arms.

He would be happy if she did either.

Lorne glared like Lott had just accused him of sleeping in on a Sunday morning. "I was not flirting with my cousin."

"It looked like it to me." Okay, it didn't, but he couldn't resist needling the guy.

"You shouldn't have been watching us in the first place."

Lott had to give it to him. Lorne had an answer for everything. "Do you ever get a word in edgewise with him, Mel?"

Melonie's eyes widened as they filled with mirth. To her credit, her voice was smooth and sounded *almost* serious. "Occasionally."

"Hmm."

"You know, there's no reason for you to act possessive of Melonie," Lorne said. "I sure don't want *her*."

Even though all three of them were good with that, Lott didn't care for how Lorne was referring to Mel—like she was something bad he'd found on the bottom of his shoe. "That don't sound very nice, Lorne."

"It's true."

"My mother asked me to bring him here," Melonie said. "Things are rather quiet at our house."

"It's been boring. I'm not sure why my parents felt the need to come to Kentucky."

"I'm not either."

"You're not much of a family sort of person, then?" Lott asked.

"We're extended family. And we have next to nothing in common."

Melonie's lips quirked. "He's not wrong."

Lorne folded his arms across his chest as he scanned the area as if some pretty girl was suddenly going to approach him with a bright smile on her face. Then he stilled. "Who is that?"

Lott glanced around. "Who is who?"

"Her."

There was a new tone to Lorne's voice. It was a little hoarse. A little breathless. Like he'd just come across the Kentucky Derby winner in the middle of Crittenden County. They all looked.

"Oh. That's Ruby Bowman," Melonie said.

"She's pretty. Do you know her?" Lorne asked.

"Of course," she said. "We all do."

"Come introduce us, then."

Melonie looked stricken. "I don't think that would be a good idea."

Lott knew why. Ruby was a year younger than Melonie and always viewed her as a rival. There was no way she would give Lorne the time of day if Melonie introduced them. Of course, Lott was fairly sure that Ruby wasn't going to give Lorne her attention no matter what. "I'll take you over there," he said.

Lorne studied him for a long moment before nodding. "That's appreciated."

This guy really was too much. Turning to Melonie, he winked. "I'll be right back."

"Please, take your time."

"What's with the two of you?" Lorne asked as they walked toward Ruby.

There was no reason to lie, especially since he didn't want this cousin of Mel's to suddenly start thinking he had a shot with her. "I've been courting Melonie."

"Do her parents know this?"

"They do. And before you ask any more questions, I'll just say that it's complicated."

"I'll say. Her mother was acting like I should court her." For once the guy didn't sound incredulous. Merely confused.

"Listen, if I introduce you to Ruby, you're going to need to not look too interested. She's used to men fawning over her."

"You've done that?"

"Nee. She's not my type." His type had wavy blond hair, big blue eyes, and the prettiest smile he'd ever seen.

Ruby stood talking with Jenn and Mary L. All three of them looked at him with curious expressions when he and Lorne approached. Lott didn't blame them. He hadn't spent any time with them after they graduated eighth grade.

"Hiya, Lott," Jenn said.

"Hi." He smiled at all of them. "This is Lorne Holst. He's in town from Ohio. Lorne, this is Jenn, Mary L., and Ruby."

Mary giggled. "No one calls me Mary L. anymore, Lott."

"Sorry, I guess not. We had three Marys in our Amish school," he explained to Lorne.

"The first time I introduced myself to someone new, I called myself Mary L.," she said with a grin.

"I'll be pleased to just call you Mary," Lorne said. "It's nice to meet all of you."

"You as well. Tell us about where you're from."

Lott figured that was a good signal to step away. "I need to go check on Melonie," he said.

Ruby frowned. "You're seeing her again?"

"I never stopped. Lorne, let me know when you're ready to leave."

"Will do. Thanks."

When the guy turned away like Lott was an annoying pest, Lott chuckled to himself and walked back to Melonie's side. He was glad that she wasn't alone. Rachel Byler, the host of the gathering, was talking to her.

After exchanging greetings with him, Rachel went on her

way, and once again, he and Melonie were alone. Just the way he liked it.

Melonie watched the four in awe. "I can't believe it, but those girls seem to be enjoying Lorne's company."

"I was surprised too, though he was a lot more personable with them."

"That makes sense. Even though I told him I wasn't interested in him, he acted as if I should've been." She groaned. "I canna believe my mother thinks we would make a good pair."

Lott couldn't either, but that was a discussion for another day. "Well, he's out of your hair for now."

"I'm grateful for that."

Her eyes were shining, making him feel all warm inside. "He asked what our relationship was. I told him that I was courting you."

"I'm sure that made him pretty confused," she said lightly.

"I don't care. All I care about is making sure you're not confused about us." He pressed his hand to her lower back. "You aren't, are you?"

She leaned against his hand for a second before looking melancholy. "I'm not confused. It's everyone around us who is."

Thinking of all the people in their lives who seemed to feel entitled to have a say in his and Melonie's future, Lott reached for her hand. "What do you think about coming over to my haus one day soon?"

"I don't know. What will your parents think?"

"My mamm and daed like you." That was the truth. "Plus, it would be good for you and Bethanne to talk some more." His sister stayed to herself too much. Spending time with Melonie would do her good.

Melonie's eyes brightened. "I'd like to see Bethanne again. Maybe one day she'll even come to a gathering like this."

"I'd like that, though I can't see that happening. She still can't seem to handle being around too many people. Especially not a party."

"It's a shame, ain't so?" she whispered.

"Jah." Taking Melonie's hand in his, he settled for holding it instead of offering any false promises or empty platitudes.

She stepped closer, smiling up at him, and relief spread through Lott.

Everything was okay at that moment. Since tomorrow wasn't a guarantee, he'd take it and give thanks.

19

Tabitha knew she was being hard on herself, but she couldn't help it. She'd been such a fool. No, it was worse than that. She'd been stupid.

She'd woken up that morning feeling like she was going to climb the walls of her house if she didn't get out for a spell. At first, she tried to ignore the feeling. Then, after lunch, she felt the pull again. By three o'clock, she didn't want to fight it anymore. So, even though she had a very good reason for staying inside behind locked doors, she'd left her house and had tea with Mary.

Her sister and the boys had been happy to see her. Well, the boys had been. Mary had seemed surprised and a little wary to have Tabitha over without Roy's permission, but she'd been cordial enough. After staying only a half hour, Tabitha still hadn't been ready to go home, so she'd gathered her courage and gone to the market for deli meat and cheese. It had been years since she'd done that.

She'd felt pretty good about her burst of bravery too. Even though Martha Brenneman had barely been civil and Ivan Troyer had taken one look at her and gone down a separate aisle in the store, Tabitha hadn't let that bother her. Especially since she'd taught Martha's daughter Daisy, who'd been a poor sport. More than once Tabitha had tried to help the child to not be so competitive and such a sore loser. Her words of wisdom hadn't done much good, though.

But when she returned home, Tabitha had realized that leaving had been a big mistake. A gift of yarn had been waiting on her front doorstep. She'd picked up the skein with a cry of pleasure, ignoring the note beside it. The yarn was spun from alpaca fur, so soft and luxurious—and no doubt expensive.

Sure that Mary had dropped it off as an apology for her less than welcoming attitude, Tabitha had torn open the card's envelope and read the note scrawled inside. And felt like she was going to be sick.

Then she knew she was.

She'd run inside, dropping the yarn and card and her keys onto the coffee table, and barely made it to the toilet in time. Only after she washed her face and brushed her teeth did it occur to her that she hadn't locked the front door before running down the hall.

How could she have been so foolish? Leon could've been lurking in the woods, watching her open the yarn and run inside. He could even be in the house now, just waiting for her to walk out of the bathroom. That thought made her feel sick all over again.

Hands shaking, she pressed the lock on the door. Enclosing her in the small, tiled space.

Her brow grew damp.

If he was there, he'd have a smile on his face. Sometimes she'd felt as if he'd almost looked forward to her doing something wrong. Then he could justify his actions to himself.

During her weakest moments, she'd almost believed she deserved to be punished too.

"Nee," she whispered. "You know better than that. You're stronger than to think such things. Plus, you never deserved his abuse. No matter what you did, you never deserved that."

She wanted to believe that small voice in her head. She really did. But years of hiding still got the best of her and she fell back into old habits in the blink of an eye.

Her keys clattered on the living room floor.

He was out there. He'd gotten in.

Tabitha clenched her teeth so she wouldn't scream. Then she heard a soft whine and a scratch at the bathroom door.

"Chance!" She'd forgotten all about the dog.

Chance whined again, this time far more high-pitched. He pawed at the bathroom door again. He sensed her distress. She knew he did.

With her shaking hand on the doorknob, she willed herself to release the lock and turn the knob. She needed to face her fears, calm Chance, and call Sheriff Johnson about the yarn and note.

She almost felt safe. Almost. But still she hesitated.

Glancing at herself in the mirror, she saw a pale face looking back at her. A line of perspiration bordered her hairline.

No, she wasn't safe here. It was an illusion. Especially since she didn't have her phone. Maybe Leon had been right, after all. Maybe she really was stupid and couldn't do anything right.

"Nee. That's not true." She swallowed. "It's not true at all," she added, her voice a bit louder.

Chance whined again.

She couldn't leave the dog alone in the hall. "I'm here," she said.

When she finally released the lock and opened the door, a waft of fresh, cooler air greeted her. She breathed in deep.

Chance pawed at her leg.

"I'm sorry, Chance," she said. "I don't seem to be myself. Are you all right?"

The hund looked up at her, his brown eyes full of compassion. His tail wagged.

She knelt down and ran her hand along his back. "It's okay," she whispered. "You are a gut dog."

Unable to help herself, she crept through the house. It was silent. She found the keys on the floor and realized the dog had probably nosed them off the table when he sniffed the yarn. After returning them to the table, she went to the front door and turned the deadbolt. And looked again at the skein of yarn and note that Leon had left for her to find.

Goose bumps formed on her arms.

She hurried to the kitchen, opened the drawer, and pulled out her cell phone. With Chance pressed close to her legs, she scanned through her very short list of contacts and then pressed the one for the sheriff's office.

A man answered on the first ring. "Sheriff's Office. This is Deputy Junior Ernst."

Fighting the urge to hang up, she spoke. "H-hello. This is Tabitha Yoder."

"Who?"

"Tabitha Yoder. I usually talk to Sheriff Johnson."

"Oh. Sure. The other day, he told me you were here and why. How may I help you, Ms. Yoder?"

"My ex-husband was here. I . . . I have a restraining order against him. He shouldn't be here."

Deputy Ernst's voice turned far more serious. "No, ma'am, he sure shouldn't be. Are you okay? Is he still there?"

"I . . . I don't think so. I left for a couple of hours, but when I came home, I found a skein of yarn and a note that he left for me."

"Where was it?"

"On my front steps. I'm scared, Deputy. Could I please speak to Sheriff Johnson?"

"I'm sorry. He's out on a call, but I'll be right there. Do you need any medical attention, ma'am?"

"No, I'm okay. Just please hurry if you can? I'm afraid he's still here. What if he's still here?"

"Are you inside?"

"Jah."

"Stay inside and keep the doors locked. I'm getting in my vehicle now. I'll be there within fifteen."

Fifteen minutes. It sounded like an eternity, but if she just took one moment at a time, she could handle it. Hopefully. "Are you sure you're on your way?"

"Yep. I promise. Keep your phone with you, Tabitha. I'll call when I'm close."

"Okay," she said. Then realized he'd already hung up.

Outside, the wind picked up. Glad that she had one or two flashlights in every room, Tabitha reached for the biggest one in the kitchen. It was a camping light and could rest on a table or floor and deliver a sizable beam onto the ceiling. The house had been so dark when she arrived.

Once again, she wished she'd had enough money to wire the house with electricity. Having lights on a timer like some of the English homes did would be wonderful—and a bright house would seem less scary.

Still shaking, she looked at her phone's screen. Only two minutes had passed. She had thirteen to go until the deputy arrived. It might as well be thirteen hours. On impulse, she called Seth.

"Tabitha?"

"Did I wake you up?"

"Wake me? Nee. It's only five o'clock. I was just relaxing after a long day at work."

"Oh. Of course. Sorry—"

"Hey. Are you all right?"

"I don't know."

"What happened? Are you hurt? Do you need something?"

She loved that he always asked about her first. Seth made her feel important and like she mattered in all sorts of ways. "Leon was here."

"What? Are you alone now?"

"Yes. I-I called the sheriff's office, but the sheriff wasn't in. The deputy answered."

"Did you tell him what happened?"

The patience and concern in his voice soothed her. "I did. Deputy Ernst said he's on his way over." She looked at the kitchen clock. "He won't be here for another ten minutes."

"I'm on my way."

Gratitude clutched her heart. "Seth, you don't have to do that."

"Tab, would you like me to come over?"

"Yes." She hated how small her voice sounded. "I'm afraid Leon is still out there."

"He better hope he's not."

She hated the idea of putting Seth in danger. "Maybe you should stay away after all. He's strong."

"I'll be careful."

"But—"

"Tabitha, I'm strong too. I'll be okay." She heard a door

open on the other end of the line. Maybe he was getting his coat? "I'm going to walk over now. Going through fields will get me there quicker than in my truck. We can talk while I head your way."

"You don't mind?" Grasping the cell phone like a lifeline, she still felt like she was asking too much of him.

"I don't mind at all. Now, tell me what you did today."

"I went to see Mary. And went to the market."

"Did you now?" There was a faint echo to his words, letting her know that he was outside. He was on his way to her.

"I even saw Martha Brenneman."

"How did that go?"

"Not too good. She would barely look at me. I pretended I didn't notice, though."

"Good for you." His voice had lifted. She could practically see him smiling. "I'm glad you didn't let Martha's bad manners bother you. Martha wasn't nice even when you were a teacher." His voice was gentle and encouraging.

"You shouldn't say that."

"I can't help it if it's true."

True. "I suppose you have a point." After walking to the stove, she put on the kettle. Then, seeing that Chance still hadn't left her side, she opened a jar and handed him a dog treat. "What did you do today?"

"I've been working on a house in Marion. The family needed a handyman, so I've been doing all sorts of things, from fixing some chewed floorboards to switching out faucets and building some shelves for their garage."

"Do you like doing so many things?"

"I do with this job. The couple is nice. The husband works at a bank. Plus, it's a happy home. I've been doing work around two kids and two Labrador retrievers." He chuckled. "There's fluff from the dogs' black fur everywhere."

"Sounds chaotic and messy."

"It is. But the kinner are friendly and don't seem to fear me, which I appreciate. I'm less than five minutes away now."

Five minutes? He had to be jogging. But she could do five minutes. "That's gut." She sat on one of the kitchen chairs, too afraid to go into the living room. Anyone could be looking inside.

"Tabitha?"

"Jah?"

"Try not to let your imagination run wild."

"I'm trying not to, but Leon could be in the yard, Seth. He could be hiding and watching me through the window."

"He could. But he also might not be, right?"

"You're not helping."

"I see your house now. Almost there. I'm going to hang up. Look for me."

Abruptly the call ended.

And just like that, her hands started shaking again. Even though she knew better, she stared at the phone's screen. Watched each minute pass. Took long, slow breaths and tried not to panic.

Chance sat down beside her chair, and she ran a hand along his soft fur. "We've almost made it."

When she heard a loud noise outside near her yard, she feared she'd been wrong.

20

Seth reached the driveway just seconds after the Crittenden County Sheriff's Department vehicle parked beside the house. He slowed his pace. He didn't know Deputy Junior Ernst well, but he'd heard that he was something of a hothead—that he supposedly had a good heart but made mistakes. That he was so eager to make a name for himself, he sometimes cut corners and then hid behind the badge when questioned.

He watched the deputy get out, say something into the radio attached to a shoulder strap on his uniform, and then shut the door and shine a flashlight into the nearby woods. The November sun set early, but it wasn't completely dark yet.

The flashlight's beam was bright, illuminating several yards of the surrounding yard and woods at a time. Each time the deputy cascaded the light in an arc, the forest floor's grasses and shrubs snapped and swayed. Critters were taking cover. The man ignored the ground noise, remaining alert and intent. Obviously taking Tabitha's call seriously.

Right as Seth thought that maybe there was more to Deputy Ernst than most folks realized, the man turned on his heel and shined the light right on him.

"Hold it right there!"

Seth stopped and raised his hands. The light was so bright he couldn't see a thing. "It's Seth Zimmerman, Deputy."

"I know who you are. What are you doing here?"

"Tabitha called me." He shifted, averting his eyes from the blinding beam.

"Don't move."

"I'll stay still if you'll stop shining that thing directly in my eyes. I can't see a thing."

"Fine." The beam lowered six inches.

"Thanks. Now, can I come forward?"

"Not until you empty your pockets."

He gritted his teeth but did as he was told. Prison had taught him that being in the right didn't always mean much. He reached into his coat's pockets and pulled out his cell phone with one hand and a candy bar with the other. "That's all I got."

"What about your pants pockets?"

Just as he reached for his keys, the front door opened. The deputy turned and pointed that blasted flashlight yet again, this time right in Tabitha's eyes.

"Oh!" she cried.

If Seth had been able, he would've wrestled the flashlight out of the deputy's hands. It was causing more harm than good.

"Sorry, Ms. Yoder." Deputy Ernst directed the beam toward the ground. Tabitha's dog, who'd been peeking out the door next to her legs, scurried away.

She stiffened. "Seth, is that you?"

"It is." He still held his hands, one holding his phone and the other the candy bar, out from his sides.

"What are you doing?"

167

"Deputy Ernst told me to empty my pockets."

She stepped out onto the porch, looking at the deputy. "Why did you have him do that? Seth is my friend. It's my ex-husband I'm worried about."

The deputy clicked off the flashlight. "Zimmerman said you called him, but I wanted to make sure. I was just doing my job, ma'am."

Concerned about her catching a chill, Seth stuffed his phone and candy bar back in his coat pockets. "Tab, you need a coat on. It's cold out."

"I'm okay." She wrapped her arms around herself.

Seth knew then that Tabitha wasn't just chilled, she was trying to hold herself together. She was used to doing that because she hadn't had anyone else to lean on. No one to wrap their arms around her and ease her fears.

But that wasn't the case any longer.

Unable to stay away another second, Seth started forward. Deputy Ernst watched him closely but didn't say anything as he moved toward the porch. The moment Seth reached her side, he pulled her into his arms and hugged her tight.

She froze for an instant, then gripped his biceps and rested her head on his shoulder. "I'm so glad you came," she whispered.

Her slight frame against him felt good. So did the faint scent of vanilla and lemons that surrounded her. "I am too. I'm glad you called."

He ran a hand along her spine, hoping it would remind her that she wasn't alone. "You're doing good, Tab," he whispered.

"Not really."

"You're on two feet, jah?" When she nodded against his shoulder, he ran his hand along her silky-soft ponytail. Her hair was such a pretty brown color. The first time he'd seen it down around her shoulders, he'd thought there was nothing prettier. Now he was fairly sure that everything about her was pretty. "I'm proud of you," he murmured. When she relaxed against him, he almost smiled.

"Ms. Yoder, are you all right?" Deputy Ernst called out.

Seth was tempted to point out that she obviously was not but held his silence.

Whether it was his support or the deputy's question, Tabitha seemed to pull up some strength from somewhere deep inside. Stepping away from Seth's embrace, she said, "I'm all right. Um. Just shaken up." Despite the tears in her eyes, she looked more at ease.

"Yes, ma'am."

"Would you, ah, like to see the yarn and the note I told you about on the phone?"

"That would be a real good idea," Deputy Ernst replied.

"All right. It's in my living room." As if she'd suddenly realized it was cold, she moved toward the door. "Please come in."

Seth opened the door and held it for her and Junior.

"Would you like something to drink, Deputy Ernst?" she asked after Seth closed the door.

"Thank you, but I'm all right." After a pause, he added, "Where are the yarn and note?"

She walked to the coffee table and pointed. "There."

"Have you touched both items?"

"Yes." Concern lined her forehead. "I didn't know who it was from. I, ah, thought it was from my sister."

"She often bring you yarn?"

"No. But she does bring me little gifts from time to time."

"Yes, ma'am." The deputy fished two latex gloves out

of a pocket and slipped them on, then picked up the note and read it aloud. "'You are mine. You will always be mine. But you have been very bad, Tabitha. Spending time with a convict has ruined you.'"

Tabitha pressed her fist against her mouth as tears filled her eyes again. "Sorry. It sounds worse out loud."

"You've got nothing to apologize about, Tab." A thousand words raced through Seth's mind, none of them suitable to share. Not caring what the deputy would think, Seth reached for Tabitha again.

She leaned close but then straightened and faced Deputy Ernst. "Do you understand why I called you?"

He looked at her with eyes full of sympathy. "I do. Sit down, Ms. Yoder." When she did, he added, "What's the significance of this yarn?"

"It's expensive yarn," she said. "It's alpaca. I . . . I like to knit, and Leon knew I always wanted something so fine." She bent her head. "I know it's wrong to be so prideful."

The deputy, who'd been writing down notes on a pad of paper, peered at her curiously. "Why do you think Leon brought this item to you now?"

"I don't know." She sighed. "Maybe to remind me that he hasn't forgotten me?"

"May I?" He gestured to a chair.

"Of course."

Seth sat down next to Tabitha. Not wanting to give the deputy anything more to question than he already had, he kept a respectable distance between them.

The deputy wrote out more notes on his notepad, then looked at them both. "No disrespect, but I think I need to know more about the two of you's relationship."

"We're friends," Seth said.

"How close of friends?"

Seth looked him in the eye. "Close friends."

"I see." He grimaced slightly. "Ms. Yoder, have you had Seth spend the night here?"

Her eyes widened. "Of course not."

Just as Seth was about to tell the deputy to concentrate on the man who had a restraining order and not him, the deputy held up a hand. "Seth, I know you're angry and want to protect her, but if you were in my shoes, you'd ask the same things. Knowing the whole situation helps us best help her. Keeping secrets only makes my job harder."

The man was right. After glancing at Tabitha, Seth said, "Deputy, until a month ago, Tabitha never even came out of her house when I visited."

"And why did you visit?"

"I chopped wood. Brought her food. Shoveled snow. You know. I did things a man would do for a woman."

He gave a few slow nods. "Why?"

"Because she needed the help."

The deputy looked at her. "You don't have anyone else, Tabitha?"

"Nee."

"I thought you had family in the area."

"My sister and her family are here. But because of my divorce, I had to leave my faith. My brother-in-law doesn't want to go against the church's beliefs, so he avoids me."

Deputy Ernst drew in a breath. "Even after what happened to you?"

She pursed her lips and nodded.

"Ms. Yoder, Sheriff Johnson told me everything the two of you talked about when you visited the other day. Is there anything else you'd like to add?"

"About what?"

"Anything about your ex-husband? Anything you might not have told anyone before but might be helpful now?" He tapped his notepad with the tip of the pencil. "He's already violated the restraining order, so we can pick him up for that. But if there's anything else you can think of that might help keep him locked up, it would be great."

Tabitha stiffened. When she cast a furtive glance at Seth, he wondered if she was finding it difficult to speak in front of him. That would hurt, but his feelings didn't matter. "Tab, if you'd like me to step outside so you can talk to the deputy in—"

"Nee." Her voice came out deep and rough, like the response had been a knee-jerk reaction. She cleared her throat. "I mean, no, there is nothing else I have to share."

Though he didn't exchange a glance with the deputy, Seth suspected the man was thinking the same thing he was. That Tabitha Yoder was still keeping something about her and her ex-husband hidden away. Something dark and painful and secret.

And that's why Leon was able to be so brazen. He had something on her, and he was content to tease and jab her with the memories. Because he knew she'd rather die than admit it to another living soul. He was counting on it.

21

It was near nine o'clock when Deputy Ernst left. After he finished questioning Tabitha, he'd gone back outside, called Sheriff Johnson, and then canvassed the surrounding area for over an hour.

When he'd said he was going to pull down the driveway but stay for a spell just in case Leon had a mind to return, Tabitha made him a sandwich and gave him a tin of chocolate chip cookies. The deputy seemed grateful for her kindness. Then, just before he left, he'd knocked on her door again and told her that the sheriff would likely be by in the morning.

He'd also offered Seth a ride home. Seth had refused, saying he had some things to speak to Tabitha about. As reasons went, it was a pretty poor one. After all, Seth had already been there for hours.

Tabitha's face had turned as hot as a morning skillet, but she didn't try to explain Seth's presence further. The simple fact was that she didn't want Seth to leave. She didn't want to be alone in the house.

The deputy had scowled at Seth's excuse but didn't argue.

After reminding her to give him a call if she needed anything, he'd walked out the door and drove back down the drive a couple of minutes later.

Seth closed the door when the vehicle was out of sight. "Alone at last," he teased.

Tabitha tried to smile but reckoned she looked anything but happy.

Looking far more serious, he reached for her hands. "Hey, you know I was just joking, right?"

She nodded.

His expression sharpened. "How are you feeling?"

"The truth?"

"Always."

"I'm rattled."

"I'm not surprised. You've had quite a day."

"I almost wish Leon had been lurking near the house. Then maybe Deputy Ernst would have gotten him and it would be all over."

"Yeah." Still gazing at her intently, Seth added, "Tab, I only refused Junior's offer because I thought he'd make me sit in the back seat of his cruiser. No way am I ever going to do that again."

That made sense. "I understand."

He looked down at their linked fingers. She did too. She'd never had delicate-looking hands. They were capable and strong. She kept her nails trimmed short, but that was the extent of care—beyond a dab of lotion every now and then— they ever received. But her hands looked small and feminine nestled in Seth's.

After a squeeze, he released hers and clasped his behind his back. "It's getting late."

"I know. I understand."

Seth looked torn. "Would you like me to stay? I'd be happy to sleep on the couch. No one will be able to get inside without going through me."

The idea of not worrying about every creak and groan in the old house was tempting. Tabitha knew she'd be able to sleep better than she had in days, as well. She trusted Seth completely. If he said he'd stay on the couch, then that's where he would be.

But if anyone found out that Seth had spent the night, her life would get even more complicated. Besides, what would she do the following night?

"I couldn't ask you to do that."

"You didn't ask me, Tab. I offered." He released his hands and used one to pat her shoulder. "I hope you know that you're safe with me. I would never do anything to hurt or scare you."

"I know."

But not only was she concerned about her reputation, she was worried about Leon. If he discovered Seth had been in her house overnight, he would react violently. Leon was possessive of her, and he hated the fact that she was living in his family's house. After taking out his anger on her, he'd find a way to hurt Seth. And as much as she feared seeing Leon again, she dreaded the idea of Seth getting hurt because of her even more.

With regret, she stepped away from him. She needed the distance to force herself to do what was right and not what all her mixed-up emotions were screaming at her to do. "Thank you for the offer, but I think it's time you went home."

He didn't budge an inch. "You look scared."

"I am scared. I mean I am a little bit."

"Tabitha, what are you worried about? Do you care so

much about your reputation that you're willing to put your safety at risk?"

"It's not just my reputation. Though, that is part of it."

"Why? A lot of the people you're so worried about turned their backs on you when you filed for divorce. You've been living here all alone. No one but me has been coming to check on you."

"That's not true."

"You're counting your sister? Mary has only visited one day a month."

"She didn't have a choice. Her husband—"

"I know. I know. Roy has decided that it's okay to practically ignore his sister-in-law. I guess that's fine with him and he has no problem sleeping at night. But leaving you to fend for yourself hasn't been right."

"I'm not saying it was right."

"But you've accepted everyone's distance?"

Feeling more frustrated by the second, she raised her voice. "This isn't about Roy or Mary or even having to leave the Amish. It's about me, and I'm telling you that I don't have a choice."

"But you do."

"Seth, do you hear yourself? You're acting as if I don't know my own mind. As if you don't value my opinion."

He shook his head. "That isn't what's happening."

"But that's how it feels to me. Please leave, Seth."

He didn't budge. "You do have a choice. You know that, right?" He lowered his voice. "Just like you had a choice about marrying Leon. Just like you had a choice about what to do the first time he hit you."

Each word stung. Not just because Seth believed what he was saying but because he obviously had no inkling about what her life had been like. "Don't tell me that. You have no idea about my choices, Seth."

"Why did you stay with Leon for so long? What did he have over you that you couldn't escape from?"

"You don't need to know."

"But you need to tell someone!"

"Fine. On my second date with Leon, we went down to Cripple Creek and drank. I was living in my family's dawdi house back then. When I woke up the next morning, my clothes were off. I didn't know what had happened. I couldn't remember anything." Still feeling embarrassed, she added, "Leon later told me that we'd had sex."

Everything in Seth's expression changed. Surprise, anger, pity . . . all of it appeared in his eyes. They were all the things she'd felt that awful, awful morning, and his compassion was almost too much to bear. A lump formed in her throat as she held on to the rest of her composure like a lifeline.

"Tab . . ." he whispered.

She shook her head. "No. Let me finish. Now that I know about such things, I . . . I think he put something in my drink. I don't know. But he blackmailed me, Seth. If I didn't agree to marry him right away, he was going to tell the school board. I would've gotten fired. My reputation would've been ruined."

"Sounds like he used the date rape drug on you. If you had gone to the police or the hospital, they would've found Rohypnol in your system. Leon would've been charged with a felony."

Tears pricked her eyes. She'd done so much to protect her reputation and she'd lost it all—and so much more—anyway.

Releasing a ragged sigh, she said, "It doesn't matter now. I didn't go to the police. I didn't tell a single person about what happened. Instead, I married Leon, soon learned what life as his wife was like, and lived in fear twenty-four hours a day. You don't know what it's like to have every choice taken from you."

"I have a pretty good idea. I was in prison."

"Yes, you were. I'm sorry for the accident and that you had to spend time behind bars, but you weren't completely innocent, Seth. You chose to get involved. You chose to fight Peter when he turned on you. You could have walked away."

"And you couldn't ever walk away?" He raised an eyebrow.

Her temper flared. "The man who promised me and God that he would care for and honor me abused me in countless ways for years. I wasn't allowed to do one thing of my own free will, Seth Zimmerman."

He closed his eyes. "I'm sorry. You're right. I shouldn't have said anything."

"No, you shouldn't have even thought it. But you did." She walked to the door and held it open. "Now will you please leave, or should I call the deputy back and ask for his help?"

"No. I am sorry, Tabitha." When she remained silent, he studied her face one long moment, then walked out the door.

The moment Seth was across the threshold, she locked the door. Then, just like she used to do, she peeked at him through the windowpane. But secretly, barely disturbing her curtains.

This time, instead of watching him approach, she watched him leave. Stared as he descended the front steps. Noticed how he strode forward, and how his pace picked up steam with each foot of distance. Like he couldn't get out of her sight fast enough.

Which made her realize yet again that she'd been such a fool. She'd thought he'd never noticed her watching him, but he had. He'd noticed everything she'd done. Just like Leon had.

But instead of judging her and finding fault with everything, Seth had encouraged her to believe in herself.

Instead of hurting her, he'd helped her heal.

Instead of ignoring her wishes, he'd honored them. Encouraged her.

She supposed he was doing the same thing now. Even though he hadn't been shy about voicing his thoughts, he'd still left. After apologizing.

Just like she'd asked him to.

Only when Seth was out of sight did she move away from the window. Turning around, she analyzed the space. The living room was neat as a pin. There was no trace of either Deputy Ernst or Seth ever being there. No, the only sign of her circumstances having changed was the bright light shining on the table. The other one currently shining in her bedroom. She needed those flashlights. Anything to feel safer.

But it was a false sense of security. She was alone.

Nerves shot through her again, clenching her stomach and tightening her throat. Like a woman possessed, she checked the deadbolt on the front door again. Then she rushed to the kitchen and double-checked the lock on the back door. Then checked every single window, already imagining Leon watching and waiting from the woods. One by one, she visited every windowpane, securing locks that were already secure. Pulling down shades that were already down.

Chance watched her. Perhaps sensing her fear, he whimpered.

"It'll be okay, Chance," she said.

He whimpered again, and she knew the dog didn't believe her words any more than she did.

After brushing her teeth and hair and washing her face, she changed into her nightgown. Finally, she lay down on her bed and curled up in a ball on her side, exhausted. Wrapped her arms around herself again. Just like she used to do when she was hurting so bad.

Just like she still did when she was scared.

She closed her eyes. The memory of Seth holding her rushed forward. The way he'd been so solid and steady. The way he'd promised her that she was going to be all right.

And for one split second, she'd believed him.

Until she'd pushed him away.

Over and over she reviewed their conversation, hating that they'd fought before his departure. Hating that she hadn't asked him to call her when he got home safe. He'd dropped everything when she'd called and then spent hours by her side. In return, she'd sent him on his way in the dark. She hadn't even offered to let him borrow a flashlight.

At a quarter to one in the morning, she allowed the tears to fall. They soaked her skin and her pillowcase and the neckline of her nightgown. Come morning, she'd likely need to wash everything.

It didn't matter, though. She'd still be all alone.

22

The pounding at the door was unceasing. With Seth still groggy, the knocking rivaled the continuous hammering inside his head. He had fallen asleep in the chair next to the fireplace. The evening before had had him so spun up, he'd lit a small fire and sat down next to it, hoping the flickering warmth would soothe his spirit. Instead, it had reminded him of Tabitha, and he'd wondered if she had brought enough wood inside.

"Seth?"

It was his sister. "Mel, stop pounding. I'll be right there." He got up and headed for the door.

"Hurry. It's cold out here."

He rolled his eyes and moved his neck from side to side. It did little to ease his headache or the tension in his neck and shoulders. He needed some pain reliever and a hot shower. And coffee.

When he opened the front door, the bright morning sun was blinding. "Come on in."

"Danke," she said as he closed the door behind her. "Gut matin."

"Whatever. I need coffee." He went into the kitchen, leaving Melonie to divest herself of her cloak and hang it on the hook by the door. His house was small but wide open, so he could easily see the front door from the kitchen.

After he turned on the coffee maker that he'd thankfully prepped the evening before, he listened to it drip as he took in the sight of his little sister. Today she had on a cranberry-colored dress and black tights. Her kapp was as neat and clean as always, and for once she didn't have a single wayward blond curl out of place. The only thing that marred her perfection was a worried frown.

"Seth, what took you so long to open the door?" she asked as she joined him in the kitchen in her stocking feet. "I must have knocked on it for five minutes."

"I was asleep." Still groggy, he peered at her. "How did you get here anyway?"

"I rode my bike." Staring at him like she had something important to say, she added, "It's ten o'clock, Seth."

"Is it? Hmm." He hadn't bothered to look at the clock. Her stare practically pierced his bones as he filled a cup with strong, black coffee.

"You look like you slept in those clothes."

"That's because I did." He closed his eyes as he savored his first sip. The taste of fresh, hot coffee never got old. He certainly never took it for granted. Not since his release from prison. Feeling his body slowly relax, he took another sip.

Melonie cleared her throat. "Aren't you going to offer me a cup?"

He adored his sister, but he was not loving her current attitude. "Didn't think I needed to."

"It's the polite thing to do."

"Help yourself if you want kaffi, Mel. You know where

everything is." Taking a seat at the kitchen table, he watched his sister pour a healthy amount of milk in a cup, then fill the rest with coffee.

Her mouth pinched slightly. "Where's the sugar?"

"Second cabinet from the right."

She opened two of the cabinet doors, located the bag of sugar, and added two heaping spoonsful. After stirring, she took a sip, added a bit more coffee, and tasted it again. Finally looking pleased, she sat down at the table.

He grinned. "I'd forgotten how much you like all that milk and sugar."

"There's nothing wrong with it."

"You're right, though I might as well be making you a cup of warm milk."

She waved off his quip. "There's coffee in here."

"If you say so."

"So, are you going to tell me why you not only fell asleep in your clothes but were still sleeping at ten in the morning?"

"Sure. I was up late reading."

"That's the story you're going to tell me?"

He figured she had a point. As lies went, it was a lousy one. "The truth is I was helping a friend last night. It was late by the time I finally got home and got to sleep." She didn't need to know he'd been up half the night wrestling with what he'd learned from Tabitha.

"Who were you helping?"

"I don't think I should share that."

"Why not?"

"Because she deserves her privacy and it's not my story to tell."

"*She?*"

Seth felt like slapping himself on the head. He knew better

than to give Melonie a single clue about last evening's adventures. "Don't worry about it, Mel."

He could practically see the wheels turning in her head. "You were over at Tabitha Yoder's last night. Weren't you?"

Well, he supposed it was ridiculous for him to even imagine that Melonie wouldn't know who he was talking about. "No comment."

"I knew it." She smiled before turning serious again. "Wait. Is she all right? Does she need anything?"

Melonie sure seemed to jump to that conclusion quickly. "Why would you ask that?"

"Beyond the fact that everyone knows you look out for her, everyone also knows she's struggling. So, is she all right?"

Seth wasn't sure what to say. The short and simple truth was that Tabitha really was struggling, both emotionally and physically. She absolutely wasn't all right. She had a scary ex-husband who had violated a restraining order, she lived by herself, and she didn't even have the full support of her family.

Adding insult to injury was the fact that Sheriff Johnson hadn't even been around the night before. No matter how much Deputy Ernst tried, he wasn't anywhere close to the officer that Johnson was.

"I'm not comfortable sharing her story, Melonie. It's private."

Melonie took another sip of her coffee before pushing it aside. "Why do you look like you've been through the wringer?"

"I tried to stay at her house last night. She didn't want me to do that."

She looked scandalized. "I can't believe you even suggested such a thing!"

"Oh, settle down. I was going to sleep on her couch, Mel. Just so she'd feel protected."

"Why does she need to feel protected?"

"Again, no comment."

His sister pursed her lips, just the way she used to when she didn't get her way. Usually he thought it was cute. Not at the moment. She was wearing him out.

He picked up his cup, saw that he'd drained it, and walked back to the coffee maker. "Mel, instead of focusing on me and my lack of sleep, how about you tell me why you're here."

"Mamm and Daed said you could come over for supper tomorrow."

Seth was glad the coffee cup was still on the counter. Otherwise, its contents would've poured down the front of his shirt. "Why do they want to see me?"

"Beyond the fact that you're part of the family?"

Hardly. "We know I'm not that anymore," he said as he joined her again.

"I think they've finally come to realize that they've been too judgmental."

"Yeah, right."

"Well, it might also be because I've been seeing more of Lott." She lowered her voice. "Please think about it."

"I'll try."

"Gut," she said, looking pleased.

"Hold on here. Tell me what's been going on with the two of you."

"Only that we've been seeing more of each other."

He rolled his eyes. "So you two are getting serious?"

Melonie looked away. "I'm not sure."

"How come?"

"Seth."

He couldn't resist needling her. "What's wrong? Don't tell me that being on the receiving end of endless questions isn't enjoyable for you."

Her cheeks turned pink. "You made your point. I shouldn't have pestered you about Tabitha. Just as you don't need to pester me about Lott. We're adults now. Neither of us should have to explain ourselves to the other one."

"I agree with what you're saying, but I'm not pestering you, Mel. I really am interested. You're my little sister and I care about you." He smiled. "Unless you'd like to chat about Cousin Lorne."

Melonie looked pained. "You heard about Lorne?"

"Yep. How he was your date at the singing and everything."

She opened her mouth to protest, then seemed to realize that he was joking. "Oh, stop. It was horrible. I'm so glad our cousins went back home."

"Let's talk about Lott, then."

"Fine." She reached for her cup, took a sip, and then jiggled her foot while she seemed to struggle with finding the right words to say. "I don't know if we're serious or not, Seth. Sometimes Lott acts like he's very serious and wants to marry me someday. Then other times . . . I don't know." Frowning slightly, she picked up her cup and put it down again. "What do you think I should do?"

"Talk to him." That was the right advice, anyway. Of course, what he was itching to do was visit Lott and order him to stop playing with Melonie's emotions. But he was pretty sure that wouldn't go over well.

"I don't know what I would even say."

"All you have to do is tell him what you told me."

The wrinkle that had been threatening to mar her forehead deepened. "But shouldn't Lott be the one to tell me his feelings first?"

For the first time in their conversation, Seth knew how to answer her. "Sorry, but most men aren't real good at sharing their feelings."

"What about you?"

He chuckled. "Obviously not. If I was better, Tabitha would have trusted me enough to let me stay there last night. Instead, I walked back here and was so worried about her I stayed up half the night debating about whether or not I should go back and camp out on her front porch."

"I hope you didn't. That would be creepy."

"I didn't." But that didn't mean he didn't regret his choice. He was still concerned that Tabitha was frightened and all alone.

"What are you going to do now?"

"As much as it pains me, I'm going to honor her wishes for at least a couple of days."

Melonie blinked. "Really?"

"I don't have much of a choice." All he had to do was remember what she told him. "Tabitha doesn't want me around." He searched for something to add, anything that might make himself sound a little less pitiful, but decided not expanding on the obvious was the best option.

Reading his silence, Melonie gazed at him. "I'm sorry."

He shrugged. "It's okay. I'm more worried about her than my bruised heart. But, hey, listen . . . if you think Lott is the man for you, don't give up on him. But don't rush into anything either. You both have lots of time."

"I'll try to remember that. Now, will you come over for supper?"

Seth wasn't sure if he wanted to. There was so much between them that couldn't be removed or forgotten. On the other hand, they were his parents and he loved them. They weren't perfect and neither was he. "Jah. Yes, I'd like that."

Melonie's smile lit up the room, and she jumped up and threw her arms around him. "I'm so glad. I'll see you tomorrow night."

Realizing that she was already heading to the door, he followed her. "That's it?"

"Jah. I've got things to do, and you need to take a shower."

"I reckon so. I probably need to eat something too."

She smiled at him. "And put on fresh clothes while you're at it."

Looking down at his rumpled clothing, he grinned. "Anything else?"

"Nee. I'm really glad you're coming over tomorrow night, Seth."

He couldn't say he was "really glad" he was going, so he did the next best thing. "I'm *really glad* you came over here today. Thanks, Mel."

Her expression softened as she slipped her feet into her boots. "Anytime. Anytime at all. I love you, Seth."

Seth helped her into her cloak and adjusted it on her shoulders. When she turned around to face him, he leaned down and kissed her cheek. "Thanks for that. And . . . I love you back."

Watching her hop on her bicycle, Seth felt like he had gained a new perspective about his relationship with Tabitha. It was time he took some of his own advice. He needed to not give up on them, which meant he needed to be more patient with her and himself. He'd waited this long for her, so he could wait longer.

There was no need to push too hard or rush into anything. A counselor in the halfway house he'd lived in briefly after being released had been fond of saying that Rome wasn't built in a day. He was pretty sure that solid, meaningful relationships weren't either.

As Seth reminded himself of those words yet again, something inside him eased. The Lord was allowing them all the time they needed. He should give thanks for that. He and Tabitha had their whole lives ahead of them. They could take their time and learn to trust each other.

Maybe he would even share more of his feelings . . . and Tabitha would give him more of her smiles. They could heal. Maybe make a future together.

Yeah, he really liked that idea. He liked that a lot.

23

Melonie had a pretty good idea that she was going to regret her decision, but it couldn't be helped. Not only was her brother's devastated expression playing over and over in her head, she was concerned about Tabitha. Melonie had never had the connection with their former schoolteacher that Seth had, though she didn't know why. Maybe it was because she'd been only a child when Tabitha had taught in their schoolhouse.

Back then, she'd been focused on her friends and playing with her dolls. She vaguely remembered when their teacher had left in the middle of the school year to get married, but it hadn't made much of an impression on her. One week Tabitha had been their teacher, and the week after that Rachel had taken her place.

She'd had no idea that her older brother had been disturbed about Tabitha's marriage. Or that Leon Yoder was considered a difficult man. Melonie had only been focused on herself. On her friends, her schoolwork, and whether or not she would get along with the new schoolteacher. Perhaps she'd also been caught up in the idea of Tabitha leaving in the middle of the school year because her husband couldn't wait to marry her. It had sounded romantic.

Years later, right about the time Tabitha had been beaten so badly that the ambulance came, Melonie ended up embroiled in her own painful drama. Seth had been arrested, and then he went to trial and was imprisoned. Her days had been filled with her parents' grief, the endless rumors surrounding Peter Miller's death, Bethanne's assertions about what had happened, and the way almost everyone in the community had taken a side.

Even after Tabitha had returned home a year after Leon was arrested, she hadn't occupied Melonie's thoughts all that much. Tabitha was no longer part of the Amish community, and Melonie had been so focused on Seth's return.

Now she regretted being so self-absorbed. Tabitha obviously needed some friends, and Seth had told her all about how long it had taken Tabitha to even open the door to him. That had been hard to come to terms with. She might not have been attached to their former teacher, but Melonie definitely remembered her being full of smiles when she'd stood at the front of their classroom.

Melonie hoped this visit would be the first of many, especially because she was sure Seth wasn't going to stay away from Tabitha very long at all.

Walking up the driveway, she noticed that while the surrounding yard and field were far from groomed and neat, they did look cared for. The closer she got to the house, the more picturesque it looked. It was white like most other Amish-owned homes in the area, but instead of having a plain white or black door, it was bright yellow. Like the colors of sunflowers in mid-July.

It was pleasing, and Melonie thought it gave her some

insight to the woman Tabitha Yoder was. As if there had always been a hidden spark of spunk but she was only lately giving that bit of boldness the opportunity to shine.

Just as she raised her hand to knock on the door, it opened.

Tabitha was wearing jeans and a loose fisherman's sweater. Her long, brown hair was contained in a high ponytail. If Melonie hadn't known better, she would have guessed they were close in age.

"Melonie, right?"

"Jah. I'm Seth's sister."

Tabitha blinked. "It's been a long time since I've seen you up close."

"Jah. I guess it has."

She smiled softly. "You turned into a lovely woman."

The compliment was unexpected. Probably as unexpected as her appearance on Tabitha's doorstep.

"Is something wrong with Seth?" Looking stricken, Tabitha inhaled. "Oh no. Did he not make it home last night?"

"He did. I mean, we don't live together. I live at home with our parents. But I was by his haus this morning. He was there." And . . . she had now made her visit sound even more mysterious.

"Oh."

Tabitha looked more confused, and Melonie couldn't say that she blamed her. "I know it might be rude of me to stop by uninvited, but I wondered if we could talk?"

"Of course." She stepped back so Melonie could enter, though her hesitation proved that she did so with reluctance.

"Danke." The first thing she noticed inside the home was the array of beautiful woven baskets in an assortment of vivid shades. Blues, reds, and yellows. Unable to resist, she walked over to the collection arranged neatly on a small table. "These are beautiful."

"Thank you."

"May I pick one up?"

"Of course."

Holding an indigo-hued square basket in her hands, she said, "I've never seen a basket like this. Not only are the sides a little longer than usual, the colors are amazing." She touched one of the slats. "Look how the light and dark shades alternate. It makes the piece seem almost alive." She smiled at her. "These would be perfect gifts."

Tabitha's brown eyes warmed. "I've thought that too."

"Where did you get them?"

"I made them."

"Truly?" Melonie looked at them more closely. Such skilled craftsmanship.

Tabitha nodded, looking a little bashful. "I purchase the wood from a supplier near Hart County and then dye the slats and finally weave them into baskets."

"That's a lot of work." Flipping over the basket, she noticed a handful of carefully crafted details. Nothing about the basket had been done hurriedly. "You should sell them, Tabitha."

"I do. It's how I make my living."

"I had no idea. I haven't seen these in any shops in Marion."

"Oh, I don't sell them in Marion. My sister comes over to pick up baskets once a month and in turn gives them to a broker. He then sells them in St. Louis and Louisville."

"How come you send them so far away?"

Tabitha peered down at the basket Melonie held. "Well, they aren't all that special. A lot of folks around here dye fabric and stain wood and turn them into handicrafts."

"A lot of women are talented at crafts, but these are special. I've never seen anything like these."

"You're sweet to say so."

"I'm being honest."

Tabitha shrugged, seeming a bit embarrassed. "Anyway, we get pretty gut prices in the big cities. It helps me since I have to pay the broker a percentage of the selling price."

"Do you ever take orders from around here?" It was all Melonie could do to not ask her about prices.

Tabitha's eyes widened before her expression turned blank again. "I . . . nee."

"Why not?"

"I never thought about doing that."

"I think you should." When Tabitha shrugged, Melonie knew that she wasn't telling her the truth. Was it because she now lived apart from the rest of their church community?

Or maybe it was something else?

She knew right then and there that it was time to talk to her about Seth. "May I sit down?"

"Of course." Tabitha perched on the edge of the couch and waited expectantly.

After she returned the basket, Melonie sat down on the edge of a chair. "I saw Seth this morning. He told me about what happened."

Wariness entered her eyes. "What did he tell you?"

"That he tried to spend the night here and you asked him to leave."

Tabitha averted her eyes. "That is true, though I'm surprised he told you."

"I'm not. Seth was pretty upset."

"I'm sure you understand my reasons," she said. "A single

woman canna be having a man over for sleepovers, no matter how innocent or well-intentioned they might be."

"No one would have had to know. No matter what you think about Seth, you've got to believe that he's a private person. He would never go out and do anything that might hurt you in any way."

"I don't think he would." Looking even more uncomfortable, she added, "But still, someone would find out, and then he or she would tell someone else. Then the rumor mill would start up and everything would get tarnished and twisted." Tabitha sounded so bitter.

"Maybe not."

"I appreciate you saying that, but things do happen. Secrets always get revealed." She waved a hand. "Just look at how you came over, and nothing even happened."

She couldn't argue that point. But Tabitha did need to know that Melonie's reason for visiting wasn't to find fault with anyone. "I didn't come over because I'm mad about Seth's relationship with you. I came over because I care."

"All right." Tabitha's tone sounded as though she doubted her sincerity, making Melonie realize that she was going to have to say more. Not just words but speaking from her heart.

"Listen, everyone knows what you've been through. I feel terrible for the way you've been treated. I'm sorry that some folks think you should have stayed with your husband no matter what he did." She took a deep breath. "But I also love my brother. I promise, despite the fact that he's been in prison, he's a very good person. He really cares for you. And I think that maybe you should consider his feelings."

"I already have."

"Then why won't you give him a chance?"

Tabitha stiffened. "Did Seth send you over here?"

"Nee."

"Does he know you're here?"

"I didn't tell him . . . but I think he had an idea that I was going to come over."

"So you're here to badger me with his blessing."

"Nee. I didn't come to badger you, and Seth didn't give me his blessing. I came over because I wanted to. It was my idea."

"After all this time?" she asked sarcastically. Looking contrite, Tabitha took a deep breath. "I'm sorry for sounding so spiteful. I'm not at my best today." She sighed. "Listen, I know you mean well, but there are things that are going on with me that you don't know about."

When Melonie tried to interrupt, Tabitha held up a hand. "While I appreciate your words about my marriage, I fear that, also, is something we shouldn't discuss. You are a young woman. My past is nothing that you should concern yourself with."

"I'm not that young."

"You're right. But sometimes it's not an age gap that separates us from each other, it's the experiences. In that sense, we're complete opposites. I think it's time you left."

Frustrated with the awful spiral the conversation had taken, Melonie got to her feet. "Is this what you meant about twisting and turning information? Because that's what you're doing right now."

Tabitha stood slowly. "All I'm doing is sharing how I feel. It's not my fault that you feel differently than I do."

"You're right. You're entitled to how you feel. You're right that I haven't been married and I probably have no idea about everything you've experienced. But that doesn't mean I don't care."

"Melonie."

She shook her head. "Tabitha, I'm sorry, but one day you're going to have to trust other people. To accept that some people really are worthy of your time. I hope and pray that one of those people is my brother."

With that said, she turned and walked out the door. And almost stepped on the bouquet of flowers and card on the doormat.

Holding the door open, she scooped up the card so it wouldn't get dirty, then called out, "Tabitha, someone brought you flowers."

"What?" She hurried to the door and stared at them like they were about to turn into a mass of slithering snakes. "Oh nee."

"Do you want me to bring them in?"

"Nee. Don't touch them!"

Alarms were going off in her head, but she didn't know why. She stepped away from the flowers, then realized the card they came with was in her hand. "Um, there's a note." She handed it to Tabitha. "Sorry. I picked it up without thinking."

Tabitha grabbed the card with one hand and Melonie's hand with her other. After pulling her inside, she slammed the door and clicked the deadbolt. "I'm sorry, but you can't leave just yet."

"Why not?"

"It's not safe. I need to call Sheriff Johnson."

Melonie whispered, "You're serious, aren't you? You really think there's something wrong with these flowers."

"I think whoever dropped them off is nearby watching."

A chill went through Melonie. Maybe she should have listened to her brother and not gotten involved.

It was too late now.

24

Her house was in chaos. Both Sheriff Johnson and Deputy Ernst arrived within an hour after Tabitha had called the sheriff's department. Soon after, the deputy had called Seth so he could pick up his sister, as well as Tabitha's sister so Tabitha wouldn't be alone.

Seth, Mary, Roy, and all four boys arrived at the same time. Thankfully Tabitha had not witnessed their meeting because she'd tucked herself in the kitchen to prepare drinks for Melonie and the police officers. When the front door opened and all seven of the newcomers greeted Melonie in the living room, the conversation confirmed that the first few minutes of the meeting had been tense.

Now Tabitha was surrounded by her nephews, Seth and Roy were outside speaking with the sheriff and his deputy, and Melonie and Mary were discussing Tabitha's baskets. Chance, after greeting everyone, was asleep on the floor in front of the fireplace.

Tabitha supposed that to an outsider, it looked a bit like a party.

The reality was anything but that. When the sheriff and

deputy had first arrived, they'd bagged the flowers and card as evidence. Then they'd spent quite a bit of time outside taking pictures and looking for evidence of footprints. She was pretty sure they hadn't found a thing.

Melonie had been nervous and withdrawn until Seth arrived. After he'd spoken with her quietly for a few minutes, she seemed to ease. Then, to Tabitha's surprise, Melonie refused her brother's offer to see her home. She wanted to stay and offer support. Seth and Roy, despite their tense meeting, were now all business as they asked Sheriff Johnson and Deputy Ernst questions.

As the minutes passed, Tabitha felt a bit like a pinball. She answered the sheriff's questions, consoled Melonie, reassured Seth that she was all right, and avoided Mary and Roy's questioning and pointed stares as much as she could. If all of that wasn't enough, her four nephews ran around in the midst of everything.

None of it was easy.

Finally, when it seemed no one was going to leave and the boys were growing restless, Tabitha pulled out a mixing bowl and some flour and sugar. She needed to do something, even if it was baking cookies in an attempt to prevent the boys from getting in the men's way.

"What kind of cookies are we having, Aunt Tabby?" Petey asked.

"Oatmeal."

"Oatmeal with chocolate chips?" he asked hopefully.

"Nee, child. They're plain oatmeal."

He frowned as he studied the contents of the mixing bowl. "Maybe you could add some peanut butter?"

She had to chuckle. No matter what his age or what the activity, her youngest nephew liked to push the boundaries a bit. "Perhaps another time, jah? Today it's just plain oatmeal cookies."

He gazed at her with big brown eyes. "What about butterscotch chips?"

"Stop pestering Aunt Tabby, Petey," Anson said. "You're being a nuisance."

Petey wrinkled his nose. "Is that bad?"

"Jah."

Tabitha couldn't deny that Petey did need to stop pushing her for the moon and the stars, but she was glad that she didn't need to be the one to chastise him. She was putty where all her nephews were concerned. "Anson, get out a cookie sheet, please. It's in the cabinet next to the refrigerator."

The eleven-year-old retrieved it without a problem. "Here you go."

"Danke."

"Anytime, Aunt Tab."

Returning to her side, Petey watched Tabitha mix the cookie dough and then place spoonfuls of it in neat rows on the cookie sheet. When she was done, he chirped, "Now they go into the oven?"

"Jah. Now they go in." Tapping his nose softly, she added, "And when they come out, you may have a cookie."

"Are you going to be giving the policemen cookies too?"

"I am."

"I don't know why they're walking around your yard again," Anson said. "Deputy Ernst told Jack and me that they'd combed the perimeter before we arrived."

"What does that mean?" Petey asked.

"It means they looked around," Anson told him before Tabitha could get in a word.

Petey scowled. "Daed says he don't trust the police."

Tabitha inwardly sighed. Of course her brother-in-law had to share an opinion. "These two are with the sheriff's department, dear. I'm sure he trusts them."

Anson shared a smirk with Jack, who'd just joined them in the kitchen.

"Well, they sure didn't look too happy walking around the yard," Petey said.

"I don't suppose they were." She wasn't happy either. Actually, she was wavering between nervous, scared to death, and confused by the company. She supposed the Lord had a reason for bringing all of them together at the same time, but she couldn't deny that she was finding it stressful. She was ready for everyone to go home.

"Did you do something bad, Aunt Tabby?" Petey asked.

"Nee."

"Are you sure?"

"Petey, you're being a pain," Jack called out. "Stop pestering Aunt Tabby."

Mary joined them. "Jack, be nice to your younger brothers."

Hurt flared in Jack's eyes. "Mamm, Petey is asking Aunt Tab all about the sheriff being here and if she was being bad and all this after he wouldn't shut up about needing chocolate chips in his cookies. You wouldn't have let me get away with any of that."

She frowned. "Is this true, Peter?"

"Kind of," Petey said in a soft voice.

Mary popped her hands on her hips. "Kind of?"

"Jah, it's true."

Mary sighed. "I'm sorry, Tabitha. Peter, go sit on the couch with John."

The boy's lip went out, but for once he didn't argue. He went to sit on the couch.

"Can I go see what the police and Daed are doing?" Jack asked.

Mary glanced toward the front door. "I suppose. Take Anson with you. But stay near the door in case they need you to keep out of their way."

"Fine."

Seconds later, the kitchen was quiet again. Tabitha walked to the sink to wash her hands and collect herself.

Melonie joined her and Mary in the kitchen. "Your boys make me smile, Mary."

"Would you like one or two of them? That can be arranged. Sometimes I wish they'd give me a rest."

Melonie giggled. "I think they're supposed to be inquisitive."

"If that's the case, then they're doing a gut job," Mary said.

Tabitha faced them. "I'm sorry the sheriff called you over here. It seems like a waste of your time."

"I'm not sorry. You canna be alone right now."

As much as she appreciated the company, she didn't want to cause any more strain for Mary. "But Roy—"

Mary smoothly interrupted. "Needed to see you."

"Why?"

"Tabitha, I know Roy hasn't been there for you. He knows it too." She lowered her voice. "I love my husband, but I haven't agreed with the way he's been keeping his distance from ya. I've told him that too. He's been so intent on doing the 'right' thing, he had forgotten what that 'right' thing was." Looking at Melonie, she added, "Furthermore, he needed to see Seth Zimmerman for himself and maybe realize that he has been too stubborn and critical with just about everyone of late." Mary raised her chin. "I've told

Roy more than once that Jesus was far more accepting than he is."

Tabitha gasped. "How did he take that?"

Mary smiled slightly. "Well, he came here today, didn't he? I think that means that my reminders might have finally made a difference."

"You didn't have to stand up for me like that, Mary. I don't want to be the reason for strife between the two of you."

"You aren't, Sister. My husband is a good man, but he needed to open his eyes and face the truth. And that truth is that he was throwing stones at things instead of forgiving. I loved him enough to push him to do better."

Tabitha checked on the cookies so she wouldn't have to say anything, but really she wasn't sure what to say. All the events of the last twenty-four hours had come as a shock. "Six months ago, I would sometimes go three or four days without speaking to another person," she mused.

Mary's gaze softened. "I bet you're wishing you could kick all of us out and return to your peace and quiet."

"I was, but now I've been thinking the opposite. That even with everything that's been going on, I've still found a reason to be grateful. I'm not alone with just my thoughts for company." She smiled at Melonie. "Peace and quiet can be overrated, I think."

When Jack and Anson started tussling on the lawn in front of the living room window, Mary groaned. "No offense, Sister, but only someone who doesn't have four boys would ever say that."

They shared a smile. Tabitha didn't have any idea what the Lord had planned for her future, but this moment was a good reminder that He hadn't forgotten her. Not for a minute.

25

After hearing at work about Seth needing to take the day off because something had been happening with Tabitha Yoder, Lott knew it was time to finally do something about his relationship with Melonie. It needed to come out in the open, which meant that he needed to stop being so worried that Anna and Wayne Zimmerman would turn him away. If he didn't stand up to them, Melonie was going to be the one to tell him they needed to end their relationship.

Lott went home and showered, then picked up the flowers he'd bought on the way home and headed over to Melonie's house.

Anna Zimmerman opened the door when he knocked. "Hello, Lott." Her smile faded when she noticed the flowers.

"Gut evening, Anna." He lifted his chin. "I came over to see Melonie. May I?"

"Yes, of course. Come in. I imagine she'll be pleased to see you." She frowned again at the bouquet in his hands. "I'll, ah, go let her know you're here."

"Danke." As he watched her walk away, Lott's mind spun.

Anna had kept looking at the flowers like they were a hornet's nest—but why? Didn't all women like flowers? And didn't most girls' mothers appreciate such a gesture?

He held up the bouquet and stared at it for a few moments. Was it an ugly floral arrangement? Was that what was wrong?

"Hiya, Lott," Wayne Zimmerman said as he strode toward him from another room. "Anna told me you were here."

Lott took a deep breath. "Jah. I have come calling on Melonie."

"It would seem so." Wayne's expression barely changed.

Lott had no idea if Wayne was about to kick him out or welcome his suit. "I know you have concerns about me, but I want you to know that I've changed my ways."

"Melonie told me that you started working at Porter Construction."

He nodded. "I'm only an apprentice now, but I aim to become a master carpenter one day. Maybe even as good as Seth."

Wayne looked at him intently. "Seth is a master carpenter?"

"He is. He's very talented and skilled. Everyone thinks so."

"That's gut to know." He eyed the flowers again. "You know, I'm not sure if—"

"Hi, Lott!" Melonie said as she joined them. "I hope you weren't waiting too long."

"Not at all." Ready to get rid of his gift at last, he thrust the bouquet at her. "These are for you."

She inhaled sharply. "Oh."

Now thoroughly confused, he blurted, "What's wrong with these flowers? Are they ugly?"

"No. Not it all." She glanced at her father, who was still hovering nearby. "I guess, um, I'm just a little sensitive where flowers are concerned right now. You see, I was over at Tabitha Yoder's today and she received a bouquet too."

"Who from? Wait, did Seth take her flowers?" Now he really didn't understand the problem. Melonie adored her brother and approved of his relationship with Tabitha.

"Oh, nee. They . . . they came from her ex-husband. He'd dropped them off at her front door."

It took him a second to remember that Tabitha's ex's abuse had led to their divorce. "Why would he do that?"

"To scare her, I think. The police wrapped them up to take to the crime lab. Deputy Ernst said Leon could've put something on them to make them poisonous."

"Truly?"

"I'm not sure if they were tainted or not, but seeing both the sheriff and deputy there was scary." As she glanced at the bouquet again, both her gaze and voice warmed. "I do appreciate the flowers. They're pretty, and it was so kind of you to bring them. It's just that seeing them was a shock."

"I guess so." He couldn't believe that he'd given Melonie a bouquet on the very same day she'd been spooked by Tabitha's. "I'm sorry. Would you like me to get rid of them?"

Her eyes widened. "No, of course not."

Her father walked over and took them out of his hands. "Don't worry about the flowers none, Lott. They are mighty pretty, and I'm sure Melonie is grateful for them."

"Yes. Yes, I really am. It was so kind of you," she said again.

"I'll put them in water in the kitchen." Wayne walked away, saying over his shoulder, "Why don't you two go into the parlor?"

"That sounds perfect." Melonie smiled at him before leading the way.

The Zimmermans' parlor was a small room. Four comfortable-looking chairs surrounded a card table, and an oak bookcase on one of the walls held a variety of puzzles, books, and games. A blue woven rug was centered under the table, and above it was a light fueled by propane. It was already on.

"This looks like a game room," he said.

"It is. When Seth and I were little, the four of us would work on puzzles together or play cards or Scrabble or something."

"Do you still do that?"

"Nee. I grew up, and Seth . . . well, now that Seth isn't here, it's not the same." She sat down at the table.

Lott took a chair next to her. "I'm glad your parents seem friendlier."

"Me too." She peeked out toward the hall. "I think Mamm's misguided attempt to play matchmaker with my cousin made her realize that she didn't know what was best for me."

Remembering how irritating the guy was, he said, "Lorne was absolutely not best for you."

She chuckled. "That's the understatement of the century."

Lott studied her face, glad that Melonie seemed more at ease. "Want to tell me about what happened at Tabitha's?"

"I will, eventually, but would you mind if we didn't talk about it right now?" Looking cute and shy, she said, "I'd rather talk about us."

"All right." Sure, he could talk, but he was feeling so relieved that all he really wanted to do was pull Melonie into his arms and hold her tight. That was definitely not a good idea.

It was a blessing that her mother appeared at the door. "Lott, Melonie's flowers are beautiful. I put them in a vase.

Would you like some hot cider and a slice of applesauce cake? Melonie helped me make it yesterday."

"Jah, Anna. I would like that very much."

"Should we go in the kitchen, Mamm?" Melonie asked.

"Nee, dear. I'll put everything on a tray and bring it out. I think the two of you deserve a few moments to relax."

"Danke, Mamm." When her mother disappeared down the hall, she reached for Lott's hand and quickly squeezed. "I'm glad you came over, Lott. Really glad."

"Me too." He brought her hand to his lips and kissed it quickly before placing his hands back in his lap. As much as he tried to think of something interesting to say, he drew a blank. All that kept running through his head was that he was going to be able to court Melonie out in the open. The way she deserved to be treated.

At last.

26

Seth's coworkers were standing in the middle of the living room of the seven-thousand-square-foot house that multiple Porter Construction crews had been working on for six months. They'd all long ago pushed aside any grumblings about the size of the home, the number of rooms, or how particular the client was. All that mattered now was that the house had turned out beautiful, it had already gotten a lot of interest from prospective clients, and it was almost finished.

As far as Seth knew, his work on the house was finally complete. He'd been in charge of the custom cabinetry in several rooms and had finished the largest job the evening before. He was pleased with how the cabinetry turned out. Even better, his boss was too.

"This might be your best work yet," Cal Porter told Seth. Running a hand along the edge of the hickory wood bookshelves, he added, "You finished these built-ins so meticulously, I've half a mind to talk to the warden at the prison and ask him to send more ex-cons my way."

Seth grinned. "If you did that, you might get more than

you bargained for. Not every man in the woodworking program does real good in group settings."

"You aren't the only skilled craftsman to come out of there, though, are you?"

"Not at all. Mr. Martin is a good teacher. He's had a hand in training some mighty skilled woodworkers. If you gave some other men a chance to prove themselves, I don't think you'd be disappointed."

"I'm going to keep that in mind." Cal opened one of the cabinet doors. "I can't wait for our clients to see all this. They're going to be very pleased."

"I hope so." Seth was trying to act modest, but he had to admit that he was proud of how everything turned out. He'd worked hard on it—all while his head was full of everything that had been going on at Tabitha's house.

She had been so shaken that it had been hard for him to leave her. He probably wouldn't have left if her sister's entire family hadn't been camped out in her living room.

He'd also felt better after he and Roy had spoken. Though Tabitha's brother-in-law might not ever be Seth's favorite person, it seemed like the man was finally going to be more involved in Tabitha's life. Roy hadn't even flinched when Seth told him that Tabitha needed people she could count on and that it was past time for him to be one of those people. When Seth had called to check on Tabitha the night before, she'd said that Roy and Mary had stopped by that afternoon to check on her. He had been pleased about that.

Returning his attention to his boss, Seth said, "Where would you like me tomorrow?"

"Anywhere but here."

"What?"

Cal slapped him on the back. "I know you were here late

last night and came back early this morning to put on the cabinets' hardware. Take the day off."

"You sure?"

"Positive. The crew is going to be finishing up the guest bathroom tile, and I've got two meetings with prospective clients. We can spare you."

"Thanks."

"Not a problem." Already looking at his phone's screen, he started toward the doorway to the next room. "See you day after tomorrow, Seth."

"See you."

Seth took another look at the finished cabinets and shelves, then picked up his tool belt and flannel shirt and headed out as well.

The early evening air had a bite to it. The sky was overcast too. Looked like they were going to get some rain and maybe even sleet. A trip to the grocery store was in order. Slipping on his flannel, he headed to his truck.

He was about to turn toward Marion when his cell phone rang.

He pulled it out of a pocket. "Yeah?"

"Seth, I canna believe that's how you answer the phone," his sister said by way of greeting.

"Melonie, I've just finished a job and am heading to the grocery store. That's as good as it's going to get right now."

"Gotcha. You're tired and you're hungry."

"That about sums it up. What do you need?"

"Well, um, I was just wondering how Tabitha's doing."

This conversation was going to take more than a few moments, so he pulled off to the side of the driveway. "I think she's all right, why?"

"You don't know for sure?"

"I just got off work, remember?" Practically hearing the worry in the silence, he gentled his voice. "Melonie, I called Tabitha last night. She sounded all right then."

"Oh. Okay."

"Honey, what's on your mind? Has something happened that I don't know about?"

"Nee. I mean, I don't think so. It's just that things were so scary when she received those flowers. I felt so bad for her. And then we all left."

Seth was tempted to remind Melonie that just a few mornings ago, she'd been shocked that he'd offered to sleep on Tabitha's couch. "I worry about her too, Mel."

"I'm thinking about stopping by her house again tomorrow but don't want to be a pest."

He made a sudden decision. "Where are you now?"

"Standing in the phone shanty by our house." She sounded disgruntled.

"How about I pick you up and we go pay Tabitha a visit?"

"You don't mind? I mean, aren't you tired and hungry?"

"I am, but I'll be okay."

"I could make you a sandwich," she blurted. "Do you still like roast beef?"

His stomach growled. "If you could do that, I'd be really grateful."

"I'll put in chips too. And a pickle!"

"That sounds even better. Thanks, Mel. I'll be there in ten."

"I'll hurry. Bye!"

Melonie trotted right out when he pulled up at the house. After waving to their mother, he helped Melonie get settled—and laughed at the small Igloo cooler she was carrying. "What is all that?"

"Two sandwiches, chips, pickles, some of Mamm's corn casserole from last night, and a half of a pumpkin pie."

"Are you eating too?"

"Oh, nee. It's all for you. When I told Mamm what I was doing, she insisted on helping. She said she knew how you liked your sandwich."

"That was kind of her."

"I know she's feeling bad that she hasn't been doing more for you, especially since your visit for supper had to get postponed because you had to work."

Not wanting to bring that up, he let the comment slide. "Thanks for putting all this together. It sounds delicious."

She grinned at him. "You're welcome."

He was still smiling when they arrived at Tabitha's house. Just as he turned off the ignition, the front door opened. She walked out in a loose-fitting denim dress, tights, and boots. Tonight her shiny brown hair fell in waves down her back. Chance was by her side, looking like he'd been taking care of her for years instead of just weeks.

"Hi!" Melonie greeted her as Seth followed her onto the porch. "Seth and I decided to pay you a visit."

Tabitha darted a glance his way before smiling at his sister. "Any special reason?"

"Because we were thinking about you," he said. Taking in her appearance again, he wished he'd taken the time to hit the shower. "You look nice. Are you going somewhere?"

"Nope. I just didn't feel like wearing slacks today. What's in the cooler?"

"Seth's supper," Melonie said.

Two lines formed between Tabitha's brows. "Ah, you came over here to eat?"

"Yeah. I mean, yes, if you don't mind," he said.

"I don't mind. Though, um, it looks like there's a lot there."

"Oh, there is." Melonie giggled. "We even have half a pie."

"Goodness. You brought pie too?"

"I'm pretty sure we have half of my mother's refrigerator." He stopped beside Tabitha and ran his fingertips along her cheek. "It's a long story."

"Come on in and tell me all about it." Brightening, she added, "I have chicken and rice soup. You can have some of that too."

"My supper just keeps getting better and better," he teased. Though it sure was the truth. He'd gone from intending to pick up a frozen meal to eating roast beef sandwiches, soup, and homemade pie.

"I'm so glad I called you." Melonie grinned at him as she stepped inside.

"Me too." He closed the door behind Chance.

They spent the next hour at Tabitha's kitchen table. While Seth ate, the women had some soup and pie and generally made everything brighter.

Best of all, Tabitha seemed relaxed and content. He hoped and prayed the Lord was giving them a taste of what their future could one day be like. Now that all the walls that had been built up around them were slowly tumbling down.

27

After almost three weeks of living on edge, barely stepping outside her door, and getting herself so worked up that she barely ate or slept, Tabitha let her guard down.

She didn't have much of a choice in the matter. Even though she was still deathly afraid of Leon returning, life continued for everyone else in Crittenden County. A string of robberies had kept Sheriff Johnson busy most every day. And when someone set fire to an abandoned trailer near Morganfield two days ago, Deputy Ernst had his hands full with that. Little by little, their concern about Leon Yoder violating a restraining order seemed to have faded. She barely saw them drive by anymore.

She didn't blame them, especially since she hadn't seen a hint of Leon again. She even began to breathe a little bit easier.

And then one moment she was on her front porch fishing out wooden slats from the cranberry dye and placing them on newsprint and the next she was grabbed from behind.

She screamed, looking for Chance. But he was in the

house. She'd taken him on a long walk that morning, and he'd fallen asleep in front of the fireplace.

The grip around her middle was so tight that she could barely breathe. It prevented her from doing much more than giving a token struggle and kick.

"Stop," he ordered.

The voice confirmed her suspicions. Leon had returned. The Tabitha of old would have frozen, too afraid to do anything to make her "punishment" worse. But that wasn't who she was anymore. She might still be weaker than him, but she wasn't afraid to try. Nothing she could do now would make her life any worse than it had been when he'd hurt her so badly that she'd ended up in the hospital.

Kicking a leg back again, she did her best to hit his shin with the heavy heel of her boot. He gasped and loosened his hold, and that was all she needed to pull away. Scrambling for balance, she ran around to the other side of the worktable.

Leon's expression burned. "You are so foolish. Do you really think there's anything you can do to harm me?"

She didn't dare answer him. Fresh memories of all the times he'd been so cruel to her, making her say and do things that were wrong just because she was too afraid to do otherwise, came back to her. Instead, she eyed the large metal drum filled with hot water and cranberries on the table in front of her. Needing to slow him down, she grabbed the side of the container and pushed it toward him.

Hot, red water shot out. The majority of it hit the center of his chest, and the rest splashed into his face and eyes.

Leon cried out and raised his hands. That was the break she needed to run as fast as she could toward the woods.

Behind her, the worktable crashed over and a chair sounded like it broke in two. Fear rose inside of her and she attempted to increase her pace. She didn't know how successful she was since she kept tripping on roots and branches.

"Stop, Tabitha!" Leon yelled. "You're only making this worse for yourself."

She used to believe every word he said. Now she knew better.

She forced everything from her mind except for her one goal: get away. Remembering the advice Deputy Ernst had shared, she repeated it over and over in her head. Her own personal mantra.

Run as fast as you can toward the road. There you'll be in the open, allowing someone to see you and preventing Leon from his primary objective, to keep his return hidden.

Spying the road up ahead, she belatedly remembered the cell phone the sheriff had made her promise to always keep in her dress's pocket. Her guard might have been let down, but not completely. Giving praise, Tabitha pulled it out. She was running too fast to dial a number, but she was able to finally dial 911.

Relief filled her. The phone would immediately ding both Sheriff Johnson and Deputy Ernst. They would be able to find her thanks to the tracking feature they'd installed on her phone.

Footsteps pounded behind her, and branches and twigs broke and popped as Leon followed.

Focusing intently, she knew Leon was breathing hard. From the sound of him, maybe even harder than she was. That shouldn't be a surprise since they'd had two very different living experiences over the last several years. Her body had gotten stronger and healthier. She was used to physical exertion and pushing herself. Leon, on the other hand, was now out of shape.

Her phone dinged with a text. She didn't dare slow down enough to see what it said. All she could do was hope and pray that law enforcement was on their way.

She soon reached the road, but there were no vehicles or people in sight. Her heart sank as despair threatened to overtake her. But then she remembered another piece of the deputy's advice. She was to run to the nearest house and scream as loud as she could. Being quiet would only give Leon the ammunition he craved to pull her out of sight.

The nearest neighbors were the Lapps. Joseph lived there with his mother and grandmother. None of them had been sympathetic to her over the years. In fact, Rose Lapp had once even gone out of her way to say cutting things to Tabitha in the middle of the market. What would they do if she showed up screaming? Would they turn her away? Worse, would they try to help Leon?

Could they be so cruel?

She used to think that wasn't possible, but experience with some people in the community had proved otherwise. Joseph and Rose were her only option, and she hoped and prayed they would help her. She couldn't keep running.

She ran as quickly as she could toward the Lapps' house. It was at the top of a steep hill, and her muscles strained on the incline. All she could hope was that Leon's poor conditioning would slow him down.

When she heard his steps quicken, that hope began to fade.

"Do you really think Joseph or Rose is gonna help you, Tabitha? They hate you! They think you're terrible because you divorced me."

Maybe they did. However, she also had to believe there was still goodness in their hearts. Had to believe that Joseph, at the very least, would step in before Leon could hurt her.

Her heart and lungs burned as she continued up the hill. Her legs were starting to cramp. "Help!" she screamed as loud as she could. "Help me! I need help!" Tabitha wasn't sure if she was crying for the Lapps to help her or for the Lord to intervene.

A window curtain moved but the door didn't open.

She was now in the Lapps' front yard. They had a big fence behind the house and some old lawn equipment in a rusty pile to one side. She had nowhere else to go.

Behind her, Leon laughed as he slowed to a walk. "You're so stupid. Did you really think they would suddenly care about you? They won't come out, Tabitha. Not for you. You're unforgiven."

No. No, Leon's words weren't true. The Lord already had forgiven her. So had Mary. So had Roy.

And now she had Seth. She was no longer alone.

Tears filled her eyes as despair threatened to take over her. She fought them back. "Help me!" she screamed again. Then, seeing a big rock at her feet, she picked it up, rushed up the three steps leading to the front porch, and threw it at the window.

The shattering of glass reverberated around them.

The door flew open, revealing Rose and an angry-sounding Doberman by her side.

"Tabitha Yoder, you've lost your—"

"Help me, Rose!" she said just as Leon grabbed her arm and wrenched her around to face him. She cried out as pain shot from her shoulder down her arm, then gasped as he yanked her again before slamming his fist into her face.

The world went black as she fell.

"Get up!" Leon yelled against a backdrop of angry barking. "Get up, Tabitha. You need to be punished."

She knew she should, but pain still radiated from her face. In addition, her shoulder burned and her wrist was throbbing. She must have landed on it when she'd fallen. Her ears buzzed from his crushing blow, and she could feel warm liquid on her face. Her nose was bleeding.

She managed to get on her knees.

As if in slow motion, Rose called for Joseph. Then out he came, wielding his grandmother's hickory cane. Tabitha ducked her head as Joseph swung it around into Leon's shoulder.

Leon yelled, but it was overpowered by the blaring of the sheriff's cruiser's siren as it tore up the drive. Both front doors opened and then men jumped out.

"Freeze!" Deputy Ernst yelled as he drew his weapon. "Leon Yoder, you're under arrest!"

Leon froze, then darted toward the side of the house.

"You run away, my dog will attack," Rose called out. "I'm serious."

The dog's fierce barking erupted again, and Leon turned toward the old farm implements.

"Don't do it, Leon!" Sheriff Johnson said as he pulled out his gun.

To Tabitha's shock, Leon smirked. "You wouldn't dare do a thing. I'm unarmed. Plus Joseph just hit me for no reason. I'm going to press charges."

Sheriff Johnson didn't move a muscle. "It's over, Leon. Don't make things worse for yourself."

Barely two seconds passed, but it felt like an eternity as all of them stared at Leon. At last, Leon put his hands up. Sheriff Johnson cuffed his hands behind his back.

"Leon, what a liar you have turned into," Rose said as she toddled outside to join them. "I feared Tabitha's words were true all this time. Now I know for sure and I'm going to make sure everyone knows that."

Realizing she was now safe, Tabitha carefully slid off her knees and turned around so she was sitting on the top porch step. The pain in her shoulder and arm was excruciating, but she could finally breathe.

"It's over," Deputy Ernst said as he sat by her side. "Looks like you're hurt bad. I already radioed for an ambulance just in case. It's on the way."

"Danke," she whispered.

Sheriff Johnson read Leon his rights as he led him toward the cruiser. "After the ambulance comes, get the Lapps' statements, Junior," he called over his shoulder.

"Yes, sir."

Rose came over. "I'll stay with her, son. Never fear."

To Tabitha's surprise, the older woman gingerly lowered herself until she was sitting beside her. "My, it's been quite a while since I sat in this spot. Feels good out here, don't it?" she asked, just as if they were relaxing on a summer's day.

Tabitha nodded.

"Any reason why part of Leon is bright red?"

It took a moment for her to realize what Rose was talking about. "It's cranberry dye," she whispered.

The sheriff faced them after shoving Leon into the back seat of the cruiser. "Dye?"

"When Leon found me, I was dyeing wooden slats for my baskets. I pushed a metal container of hot dye water on him so I could run away."

"Now ain't that something?" Rose murmured. "That was mighty quick thinking, girl."

"I had to do something. I promised myself I'd never be hurt by him again. Not without a fight, anyway."

"Sounds like the Lord heard your promise and helped you out."

Thinking of how heavy the metal container had been and how hard it usually was for her to empty it, she had to agree.

Sheriff Johnson returned to her side just as the sirens from the ambulance approached. "We're going to get you loaded up and on your way to the hospital right now. I'll stop by there later to see how you're doing."

He'd also no doubt ask her a lot of questions.

"I understand."

"Who would you like me to contact for you?"

She supposed the best person would be her sister, but she didn't want to involve Mary and Roy just yet. Besides, there was only one person who would truly understand how she felt. Only one person who she could trust to help her but not pester her with a dozen questions about the day's events.

Oh, who was she kidding? While all that was true, the main thing was that there was only one person who she trusted with her heart . . . just like he trusted her with his. "Would you call Seth Zimmerman?"

"Seth?" He sounded surprised but then nodded. "I'll call him now."

An ambulance pulled up with a parade of flashing lights.

"Thank you. Oh, and Sheriff?"

"Yes?"

"Thank you for everything."

"Anytime. But don't forget that you helped yourself today. You fought, ran, and called for help. You should be real proud."

She was glad that was the last of their conversation. Her arm and shoulder really hurt and it was getting hard to see out of her one eye. She closed her eyes as the paramedics spoke to Sheriff Johnson.

"Tabitha, my name is Kurt. Can you hear me all right?"

She opened her one good eye. "Jah."

Kurt had a kind look about him. His cheeks were full and looked as if he only needed to shave every couple of days. His blue eyes were bright and framed by light brown eyelashes. "Looks like you've got some bruising on your face. What else is hurting?"

"My shoulder and wrist."

"Anything else?" he asked as he took her pulse.

"I don't think so," she said.

He shined a light into her pupils and then scanned the rest of her body. After immobilizing her arm, he said, "Okay. Billy and me are going to help you onto the stretcher and get you loaded in the ambulance."

"All right." She closed her eyes again as the two men spoke to each other and carefully lifted her onto the stretcher.

She was vaguely aware of the sheriff speaking with the Lapps, no doubt telling Rose that someone would be over to help board up the window she broke. When Tabitha was situated in the ambulance, Kurt asked her more questions as he pricked her good hand and started an IV. Then, the next thing she knew, they were on their way to the hospital.

Maybe she should be worried about what the doctors were going to do, or be thinking about how she was going to pay for the services, but all she could concentrate on was that Leon had been apprehended. She was safe again.

Just as important to her was the knowledge that she'd fought her ex-husband and run instead of cowering at his demands. She'd gotten stronger.

"We're almost there, Tabitha," Kurt said. "You hanging in there for me?"

"Jah."

"That's good. You sure are a lot tougher than you look."

Kurt might not realize it, but that was one of the sweetest things someone had ever said to her.

28

Seth braked hard on the turn, causing his sister to clutch the edge of his truck's bench seat.

"Hang on," he murmured as he passed a delivery truck parked on the side of the road. Pleased to see no one ahead for miles, he sped up.

"Seth!" Melonie gasped.

"What?"

"Bruder, I think you're driving too fast."

That's because he was. All he could think about was getting to Tabitha's side. Even though it made no sense, he felt responsible for what had happened. If he couldn't have prevented Leon from showing up again, he wished he could have been there instead.

He tapped on his brakes at a stop sign, turned left, and edged closer to the vehicle in front of them. The moment it was safe, he passed the white sedan. "We're almost there."

Melonie cleared her throat. "I don't know if you should be driving. I think you're too upset to be behind the wheel."

"I may be upset, but I'm fine." Saying he was upset was

an understatement, though. He was angry and worried and guilt-ridden too. All at the same time.

"Prove it."

Prove it? "What are you talking about?"

She waved off his confusion. "You know what I mean. Slow down."

"Melonie, I have enough going on in my life without you being a back-seat driver."

"But I'm not. I'm sitting in the front seat with you," she said without missing a beat. "I think that means I'm allowed to give you my opinion about things."

"Of course you're allowed."

"What I mean, Seth Zimmerman, is that you are also supposed to listen to me."

Glancing at his sister, so spunky and full of herself, he tapped the brakes. His truck settled closer to the posted speed limit. "I hope Lott knows what he's getting into," he murmured.

"If you're suggesting that Lott won't be getting a quiet wife if we do get married . . . you're right. And, just to let you know, he likes me the way I am." Melonie sounded so secure.

"Married? How serious are the two of you?"

"Serious enough for him to be officially calling on me now. Mamm and Daed seem to like him fine."

"Hmm." He glared at the line of vehicles in front of them and tapped his steering wheel impatiently.

"Seth, I'm telling you the truth."

"I believe you. But . . . you're awfully young, Mel."

"You're only saying that because you think of me as your little sister. I'm not that young. I'm certainly old enough to realize that Lott makes me happy."

As they approached another traffic light, he glanced her

way. Melonie's chin was up and her eyes were bright. She felt comfortable in her skin and with her relationship with this boy.

There were so many things Seth wanted to say about that. He wanted to tell her he was proud of her for being the type of woman she was. That he'd been wrong about his prejudices against Lott. Most of all, he wanted to tell Melonie that he was grateful to her for never giving up on him. For writing to him while he was in prison and always choosing to see him—even when their parents had kept their distance.

But his nerves were so frayed at the moment, he was afraid he would either start crying or say too much and make her cry. So he'd save that conversation for another day when he wasn't feeling so emotional.

"Seth?" she asked in a tentative voice. "Are you okay?"

"Jah. I'm sorry." He turned into the hospital parking lot. "There's a lot I want to tell you, but I can't do that now. I fear anything I say is going to come out in a jumbled mess."

"Good things or bad?" Her voice sounded timid and sweet. Exactly the way it had always been, even when she'd been a little girl and following him all around.

It made his voice gentle. "Good. All good," he said as he maneuvered his vehicle into a narrow space in the back of the lot.

As soon as they got out, Melonie came around the truck and wrapped her arms around him. "You're not alone, Seth. God is with you and Tabitha. I am too."

"I know that. Danke."

"I know Mamm and Daed love you and care about you too."

He pressed his lips to her brow. "I know, Mel."

She smiled at him. "Let's go on in, then."

227

He'd been inside the hospital only one other time. Now, walking through the emergency room doors, he was inundated with the sounds of a baby crying, a television that droned from its place on the wall, and about a dozen conversations. The lights were bright, and there was an astringent smell in the air. Several people stood in lines near the front of the room. Some of them didn't look happy at all.

Beside him, Melonie wrinkled her nose. "It's not like I thought it would be. Where do you think we go?"

Seeing that a man was standing behind a sign that said "Reception," Seth figured that was a good place to start. They joined the other six people in line. Unable to help himself, Seth kept looking at where the nurses were, hoping to see some sign of Tabitha.

Several minutes later, they'd finally reached the reception desk.

"May I help you?" the man asked without looking up from his computer screen.

"We're here to see Tabitha Yoder," Seth said.

"How was she brought in?"

"By ambulance."

The man raised his head. "Sorry. You're in the wrong place." He pointed to another line on their right. "Someone over there will help you out."

Seth gritted his teeth but nodded. "Thank you."

Melonie glanced at him out of the corner of her eye. "You handled that well."

He wasn't sure if he had or hadn't. All he did know was that he wasn't going to do anything to jeopardize his chances of seeing Tabitha as soon as possible. "Nothing one can do about it, jah?" he said as they went to the end of the next line. "Complaining won't change things."

"I suppose." She sounded as doubtful as he felt, though.

Seth sighed in relief that she didn't say anything more. He didn't like to admit how much his incarceration had changed him, but there were times when he realized that his experience had a lasting effect that wasn't completely unwelcome. He'd learned patience in prison. Patience and the benefits of keeping one's mouth closed instead of complaining.

Ten minutes later, he was speaking to yet another hospital representative wearing a pair of light blue scrubs and staring at a computer. "We're looking for Tabitha Yoder. She was brought here by ambulance."

The lady tapped on her keyboard. "She's being seen now. Are you family?"

"No."

The woman looked sympathetic but firm. "I'm sorry, but you'll have to wait in one of these seats. I'll try to have someone come out to give you updates on her condition."

Seth nodded, but the disappointment was crushing. He needed to be there for Tabitha. She had to be in pain, and he was closer to her than her family. Plus, he wanted to be the one to comfort her. "Do you need my name?"

"Oh. Sure." She picked up a pen and a block of sticky notes. "What is it?"

"Seth Zimmerman. And my sister, Melonie."

The woman scribbled their names in such a way that he doubted she was going to look at them again. "All right. Like I said, someone will fill you in as soon as we have some information." She was already looking at the person behind them.

"Thanks," he bit out as he turned.

"Nee. Wait a minute," Melonie said. "My brother isn't Tabitha's family, but he's her closest friend."

"I'm sorry, miss. Rules are rules."

"Listen, Tabitha's sister isn't going to come here. She's got four young boys and a stickler of a husband. Tabitha is going to want Seth. Him," Melonie added, gripping his arm.

A bit of the woman's harried, businesslike demeanor evaporated. "Miss, I know you're upset, but rules are rules. They're in place for a reason."

"It's okay, Mel," he said.

"Nee, wait!" Melonie turned to him. "Seth, didn't the sheriff call you?"

"He did."

With a look of triumph, she lifted her chin. "See? The sheriff asked Seth to come here to the hospital so he could be with Tabitha. Couldn't you call and ask if she's waiting for Seth Zimmerman?"

The pair of men behind them sighed.

Just when the receptionist seemed about to threaten to kick them out, Melonie whispered, "Please? Tabitha was attacked by her awful ex-husband. She needs a friend right now. Are you really going to refuse her that?"

The woman's eyes darted from Melonie to Seth. Whatever she saw there—combined with Melonie's earnest speech—must have swayed her because she picked up the sticky note. "I'll be right back."

When the men behind them sighed again, Seth lost his patience. "You got a problem?"

Whatever one of the guys saw in his eyes made him take a step back. "What? No. Sorry, man."

Turning back to Melonie, Seth leaned close. "When did you get so bossy?"

"You're not the only person who's changed a lot during the past six years."

"I'm beginning to see that."

The receptionist returned with a woman wearing pink scrubs. "Mr. Zimmerman, Donna will escort you to the back."

"Thank you, " he said.

"I'm sorry, but you'll need to stay out here," the woman in scrubs told Melonie apologetically. "There's not a lot of room back there, and Mr. Zimmerman is who Tabitha is requesting."

"That's fine with me." Looking like a fresh-faced Amish woman again, Melonie squeezed Seth's arm. "Tell Tabitha that I'll be praying for her."

"I will. If it's going to be a while, I'll send word and call for a driver for you."

"Danke, Bruder."

Next thing he knew, Seth was walking beside the nurse.

"We're sure glad you're here," she said, glancing up at him. "Your girlfriend has been asking for you."

The new title caught him off guard, but he couldn't deny that it felt right. "I got here as soon as I could. How is she?"

"Fortunately, her nose isn't broken, but she's sustained quite a few other injuries. Her shoulder was dislocated, and the way she fell injured it further. She's already had X-rays and is waiting for a CT scan. That'll show if anything has torn."

"If there is?"

"That's for the doctor to say, but surgery is a possibility." She hesitated, then added, "Oh, and her wrist is broken as well."

"The same arm?"

"All on her right. Is she right-handed?"

"I think so." How did he not know that?

They walked through silver doors that opened automatically. The atmosphere was buzzing in the ER. Curtains and cubicle walls divided each patient area, and there were wheeled stainless-steel carts of equipment parked in the hall. Orderlies were either standing next to gurneys or pushing patients down the hall, and nurses and doctors were speaking in soft tones, glancing at computers or at phone screens. It reminded him of an ant farm. Everyone had a job and was focused on it.

The nurse stopped outside a curtained partition. "She's just in here, Mr. Zimmerman." She lowered her voice. "She's got a black eye, but it looks worse than it is. Try not to worry about that. Also, we've given her pain medication and a mild sedative. She might seem a little groggy, but that's to be expected."

He nodded. Then, after bracing himself, he pushed aside the curtain, peeked in, and saw Tabitha.

She wore a blue-and-white hospital gown and had several monitors attached to her. She was sitting up, though, and awake.

When she caught sight of him, tears filled her brown eyes. "You came."

"Of course I did," he said as he approached. "I'm sorry it took me so long."

"That's you, Seth. Always attempting to take on the burden of things that aren't your fault." She swiped at her eye with the side of her left hand.

"Hey now," he murmured. "Everything's going to be all right. Leon is in custody."

"I know." She hiccupped. "I don't like being here, though. I hate this place."

Unable to help himself, he ran a hand along her cheek.

There was a faint bruise near her mouth. And her left eye was swollen and a horrible dark purple color. He was glad the nurse had prepared him for how she'd look. "I can understand that. Hospitals can be scary places."

"I think being here again is bringing back memories of when I was here the last time." She swiped her cheek again. "Of course, I don't even remember being in the ambulance last time."

"You're hurt, but you'll get better."

"You sound so sure."

"That's because I am, because I'm going to help you." He hoped she understood everything that he wasn't saying—that he was willing to do whatever it took to make sure she felt safe, secure, and as pain-free as possible.

"I know you will."

The curtain slid to the side a bit, and then Donna led in a doctor who wore scrubs and a stethoscope around his neck.

"Hello again, Tabitha." He smiled at Seth. "It looks like you've got some company."

"Jah. This is Seth."

"And you are?"

"Her boyfriend."

Tabitha's eyes widened but she didn't correct him.

"I'm Dr. Kintz." He held out his hand. "Good to meet you."

"Same," Seth said as they shook hands. "Thank you for allowing me to be by her side."

The doctor turned his attention to her. "How are you feeling now, Tabitha? Still in a lot of pain?"

"Some, but it's bearable."

Donna, who'd been looking at the monitor and checking the bandages on her hand, said, "How would you rate it on a scale of one to ten?"

"Maybe a six?"

The nurse looked at the doctor.

"Tabitha, I requested the orderlies to take you for a CT scan, then they're going to transfer you to your room. As I told you before, we need you to stay overnight."

She looked crestfallen. "You're sure?"

"It's safer for you. We'd like to keep an eye on you."

When she looked like she might protest, Seth reached for her hand. "The doctor wouldn't recommend it if he didn't think it was necessary. Besides, it will give us time to clean up your place."

The little bit of color that had appeared in her cheeks faded. Her eyes were filled with fresh pain as she clung to his hand, her fingers gripping his own. "I hadn't thought about my house."

He bit back a curse at himself. He should've known better than to bring up her house. Of course she would be afraid to be by herself at home once again. "Please don't worry. By the time you get released, everything will be set to rights. I'll find someone to stay with you too." Even if it was himself.

"Okay, we're all settled, then," the doctor said. "Tabitha, either I or the attending doctor will be in later to let you know about the test results."

"Will Seth be able to stay with me?"

"Of course, honey," the nurse said. "The police will no doubt be stopping by to talk to you and take your statement. It will be good to have him by your side when that happens."

She nodded. "Danke."

"I might be overstepping, but I suggest that you allow this guy to look out for you," Dr. Kintz said in a kind voice. "Take it from me, there's nothing wrong with leaning on someone who cares about you. It can only help."

Tabitha smiled softly at Seth. "That's good advice, Doctor. Thank you."

Seth knew he should thank the doctor too, but he didn't want to do anything but sit with Tabitha and think about everything that was suddenly within their grasp.

29

The driver Seth had called to pick up Melonie at the hospital was a retired lady named Paige who enjoyed driving the Amish around to help supplement her income.

Melonie reckoned she was nice enough, but the friendly chatter grated on her nerves. She was tired, and the visit to the hospital with her brother had taken a toll. Even though she hadn't been able to see Tabitha, just hearing about some of her injuries from Seth had been difficult. Melonie had heard stories about Leon's abuse, but now that she knew Tabitha better, this latest incident brought her to tears. Especially since Seth had looked crushed when he came out to walk her to the driver.

Melonie was coming to the conclusion that she'd never wanted to completely imagine what Tabitha had been going through.

Tabitha was so alone in the world, and Seth was the most important person to her—and he had been unforgiven as well. Everything about what was "right" and "wrong" was a mixed-up muddle in her head. She knew she'd be asking the Lord some hard questions when she said her prayers that night.

"Did you hear me, miss?" Paige said, bringing her back to the present.

Sitting in the back seat of the van, Melonie shook her head. "I'm sorry. I . . . I think my mind drifted off. What did you say?"

"Do you have a beau? A pretty young girl like you probably has scads of boys calling on her, hmm?"

Thinking of Lott, she smiled. "I do have a beau."

"Well, tell me all about him. What's his name? What does he do? How did you meet?" She chuckled softly. "What does he look like? I can't wait to hear all the details. It's been ages since I've been in love."

Love? Was Melonie in love? "We . . ." No. No, she wasn't going to do this. She wasn't going to talk about Lott to this nosy Englisher stranger, and she wasn't going to pretend that she didn't mind being asked something so personal. "I'm sorry, I'd rather not talk about him."

"Oh."

Even though she didn't owe the driver an excuse, she said, "It's, um, still new."

"Hmm." Paige drummed her fingers on the steering wheel. "Well, we've got another ten or fifteen minutes at least. What would you like to chat about?"

"Nothing. I don't want to talk at all. Perhaps you could put on the radio?"

The driver inhaled sharply but did as Melonie asked. Seconds later, a country western station was on and a man was singing about beers and trucks. Paige peeked in the rearview mirror at Melonie, waiting for her reaction.

Melonie hid a smile. She was pretty sure that Paige thought

she would be offended by the song, but it only amused her. After all, it wasn't like she didn't know a thing about beer or trucks.

Now that she had a moment to relax and quiet her mind, she was able to take a moment to pray for Tabitha's healing and ask the Lord to continue to look after her and Seth's relationship. And then, at long last, she concentrated on her and Lott.

Lott Hostetler was such a mess of contradictions! Now that he was calling on her, things between them seemed more solid. But instead of acting more at ease, he had become almost formal. He took care not to sit too close to her when he visited and didn't even try to kiss her cheek. Her mother was thrilled with his gentlemanly ways.

Melonie felt differently. It might have been bad, but she kind of missed the way he'd been when they were sneaking around together. That embarrassed her. Shouldn't she want him to be reserved and proper when they were alone? Why was she missing his heated looks and all the secrecy? Why had that made her feel so alive?

Maybe she was more like her brother than she'd realized, Melonie mused. Seth was filled with good intentions but hadn't always thought of the consequences or repercussions before he did things. His fighting Peter Miller was the obvious example. But so was looking after Tabitha Yoder for so long . . . and now falling in love with her.

Was that what love was? Was it impetuous and vibrant? So much so that it filled one's heart with barely any room left for doubts and regrets? She kind of hoped so.

"You still doing okay back there?" Paige asked.

"Yes. Thank you."

"We're almost there."

"Yes. I'm glad."

238

Paige glanced at her in the rearview mirror. "I've never known an Amish girl to be so quiet."

Melonie looked up and gasped. "The buggy!"

"What?" Paige looked back at the road and swerved the vehicle to the left, narrowly missing the horse and buggy by just a few feet.

The horse reared and the buggy weaved as the driver tried to gain control.

Paige heaved a sigh of relief. "That was close."

Melonie turned to look out the back window. The driver had pulled off to the side and climbed out to calm the horse. "You almost hit them!"

"Don't get so excited. I didn't."

"The driver is having to calm down his horse! You caused that! The buggy could have overturned and killed him or the horse—or both."

"But they're both all right. Stop talking about what-ifs and almosts. Everything is just fine. Honey, sorry, but I don't need to hear any more complaints. I bet you've never driven a car. You have no idea what you're talking about."

Melonie didn't appreciate Paige's cavalier attitude or dismissal of her concerns. She was tempted to give her a piece of her mind but suspected it would do no good. And maybe the Lord had been giving Melonie another example of how two viewpoints could be drastically different.

It happened all the time. Sometimes there really was someone in the right and someone else in the wrong. But that didn't seem to matter. People believed what they believed and didn't want to be swayed no matter what evidence there was to the contrary.

"Is it this one?" Paige asked as the van neared the Zimmermans' drive.

Melonie looked out the window. "Yes."

Paige pulled into the drive, and both of Melonie's parents came out to greet her.

Relieved, Melonie exited. "Thank you for the ride," she said to Paige.

"Aren't you forgetting something?"

"Nee. I know my brother paid you."

"What about my tip?"

"You almost hit a horse and buggy. You would've done so if I hadn't called out to you. As far as I'm concerned, you should be giving me a refund."

Paige scowled at her but didn't argue.

As the van backed out onto the road, Mamm said, "What was that all about?"

"The driver wasn't good. She almost hit a horse and buggy."

Daed shook his head. "People drive too fast on these roads, and that's the truth." Smiling softly, he gave her a hug. "I'm glad you're home. How is Seth?"

"Worried about Tabitha. I canna believe Leon hurt her so badly yet again. Seth told me that she'll likely be in the hospital overnight."

Her parents exchanged a look. "I wish Seth hadn't involved you, Melonie," Mamm said.

"What are you talking about? I'm not involved."

"I'd prefer it if you weren't even aware of what happened. You shouldn't have to worry about things like that."

"About real life?"

Her parents glanced at each other again. "You know what has happened to Tabitha Yoder is not what married life is usually like," Daed said. "I don't want you to worry about that."

"But I am worrying about her, Daed. And Seth, because he loves her."

"How can that be? They hardly know each other."

"That's where you're wrong. They know each other very well. I know Seth has fallen in love with her and believes their love is real. Besides, who are we to judge?"

Her parents exchanged looks again. "Let's go inside, dear," Mamm said. "You can help with supper."

That was the last thing she wanted to do, but Melonie knew better than to refuse to help. "All right."

Just as she was lamenting how everything was terrible, her father said, "Just because Lott Hostetler is joining us is no reason to get into a tizzy."

"Lott is coming over?"

Mamm smiled. "He certainly is. When I saw him at the market, I asked him over. He accepted immediately."

Her father chuckled. "He thinks the world of you, Melonie. I'm sure of it."

"I . . . I hope so."

"Come now," her mother said. "Settle down. I thought having him over would make you happy."

"It does."

"Then I'm glad, child. We want you to be happy."

She smiled at her mother as they walked inside. After agreeing that she'd be in the kitchen to help in ten minutes, she went to her bedroom. Praised God and gave thanks for the many blessings she'd been given.

And then hurried to freshen up so she'd look her best.

She might have some new attitudes about how she wanted to treat people and how people should be treated . . . but some things were still the same.

She was okay with that.

30

Tabitha hadn't wanted to stay overnight in the hospital, but she hadn't put up much of a fight. She'd been shaking and hurting and needed to feel safe. The nurses and doctors had done a good job with that. In addition to letting Seth stay by her side past regular visiting hours, almost every hour someone had come in to check on her.

When she'd woken up bleary-eyed and exhausted this morning, she'd been ready to go home. She knew she'd be a little frightened there, but she had good locks on her doors. She would be all right.

Then the doctor surprised her by recommending that she stay another night. It seemed they were still worried about a possible concussion since she'd almost passed out when she'd tried to walk to the bathroom.

She was just glad to not have to be alone just yet. Even though Deputy Ernst had come in and promised that Leon was behind bars and wasn't eligible for bail, she wasn't sure if she completely believed it.

So, maybe it was good that she was in her hospital room. But as she tapped a button on the TV's remote control and

242

watched the variety of stations flicker across the screen, Tabitha knew that while she might feel safe, she was also going to be very bored. And uncomfortable. Her hospital bed's mattress was hard and unforgiving. Not very comfortable at all.

When her door opened after the briefest of knocks, she turned toward it in time to see Seth come in. "Seth. You came back."

He crossed the room, then leaned down and kissed her cheek. "Of course I did. I told you I would. Were you wondering where I was?"

She had been, but admitting that would tell him too much. "No. I'm just pleased to see you."

He glanced at the clock on the wall. "Sorry, but I had to wait until visiting hours began. I didn't think the nurses would let me come early after they let me stay here so long last night."

"I understand."

"Do you?" He frowned as he sat down. "Then why am I getting the feeling that you're surprised to see me?"

"I don't know."

"Tabitha, talk to me."

Feeling foolish, she said, "I guess I just thought you'd be ready for a break from me."

His steel-blue eyes seemed to look all the way inside her heart. "I didn't want to leave your side last night. Did you not think that meant something?"

"I knew it did." She was at a loss for words and feeling flustered. That feeling only got worse when he remained silent, waiting for her to continue. She waved her good hand. "I don't know what else to say." It was a miserable thing to admit but the truth. Seth seemed to turn her mind into mush.

"I happened to see your nurse in the hall. She said they've recommended you stay another night."

"Yes. The doctor thought it would be a good idea." No way did she want to admit to Seth that she feared everyone knew she was afraid to be home by herself.

"Honey, I'm glad they're keeping you here. You'll be able to rest." His eyes were filled with compassion. "And let's not forget your broken wrist."

He'd called her honey. She mentally tried it on for size and decided she liked it. "I haven't forgotten my wrist." She frowned down at her arm. The bandages were bulky, and her wrist was throbbing. Actually, she was so bruised and sore, she didn't know how she was going to do a single thing when she got home. She couldn't even imagine getting dressed by herself.

"Are you in pain?"

"My shoulder and wrist hurt." Actually, pretty much every part of her body hurt. Besides the black eye and her shoulder and wrist, she had an assortment of bruises and abrasions all over her. The doctor had reminded her that recovery was going to take time. Maybe even weeks before she felt like her old self.

Seth pushed a button beside her bed.

"Yes?" a woman's voice said.

"I'm here visiting Tabitha Yoder. She's in a bit of pain. Can you help her with that?"

"I'll come right down."

When Seth leaned back with a satisfied expression on his face, she shook her head. "You didn't have to call the nurse."

"Of course I did. I could see you weren't about to call for help yourself."

"I hate to be trouble."

"You're here because the doctors and nurses feel that you need help, Tab. Asking for pain medication is not too much trouble. It's why you're here, jah?"

"Jah."

"Hello, Ms. Yoder." The nurse in yellow scrubs who came into the room a few minutes later was one Tabitha hadn't seen before. "I'm Monica. I understand that your man here said you're in some pain?"

Her cheeks heated in embarrassment. The nurses thought Seth was "her man." "Yes."

"How bad is it on a scale of one to ten?" she asked as she reached for Tabitha's good wrist.

"Seven?"

"That's not good." Monica took her pulse and entered it on the computer screen. Next, she clicked on another icon on the flatscreen. "It's been a while since your last dose. I'm glad you said something. You've got to stay on top of it."

"Okay."

Monica picked up her syringe, double-checked the amount and name, and then inserted it into Tabitha's IV. "You should start feeling some relief before you know it. Ten minutes at the most."

"Thank you."

"If there's no improvement, buzz again, okay?"

Tabitha nodded.

"Now, do you need anything else? More water? Maybe some juice and crackers?"

She glanced at Seth. He didn't say a word, but she knew what he was thinking. "Juice and crackers sound good."

He reached out and gently ran the tips of his fingers along her forearm. The soft touch encouraged the hair on her arm to stand up and chill bumps to form. Had her body ever reacted like that before? She couldn't remember. She'd never responded like that to Leon, not even when he'd been courting her and had seemed so kind.

She knew now that her feelings for Leon had never been about love. At first, she'd been flattered by his regard, but then that had slowly disintegrated into a desire to please him. Then that had turned to fear. If she'd ever gotten chill bumps with him, they'd been from trepidation, not desire. Not love.

Was that how she felt about Seth? Had she fallen in love with him? Did she even know what love felt like?

And did he feel the same way? Or was he simply trying to take care of her because he knew she was alone? Worse, maybe he pitied her? How mortifying would that be, to realize that she loved Seth but he only felt pity for her. Feeling confused, she drew her arm closer to her body.

"Did I do something wrong?" he asked.

"Nee."

"You sure about that?"

"Yes."

Looking concerned, Seth leaned closer. "Tabitha, tell me what you're thinking. You don't have to be afraid to be honest."

"I . . . I don't know what you want me to say." Her cheeks burned. She was starting to wish the nurse would've asked him to leave. Or that Monica would've given her a stronger painkiller that would make her too tired to visit. Then, at least, her nerves wouldn't feel so frayed and worn. But she'd also be alone with her thoughts when she woke up again.

She released a ragged sigh.

"How's the pain? Have you noticed any difference?"

"Jah. It is better." He didn't need to know that she was only just now realizing that the pain had subsided to a dull ache.

Seth smiled. "I'm glad."

"Perhaps it would be best if you left now."

A line formed between his brows. "Why?" His voice lowered. "Tab, what's going on?"

"Nothing. It's just that I'm sure you have other things you'd rather be doing."

"Being here beside you is the only place I want to be."

His words were captivating. His voice was so sincere. But she wasn't sure about his reasons. "Why?"

He looked nonplussed. "Why?"

"Yes." She was embarrassed, but she needed to know the truth. "Are you here out of pity?"

"Pity? Ah, no." Seth shifted, edging closer. "Tabitha, maybe we should talk about a couple of things when you get out."

"Like what?"

"Well, I want to make some changes. As long as you're good with them."

"Changes?"

"I'll be clear, then. First off, I'm going to be coming over to your place a lot."

"There's no need for you to do that. I'll be fine. I mean, the sheriff promised me that Leon won't be getting out anytime soon."

His expression warmed. "I won't be visiting for your safety, honey."

There was that word again! Her skin tingled. Afraid to misread what he was saying, she blurted the first thing that came to her lips. "I have a lot of firewood."

A smile touched the corners of his mouth. "Sorry, but I'll not be coming over to chop wood." He paused. "Or to shovel your driveway or gather eggs or clean your house."

"R-Roy said he would come over more often. Actually, they all will. Mary told me that all of them want to spend more time with me." When Seth didn't look like that made a lick of difference to him, she added in a whisper, "I won't be so lonely."

"You're right. You won't."

"Seth?"

He chuckled. "I guess you're going to make me say it, huh?" Reaching out, he wrapped his fingers around the top bar of her bed's side railing. "Tabitha, I'm going to be coming over and spending time with you because I've fallen in love with you."

She could practically feel the blood rushing out of her head. Her vision swam a little like she might faint.

"You look pale as a ghost!" Seth pushed the button on her bed so she was sitting up more and handed her a plastic water bottle. "Sip."

She swallowed some of the icy water. It did help, but she still felt discombobulated.

"Tab, what's wrong?" Looking crushed, he said, "Do you not feel the same way?"

"Of course I do. It's just . . . I guess I'm still afraid to trust."

"There's no reason to be afraid. We've got time. We've got all the time in the world. We'll take things as slow as you want. I'm not going anywhere."

"I'm damaged, you know."

"You'll heal."

"I mean my heart is damaged."

"I was talking about your heart. It's going to heal, Tab. Before you know it, your heart is going to heal and you're going to trust falling in love again." He lowered his voice.

"If you want to know the truth, I think there's a very real possibility that you love me too. But you're just scared."

Maybe she was, maybe she wasn't. "There's nothing wrong with being scared."

"I don't think so either, honey. Because I'm going to do everything I possibly can to make you want to love me."

"And until then?"

"Until then, I'll love you enough for both of us."

While she gaped at him, Seth stood, leaned down, and carefully pressed his lips to hers. "Relax, Tabitha," he whispered and kissed her again.

The kiss was sweet. Tender. Filled with tamped emotion.

Chill bumps appeared on her arms again, but she pretended not to notice.

31

Look who the cat dragged in!" Cal Porter called out. "I'd given up on seeing you today."

Seth inwardly winced. His boss was a good foreman and he'd been really understanding about Seth's need to be near Tabitha for the last week. Though Seth didn't regret a second that he'd spent by her side, Cal was counting on him to help get the finish work done so the new owners of the house could finally move in.

"Sorry about being gone so much. It couldn't be helped."

Cal slapped him on the back. "No apology needed. Lott told me you were visiting your girl at the hospital."

Surprised to hear that they'd talked, Seth scanned the front yard of the house until he found Lott's lanky form next to two of the more seasoned members of their crew. Some of the awkwardness he'd displayed when he'd first started his apprenticeship had faded. He now fit in.

"She's not a fan of hospitals."

Cal nodded. "That was where you needed to be." His voice lowered. "How's she doing?"

"She's better and home now." Mary had stayed with Tabitha her first night home. Now Melonie—and their mother—were over at Tabitha's. Seth couldn't believe how many things had changed so quickly. Or maybe it shouldn't have been such a shock. For years now, they'd all been in something of a holding pattern. It was like they'd all been waiting for the right moment to move forward. Though Seth would've preferred that Leon had never resurfaced, he was thankful for the changes that had occurred.

"That's good. Praise God."

"Yes." Glancing back at Lott, Seth noticed that he was grinning at one of the other guys. "How's Lott doing?"

"He's making progress. I received some good reports about his first weeks apprenticing, so I asked him to come to my house for the last three days."

"Yeah?"

"I wanted to spend some time with him before giving him more responsibilities."

"I hope he didn't let you down."

"Not at all. He worked hard and listened. Plus, he was good company. We got to know each other pretty well."

That was a surprise, but a welcome one. "I'm pleased."

Cal's eyes twinkled. "I hear he's courting your sister."

Seth groaned but figured he might as well get used to a little bit of gentle ribbing about Lott seeing Melonie. "Yeah."

"And how's that going?"

"I couldn't say."

"No?"

"My sister's not going to give me details, and Lott knows better than to say anything other than that he respects every last hair on Melonie's head."

Cal laughed. "Sounds like my family. We love each other but know our boundaries."

Seth grinned, liking the idea that the Zimmermans might

start thinking of themselves as a family again too. "Boundaries are a good thing."

"You ready to work?"

"Yes, sir." Looking at the beautiful house that was almost complete, he said, "Where do you need me?"

"In the pantry." He waved a hand. "The owners got to thinking and decided they wanted to fancy up the space. More woodwork and new glass cabinet doors."

"I see."

"The lady has some kind of fancy pottery collection she wants to show off."

"Gotcha." The crew hadn't done anything but the basics in that room, on account of the owners wanting to keep at least some of the costs low. It seemed they had changed their minds. People always did, he reckoned.

Inside the house, everything was essentially finished. When they reached the pantry, he had to agree with the homeowners. It looked too basic and plain when compared to the rest of the house.

The room was little more than an enclosed hallway, about five feet wide and ten feet long. Cabinets covered most of one of the walls. On the floor were the replacement cabinet doors and baseboards. To his relief, they all had been coated with primer.

"What do you think?"

"It all looks easy enough."

"How soon can you finish it?"

"Tomorrow, most likely."

"I'll give you a bonus if you can do most of it today."

"Seriously?" Seth couldn't care less about the bonus. What he was concerned about was the fact that Cal was expecting him to work a miracle.

Cal grimaced. "I know you don't like to work so quickly, but I can't help the homeowners changing their minds all the time."

"You're right. I know it's out of your hands. I'll get to work. I could use an extra hand, though." Wanting to connect with Lott again, he said, "Any chance I could have Lott? He could help me get some of the prep work taken care of."

"That's not a problem. I'll send him in."

"Thanks, Cal."

Seth had just knelt down to look at the baseboards they were going to pull off when Lott walked into the room.

"Hiya, Seth. Uh, Cal told me to come help you."

"Yep. I asked for you."

"What would you like me to do?"

"Come here." Picking up the crowbar, he showed him how to carefully pull the existing baseboards from the wall. "See how I did it?"

"Jah."

"Go slowly, okay? We'll be able to use the baseboards someplace else in the future."

"We can't just pull them out and put them in the dumpster?"

"Nope. After you get the pieces off, remove the nails and clean the area. I'll work behind you and start putting the new ones in."

"All right." He removed a couple of nails and stopped.

"Hey, we've got to move a little quicker than that," Seth teased.

"Yeah, I know." Exhaling, he lifted the hammer again.

"Hold on." Moving closer, he placed his hand on Lott's shoulder. "Something's going on with you. What is it?"

"Nothing."

Keeping his voice low and steady, he said, "Care to tell me again?"

Lott met his gaze, then looked away. "Nothing. I . . . I just don't want to mess up."

"I can understand that." He suspected Lott wasn't just talking about their current project, that he was talking about his relationship with Seth and his relationship with Melonie too. Since connecting with Lott was the reason he'd asked for Lott to work by his side, he figured it might be time to do just that.

Once the kid settled down a bit.

"Let's get started. After we make some progress, we'll talk."

Instead of acting relieved, Lott looked a little sick. "Okay." He picked up the crowbar, slid it into the small gap between the baseboard and the wall, and pulled hard.

The wood splintered and broke.

"Sorry."

"Do you see what you did wrong? I told you to go easy."

"I thought I did."

"Slow and steady, Lott. Try it again."

Lott slid the crowbar into the gap farther down and pulled with too much force again. The wood released in one piece, but just barely.

"Lott, you're not listening to me."

"I'm trying, but Cal told me that I needed to work fast."

"You need to work efficiently. That's different." Seeing that Lott still looked obstinate, Seth held out a hand. "Hand me the crowbar." When Lott did, he showed him how to gently pry the wood. "You see the difference?"

He frowned. "I guess."

Seth stood and pointed to the next section. Even though

part of him wanted to take over the project, he knew that Lott needed to learn. He also needed to see that Seth believed in him. "Try it again. You'll get it."

It took another ten minutes, but finally Lott followed directions enough to get the next section of old baseboard up and the nails removed.

"Good. Now keep going."

Lott looked frustrated but nodded.

Ignoring Lott's attitude, Seth concentrated on measuring and using the miter board to cut the new wider baseboards. After another hour went by, all the old boards were stacked neatly, the area was clean, and Lott was helping him nail in the new boards.

"This looks better, doesn't it?" Seth said.

"Jah. I thought it was a waste of time, but I guess it wasn't."

"It wasn't. Rushing through things is rarely the best option. To do them right takes time."

Lott glanced at him. "Are you talking about just woodwork?"

"I might be talking about courting my sister too."

"I'm being careful with Melonie. I like her a lot." Blushing slightly, he stared down at the floor. "More than that, even."

"I'm glad. She's special."

"I agree."

Feeling like the words he said were going to matter, Seth added, "Just so you know, Melonie doesn't give her heart easily. Take care with it, okay?"

"I'm doing my best. I'm only calling on her properly so your parents don't get mad."

"I see."

Lott looked at him. "You aren't acting like that's a good thing."

"Oh, I'm sure it is. But, um, don't forget that she's still Melonie. Even though I'm not supposed to know about it, she's still the girl who snuck out to see you when my parents weren't happy about you calling on her."

"You want me to sneak around with her again?"

"No, but, um, if she needs you to sit in her living room on a formal call, then that's what you should do. And . . . if Melonie needs you to talk about your feelings, then you're gonna need to do that too. Women like that sort of thing."

"Does Tabitha?"

"I think so." Feeling Lott's gaze on him, Seth swallowed hard. "I'm still trying to figure out a way to be the person Tabitha needs me to be. But I'm willing to try. And if I fail, I'm willing to try again."

"Falling in love is hard, isn't it?"

It hadn't been for him. He'd crushed on Tabitha when he was fourteen, ached for her when she was married, and spent the last two years building a new, more solid relationship between them. All of that had been hard.

Everything except falling in love.

"I think relationships are hard, Lott. Good ones, at least. I reckon that deciding who to marry is the most important decision in a person's life. The person who's beside you is going to help you be the man you want to be. She's also going to help you when you aren't." He grabbed the level, made sure the board was straight, and then added, "That's not just for now but for years and years, Lott."

"I never thought about marriage like that."

"Like you've pointed out a time or two, I'm no expert when it comes to a lot of stuff. But prison gave me some time to really think about things."

"Sometimes you act like going to prison wasn't the worst thing in your life."

Seth knew Lott was studying him carefully. "That's because sometimes it wasn't. Not every hurt is obvious to others, you know? Everyone's got something that aches that they don't like to mention."

Lott's eyes widened, then he nodded. "What's next?"

"Grab the screwdriver and start taking down the old cabinet doors."

Seth was pleased that the boy was now following his directions without question. Maybe the two of them were figuring out a lot of things about each other at last.

He reckoned that was a very good thing.

32

The Zimmermans' house was quieter than usual. According to Melonie, her father was late coming home from a horse auction and her mother was in bed with a migraine. Good manners would have been for Lott to tell Melonie he understood that it wasn't a good evening for a visit and go home.

He stayed.

Melonie seemed pleased that he didn't take off. Though it was probably a mistake, he walked right in when she held open the door. All day long he'd been thinking about this visit. Debating about whether he should stop by or not.

"It's gut to see you, Mel." That was the truth too, though he feared he might wish he'd been more circumspect when her father realized he'd sat with Melonie unchaperoned.

She smiled at him. "I didn't think you were coming over today. Did we have something planned that I've forgotten?"

"Nee." He followed her into the kitchen. "To be honest, I wasn't planning on coming over, but when I was walking home I changed my mind."

"How come?"

Lott debated his answer but decided that the truth was

probably the best course of action. "Because I was with your brother most of the day and he got me thinking about us."

Melonie didn't bother to hide her surprise. "You were working with him today?"

"Jah. When I reported in today, I thought I was going to be cleaning and sweeping, but Mr. Porter told me he had something else planned. Next thing I knew, Cal was driving me over to a fancy house on the outskirts of Paducah and I was working with Seth in some lady's pantry."

"Wow. What did you do?"

"Helped your brother pull off old baseboards and install new baseboards and fancy cabinet doors." He exhaled. "It took all day." Sure, he might have been exaggerating his contribution a touch, but he was too full of pride not to take advantage of it.

"So you talked to my brother and then decided to come over here?" She opened the refrigerator and pulled out a section of roast beef, which she set on the counter.

"Pretty much."

"Ah."

Lott watched her open a container of bread, slice two pieces, and then carve a good bit of roast beef. His stomach growled, but he pretended he wasn't hungry. Though he'd be lying if he wasn't a little hurt that she had no problem making a snack for herself in front of him.

Then he remembered her mother. He cleared his throat. "I'm sorry your mother has a migraine."

"Emph." She raised a shoulder as she pulled lettuce, cheese, and mayonnaise out of the refrigerator. "She gets them from time to time. I'm used to her being indisposed."

That didn't sound good. "I guess she's seen someone for them?"

"Not exactly." With efficient movements, Melonie slathered mayo on a piece of bread, added swiss cheese and meat, then topped it off with two perfect pieces of iceberg lettuce. When it was complete, she sliced the sandwich in half and placed it on a plate. "My mamm gets headaches whenever she feels overwhelmed. She gets overwhelmed a lot."

"I see." He didn't, though. Here, he'd thought that the worst thing for the Zimmerman family had been Seth's incarceration. And maybe it had. But maybe having her brother in prison hadn't been the only difficult thing in Melonie's life. Had he been so consumed with concern about Bethanne that he'd minimized everyone else's problems?

"Do you want milk or water with that?"

Realizing he'd been staring into space, he glanced at her again. "Hmm?"

She carried the plate to where he sat at the table. "I made you a sandwich. What do you want to drink with it?"

"Oh. It's not for you or your mamm?"

"No, silly. It's for you. Now, what would you like to drink?"

"Water, but I can get it." He moved to stand up, but she was already filling a glass with cold water from a glass pitcher. Sitting back down, he reached for the glass she held out. "This is kind of you."

She rolled her eyes. "It's a sandwich and a glass of water, Lott."

"It's still sweet. You're sweet."

"I'm a lot of things, but I don't think sweet is one of them," she said. She sounded pleased, though.

"I disagree."

She sat down and motioned for him to eat. After he'd bowed his head in silent thanks, she spoke again. "When

I think of sweet people, I think of your sister. Bethanne is close to being an angel."

He laughed. "She can be nice, but she's human too. I wouldn't say my sister is always angelic." Immediately feeling guilty, he added, "I don't suppose anyone is, though."

"I suppose not." She motioned with her hand. "Eat, Lott."

He dug in, surprising himself with how hungry he was. "Tell me about your day," he said after swallowing his second bite.

"Hmm? Oh. I worked around here. Prayed for Tabitha Yoder."

"I thought she was doing better. Is she not?"

Watching him eat, she shrugged a shoulder. "Oh, she is, but I've been more concerned about her feelings. Seth told me how she used to be practically afraid of her own shadow. At first, she wouldn't even come out of the house when he would leave her food or chop wood."

"Do you think this attack is going to make her be afraid of everything again?"

"Maybe. How could it not? She was dyeing wood on her front porch when Leon attacked her. If she hadn't run, he could have held her hostage in the house."

"It's good she ran."

Looking pensive, Melonie nodded. "I think—" She stopped abruptly when footsteps sounded down the hall.

"Melonie, who are you talking to?"

Staring at him, Melonie answered. "Lott, Mamm. He paid us a surprise visit tonight."

And . . . now he was sitting at their table eating a sandwich. Not exactly the best way to ingratiate himself with her mother.

Her mother shuffled in. Her dress was a little rumpled

and her eyes a bit strained. Her hair and kapp were neatly arranged, though. "Hello, Lott."

He stood up. "Hi, Anna."

She looked at them curiously. "You're hosting him in the kitchen, Mel?"

He answered quickly. "Your daughter was kind enough to make me a sandwich."

With a distracted glance, she eyed his plate before focusing on Melonie. "Did you tend to the animals in the barn?"

"Nee. I made you some chicken and rice, though."

"Danke." She turned and wandered back into the hallway. "Don't forget to tend to the animals."

His mouth was dry as he realized he'd finished the rest of the sandwich while Melonie had answered her mother's questions. Now that they were alone again, she seemed flustered.

He stood up and held out a hand. "Come on."

She looked at him curiously as she got to her feet. "What do you want to do?"

He smiled slightly. "If I said run away to the beach, what would you say?"

"I'd ask if I had to pack a bag before we got out of here."

He wished he could offer her that. A break from everything sounded wonderful. No, it sounded like relief. They needed a little bit of that. "Since I haven't bought any bus tickets, how about we settle for going to your barn and tending to the animals?"

"That's not necessary. I can do it."

He couldn't deal with the distance between them anymore. No, he couldn't handle the idea of her standing alone, trying so hard to be strong. "Come here," he murmured, though he didn't really give her a choice. He pulled her into his arms, and Melonie hesitated a mere second before relaxing against him.

The best choice would be for him to offer comforting words and pat her upper back. Like a brother would. But Lott rarely made the right choice.

Cupping her face in both of his hands, he kissed her. Gently nipped her bottom lip, encouraged her closer, and finally kissed her the way he'd dreamed about in the middle of the night. For her part, Melonie didn't hesitate. She kissed him back, clung to him like he was her lifeline.

On and on their embrace continued, and he savored every second of it. Melonie was responsive, and so good that he could practically feel all of that goodness seep into him. He pulled away before he did anything more.

Startled, she gazed up into his eyes. Her lips were parted and she was breathing heavy.

"I'm not going to apologize," he said.

Her lips closed. She blinked. Stepped back. Giving them additional space. Breathing room. "Good," she said at last.

When she headed for the back door, he followed. Lott loved her so much, he'd follow her anywhere.

33

He'd come over again.

Standing next to the window of her living room, Tabitha watched Seth take a bag of salt from the back of his truck and sprinkle it on her walkway. It was December now and the weather reflected it. Last night they'd gotten a light layer of snow and ice. The sugar maple's branches glistened in the afternoon sun, and the worn cement path leading up to the door fairly gleamed. It was treacherous to walk on, though—especially for someone with a cast on her arm.

Ever since she'd gotten home from the hospital, Tabitha's life had felt different. Gone was the constant grip of fear that surrounded her. In its place was a sense of peace. Leon was in jail awaiting trial and therefore no longer a threat. Ironically, his latest attack had seemed to remove the last bits of reticence from the community. Tabitha supposed, if she had a mind to do it, she could possibly become Amish again. Sure, it would involve a lot of conversations with the bishop and a lot of prayers, but it could happen.

She didn't think she'd be able to do that, though. As much

as she loved the Lord and found many, many things about the Amish way of life comforting, there were too many bad memories of striving to be Leon's gut frau mixed in. It was better for her to move on.

Tabitha liked to think the Lord was okay with her decision too. She was closer than ever to her family. Why, Mary, Roy, and the boys had even come over for supper the other night. Melonie and her parents had stopped over as well. And then there was Seth, who seemed determined to follow through on his promise of loving her enough for the both of them.

Still watching him from the window, Tabitha smiled. No matter how busy he was, he stopped by to see her at least once a day. Sometimes they shared a meal. Sometimes they sat in front of the fire and chatted. And every so often, he helped her climb into his truck and they went for a drive. Once they even went to St. Louis so she could see her baskets displayed in a fancy shop. That had been incredible.

But then, so was Seth.

Tired of being so far from him, she opened the door and stepped out. "Seth, come on in!"

He turned to her. Then scowled. "Tabitha, get inside. You don't even have shoes on your feet."

"They're fine. I have on socks."

"They're not fine. You could slip. I'll be in as soon as I'm done."

"Soon?"

His expression softened. "Soon."

Needing something to do, she added, "I'll make coffee."

"Sounds good."

Pleased to have a job, she hurried back inside and started a new pot on the stove. Then she heated up some drop biscuits she'd made early that morning and pulled out jam too.

When Seth came inside a little while later, bringing with him the slight scent of snow and evergreens, butterflies flitted in her stomach. No longer worried about her reaction to him, Tabitha appreciated every sign. It was as if her body had believed in their love before her heart or mind had.

"What's that smile for?" he asked.

"I'm just glad to see you."

He pulled her into his arms. "I like seeing you watching me out the window." He winked. "It reminds me of old times."

She supposed it did, though her actions then had been more those of a scared rabbit than those of the woman she was now. "I couldn't help myself."

"No?"

"No." She smiled, telling him that at long last, she was sure of her heart. "I love you, Seth Zimmerman."

Warmth filled his gaze as he ran a hand along her cheek. "Does this mean you'll marry me?"

"Seth! Are you being serious?"

Looking put upon, he stepped back. "I suppose I should do this right, hmm?"

She gaped as he reached in his jeans pocket, pulled out a small cloth bag, and got down on one knee. "Seth?"

"Tabitha Yoder, I've loved you for years. Ever since we were both teenagers. Even when we were both Amish. And then not Amish. I loved you even when you were afraid and I didn't think I was good enough."

"Even when I was too afraid to speak to you?"

He nodded. "Even then." Carefully, he opened the pouch in his hands and pulled out a ring. A white gold band with one perfect diamond. He held it out toward her. "Please say yes."

"You . . . where did you get this?"

266

"I bought it, honey."

Still stunned, she shook her head. "I mean, when? How come it was in your pocket?"

"I've been carrying it around for two weeks, Tabby."

"Really?" It was hard to imagine.

"Yep." Looking right proud of himself, he smirked. "I've been holding it for you since that day we talked in the hospital."

"You should have said something."

"I didn't mind waiting. I knew one day the time would be right." Studying her face, he murmured, "This seems like the perfect moment."

She looked down at him, feeling the way his lovely, lovely words affected her. "I . . . I guess it is."

"So what do you say?"

She laughed. "Yes. Yes, of course! But you have to stand up to give the ring to me. With my wrist, I'm afraid to join you down there on my knees."

With a look of triumph Seth rose to his feet, reached for her left hand, and then slid the ring onto her fourth finger. It looked perfect.

Gazing down at the glistening diamond gracing her hand, she murmured, "I never thought I'd ever wear a ring, but I like how it feels."

"I like how it looks on you."

"I won't ever take it off." She wrapped her good arm around him and kissed him with all her heart.

Seth held her close, telling her how pleased he was without words. When they finally broke apart, Tabitha had to lean against him to catch her breath.

It seemed Seth Zimmerman had taken her breath away. Yet again.

Epilogue

Only God knew how the five of them had ended up sitting together on the back field of Seth and Tabitha Zimmerman's property on Independence Day.

A year ago, Tabitha wouldn't have imagined that she would leave the safety of her house, let alone be in the company of Seth Zimmerman, his sister, Melonie, her fiancé, Lott, and Lott's sister, Bethanne.

Obviously God had had other plans.

At one time, she'd been their teacher. Now she was married to Seth and living in the house that she'd been both afraid to leave and afraid to stay in for the rest of her life. Smoothing the red-and-white-checked tablecloth underneath her, she leaned back on her hands and watched the sun slowly make its descent in the west. Chance, who was sprawled out by her side, stretched a paw.

"You look awfully pensive, Tabitha," Melonie said. "What's wrong? Did you forget something in the house?"

"She couldn't have done that," Seth quipped. "We have half the kitchen out here."

Seth was right. They'd made BLTs and fried chicken for their picnic. There were also three carafes of fresh lemonade, two bags of potato chips, a container of pickled cucumbers, thick slices of watermelon, and giant chocolate-cherry cookies individually wrapped in waxed paper. With the cheese, crackers, apples, and cold cider Melonie and Bethanne had brought, it was a feast.

"My husband's right," Tabitha said, feeling her cheeks heat. They'd only been married one month, and she was still a bit giddy that Seth was hers.

"I like how that sounds," Seth teased.

She chuckled. "What I was actually thinking about was how different my life was last year at this time."

Melonie nodded. "A lot sure has changed in a year." She reached out and squeezed Seth's arm. "A year ago, I barely spoke to you."

"Or me," Lott said. "And now you're my fiancée, Mel."

She giggled. "Sometimes I think my mother's head is spinning."

Turning to Seth, Lott added, "Years before that, I was so messed up, I actually told Bethanne that she shouldn't be writing to you in prison. Even though the reason you were there was because you saved her."

Tabitha tensed, half worried that Seth would be upset that Lott brought up his incarceration, but Seth shrugged it off.

"I'm glad you wrote me that note, Bethanne, though I still say you didn't owe me anything. You never did."

"And I still think differently," Bethanne said.

"How about this? I'm glad to call myself your friend."

"Me too," Tabitha told her.

"Me three," Melonie said with a smile.

"I'm glad too," Bethanne whispered.

Remembering something Bethanne had mentioned last

time they'd talked, Tabitha said, "Are you still thinking about moving?"

"I am."

Lott grimaced but didn't try to interrupt.

"Where are you going to go?" Melonie asked.

Bethanne shrugged. "I don't know. I haven't thought of any details yet. I'm feeling the need for a fresh start, though."

"Is it because the memories here in Crittenden County are too difficult?" Seth asked.

"Oh no." She paused, then seemed to find her voice. "It's because no one seems able to look at me without remembering the worst day of my life. Or the fact that I'm more than that, you know? Everyone likes to see me as a victim. I don't want to be a victim anymore."

Tabitha knew exactly how that felt. "I can understand you feeling that way."

But instead of accepting Tabitha's words and moving on, Bethanne shook her head. "I appreciate your kindness, Tabitha, but I have some responsibility for what happened between me and Peter. I should never have walked off with him. If I had followed the rules, Peter would have never attacked me."

Lott glowered. "Don't put Peter's actions on your shoulders, Bethanne."

"Your brother's right," Tabitha said. "Bethanne, you need to forgive yourself."

Bethanne stared at her intently. "Is that what you did?"

"I think so. But I think I finally heard God's words one day at home. I was standing at my window, watching Seth chop wood and wondering why so many people couldn't forgive me for divorcing Leon. But then God whispered that instead of wondering why other people weren't forgiving me, I should be wondering why I hadn't forgiven myself." Remembering that moment like it was yesterday, she added, "It was pretty powerful."

"But you didn't do anything wrong," Bethanne said. "What did you blame yourself for?"

"I made some hasty decisions. Getting married so fast. Trusting my parents' judgment more than my own. And I stayed with Leon for longer than I should have."

"What did you say to God?"

"I told Him all that . . . and then He quietly reminded me that He's already forgiven me for my transgressions, so I should do the same." Thinking about just how far she'd come, Tabitha added, "Bethanne, I don't blame you for wanting a fresh start, but you might want to remember that the Lord has already offered you one."

Her expression softened. "Maybe one day I'll be able to accept that. I hope so."

"Me too."

Melonie stood up. "The sun has set. I think we should all get ready to watch the fireworks."

Lott chuckled. "You're right, Mel. Let's think about brighter things."

Right away, they all got busy. Tabitha and the other women put the empty containers in the picnic baskets while the men gathered their trash and put it in the garbage bag they'd brought.

And then the first burst of fireworks lit up the sky.

"Come here, Tab," Seth said as he stretched out on the tablecloth.

As Chance shifted again, she lay down on her back beside him as Melonie, Lott, and Bethanne got situated too. Then there was only silence. Everything was dark and so still.

Seth reached for her hand. For a second, Tabitha felt as if they were alone. No, more than that. As if she and Seth were the only two people in Crittenden County. Only them, the warm air, and the solid ground beneath them.

But then a huge red and gold starburst lit up the sky.

All five of them gasped.

It was beautiful and so vibrant.

Amazing.

But as the starburst slowly fizzled into golden dots and then vanished from sight, it became just a memory.

Just another memory to hold on to while darkness surrounded her again.

No, that wasn't right. She was surrounded by friends and holding her husband's hand on a piece of land that she'd fought hard to keep. Her stomach was full and her heart was fuller.

But even more importantly, her focus was on the sky above.

Just waiting for the next glorious thing to appear.

Anticipating it.

She reckoned that was a fitting metaphor for life. For everything.

Turn the page for a *sneak peek* at

SHELLEY SHEPARD GRAY'S

next suspenseful Amish read

AUGUST

Wonders never ceased. Bethanne Hostetler had seen a lot of things and had even experienced some surprises. That said, the scene playing out in front of her was like nothing she'd ever imagined. For sure and for certain.

Right there, up on the fairground's amphitheater stage, stood her cousin Candace. Her dark blond hair was curled and shiny and flowing down her back. Eyeliner accentuated her hazel eyes and red gloss stained her lips, making her lovely face even more beautiful.

As the crowd clapped, Candace stood as still as a department store mannequin. Her satin gown had a sweetheart neckline, hugged her curves, and skimmed the stage's wooden floor. The toe of one of her silver high-heeled sandals peeked out whenever a faint breeze caught the dress's hem.

All in all, Candace looked nothing like the little girl who used to follow Bethanne around at holiday get-togethers years ago. Honestly, some folks might even say that Candace Weaver was the complete opposite of her Amish cousin Bethanne Hostetler.

They might be right too.

"Ladies and gentlemen, let's give these ladies one more final round of applause while they exit the stage," the announcer said over the loudspeaker. "But don't y'all go anywhere. We'll announce this year's Miss Crittenden County in just a few minutes!"

Applause and cheers rang out from all around her. Just like they had for every entrant from the preteen to the "Mrs." category. In response, all seven women on the stage moved to stand side by side. They linked hands and smiled.

Every one of them was pretty and graceful. There was no doubt about that. But as Bethanne gazed at the line of ladies, she couldn't help but think that not a one of the others could hold a candle to Candace. She was graceful and gorgeous. Even better, she was as sweet as spun sugar.

When Candace caught her eye, Bethanne waved and smiled while her brother Lott whistled. Candace's beatific smile widened.

"What do you think her chances are?" Lott asked as the applause started to die down.

She shrugged. "About as good as anyone else's, I reckon."

Her brother frowned. "Really?"

As the women exited the stage in preparation for the judges' final vote, Bethanne shifted in her seat to face him. "Lott, you know this is the first beauty pageant I've ever watched. I'm still trying to get my head wrapped around the fact that my English cousin is up onstage wearing makeup and high heels."

"Me too, though Candace has always been a pretty thing."

"That she has." Bethanne smiled, though a part of her was feeling a pinch of melancholy. Many years ago, she, too, had found comfort in the gifts that the Lord had given her. Now she realized that it hadn't served her well. But maybe that had more to do with her actions than her looks. No, most likely it had everything to do with her actions.

Hating the dark thoughts that threatened her happy mood, she shook her head.

"Hey, are you going to stay here for a little while?" Lott asked.

She crossed her legs. "Probably. Why?"

"No reason."

"Lott."

"Fine. Melonie is here and I wanted to walk with her a bit."

"Go ahead. I'll be fine."

"You sure?" He scanned the crowd. "Mamm and Daed are around here somewhere. I thought they were going to sit with Candace's parents, but I don't know . . ."

"They're around, but I don't need anyone looking after me. I'm fine." In spite of her best intentions, her smile trembled, betraying her emotions.

Her younger brother noticed. "Bethy."

"Nee, it's not you. It's . . . I was thinking about something else. I'll see you later." She hated that her younger brother felt obligated to look after her. She also hated that until very recently she would've clung to him like a parasitic vine.

He didn't move. "You know what? I can take Melonie out—"

"Now." She finished. "Please, Lott. Don't worry about me. I'm fine." Noticing Melonie now stood a few yards away, Bethanne shooed him off. "Go on, now."

"When do you want to meet?"

"Two hours?" They'd been at the fair most of the day already.

"Sounds good. I'll meet you at the entrance."

"Perfect. Go, now. I'm going to wait here for the winners to be announced."

"Tell her congratulations for me."

She laughed. "If she wins, I sure will."

"She'll win. I know it," he called out over his shoulder.

Feeling like an odd combination of wallflower and doting aunt, she watched her brother rush to Melonie's side and barely refrain from clasping her hand. Less than two minutes later they were out of sight.

Sitting back down on her chair, Bethanne placed her purse neatly on her lap. If it wouldn't look so odd, she would pull out a book. That's what she usually did whenever she had the chance.

But about six months ago she'd decided that she needed to change her life. She determined to stop worrying about the past and start thinking about what she wanted to do with the rest of her life. She was only twenty-three. It was past time that she got over Peter Miller's death. And the fact that he'd attempted to rape her and would have if Seth Zimmerman hadn't heard her cries and come to her rescue. Why the Lord had then allowed Seth to hit Peter hard enough for him to fall, hit his head, and die was a mystery. But still it had happened, and she'd survived. Seth had too, even though he'd been sent to prison for a time.

"If Seth Zimmerman can move forward, you certainly can too," she whispered to herself. "You have to." Which meant that she needed to stop dwelling on such dark memories. Hadn't her counselor told her more than once that she needed to make peace with her memories instead of trying to forget them?

"Hey," Jay Byler said as he sat down. Right next to her.

Her whole body tensed, even though Peter's best friend had never done anything to harm her. Though, he did know that she tried to avoid him whenever their paths crossed.

"What are you doing?" she hissed.

"Do you mean I should be doing something other than waiting to see who is crowned this year's Miss Crittenden County?"

"Come on. You don't care about such things."

"How would you know, Bethanne? It ain't like you've given me more than a few minutes of your time in years."

Even though his words were true—and even sounded innocuous—they still hurt. Everything about him made her hurt. Though tempted to stay silent, she couldn't. "You know why I haven't talked to you."

"Of course I know." His voice softened. "But that doesn't mean it's okay with me, Bethanne. We were once friends."

Were they? She didn't remember much about their interactions beyond the obvious—he'd been best friends with Peter and she'd had hopes to be Peter's girlfriend.

"I don't want to talk about you and me. Or our past. Ever."

"Fine. Let's talk about the beauty pageant." He waggled his eyebrows. "I know you're rooting for your cousin, but who else do you think has a chance?"

Jay was as Amish as she was. "Why are you so interested? Are you hoping to take one of the girls out?"

"Of course not."

"Then?"

He pulled at the collar of his white shirt. "You know putting me on the spot isn't fair."

"No, I know you choosing this moment to speak to me isn't fair." If she got up and left before the winner was announced, she'd feel terrible.

"Come on. I've been trying to talk to you for a year. Longer, even." Frustration filled his tone. "But . . . every time I come around, you run away like I've got the plague."

"I've hardly been that bad."

"Close, though." Gentling his voice, he said, "Bethanne, please. Won't you let me be your friend again?"

"Why?"

Blue eyes blinked. "Why?"

"Jah. Why do you want to be my friend so badly? Why do you keep trying even though I keep pushing you away?" She stared at him, silently willing Jay to speak the truth. To share what was in his heart.

"Because you're worth it."

Her pulse seemed to slow. "Worth what?"

"Everything."

Jay had almost whispered that one word. She turned to stare at him. "Jay?"

"The decision's been made!" the announcer said over the loudspeaker. "Everyone, get on your feet and welcome these beautiful ladies back onstage!"

Bethanne had never been so happy to hear the roar of a crowd.

• • • •

Only by sheer force of will did Jay remain where he was while Bethanne scooted down the aisle of chairs and hurried toward the stage where her cousin Candace was getting her picture taken.

Candace Weaver now had a white satin banner arranged over her gown and a silver and rhinestone tiara perched on the top of her dark blond hair. She was pretty, there was no denying that. She looked like the beauty queen she now was.

But he only had eyes for her cousin Bethanne.

Bethanne was standing off to the side, looking as perfectly beautiful as she always did. Her skin was smooth and creamy, there was a touch of pink in her cheeks, and her brown hair was neatly arranged under a white kapp. Even her light blue dress was spotless and crisp looking. That was a minor miracle in his estimation. Everyone attending the Crittenden County Fair had to walk on dirt, grass, and gravel.

But that was Bethanne, at least by his estimation. No matter her age, she'd always managed to look serene and in control of both herself and her surroundings. Most people thought she always did the right thing. And she did. Just not 100 percent of the time.

He knew that better than most, he reckoned.

Peter Miller, his best friend in school, had always been smitten with her. When they were young, Peter would tease and joke around with Bethy. He'd do the most outlandish things just to make her smile or laugh. Peter had once told him that he got a kick out of pushing Bethanne out of her comfort zone.

Jay had never thought that was necessary.

After they'd all graduated eighth grade and begun apprenticing or working, Bethanne had finally let down her reserves around Peter and had started spending a lot of time with him. That hurt. Jay had longed for her for years but had been forced to keep his distance on account of Peter's interest. But he'd known deep in his heart that Peter wasn't right for Bethanne.

Worse, he'd also been pretty sure that Peter wasn't good for her. Back then, he'd believed that Peter had some good qualities but that he sometimes let his impulsive ways get the best of him.

Jay hadn't known the half of it.

Jay would have never guessed that Peter could do something so horrible. Which was part of his problem, Jay knew. Why hadn't he known that Peter was capable of rape?

He could barely handle the guilt.

"Ain't it something?" the woman sitting next to him called out over the roar of the crowd. "That girl is from right here in Marion. Candace is one of our own!"

Jay forced himself back to the present. "Jah. It is something indeed."

He joined the clapping as Candace finished a brief speech, then he stood up when everyone else started to leave. He barely had time to watch Bethanne hug her cousin before it was time to join the others around him and walk out of the amphitheater.

"Never pictured you to be a fan of beauty pageants, Jay," Walker Burkholder said when Jay made it to the main aisle. With a grin, Walker clapped him on the back.

"I'm not. Not really."

"You just ended up here, then?" His eyes were filled with mirth. "Not that I blame ya, of course. Nothing wrong with wanting to look at a pretty girl . . . or six." He chuckled at his own joke.

"You're right, but, ah, I mainly just sought some shade. It's covered and there are chairs."

Something eased in Walker's expression. "Jah, that is true."

"What about you? Why are you here?"

"One of the contestants is one of Peggy's former students." Looking over at his wife, he said, "Peggy wanted to cheer her on." Chuckling to himself, he added, "And where Peggy goes, I go."

"I knew you were a smart man."

"Of course I am. I hired you, didn't I?"

"I'd say that was a sign of your brilliance, but we both know I didn't give you much of a choice in the matter," Jay joked. "I begged and pleaded for that first job."

"And since then, you've proven yourself to be outstanding. You've deserved your promotions, Jay."

"Yes, sir. I'm thankful."

"Sam treating you all right?"

"Yes, sir."

Walker was the president of one of the biggest sawmills and lumber manufacturers in the county. He was as honest as they came and had been good to Jay from the day he'd signed on to work in the mill. His new manager? Suffice it to say that Jay did not hold the man in the same esteem.

"Walker, are you ready to head to the arena?" his wife called out. "The boys are about to show their calves."

"Sure thing, Peg. I was just catching up with Jay here."

Jay tipped his hat as she approached. "Gut day, Peggy."

"And to you as well, Jay. Enjoy the fair and don't forget to go on some of the rides on the midway tonight." She winked as they walked off.

Just in the nick of time too. The last thing he wanted to think about was going on the Ferris wheel alone. Or with anyone other than Bethanne Hostetler by his side.

That wasn't going to happen, though. Not when she hated him.

"Jay, there you are!" his brother Tommy called out. "I've been looking for you everywhere."

Tommy had been his parents' surprise baby. Twelve years younger than Jay, Tommy was twelve, had red hair and freckles, and was built like their father's grandfather. He was large for his age and would've been a great football player if he was English. As it was, he was simply a good farm hand and one of Jay's best friends. He loved Tommy.

"You found me now. What's going on?"

"I'm starving. Want to get something to eat?"

"I could eat. What are you hungry for?" He grinned. The kid was always hungry.

"They've got a food truck with tacos. How does that sound?"

"Sounds good. Let's go."

The food trucks were off to the side, just before the carnival games and the tent housing all the food and handcraft entries. "What have you been doing?"

"Hanging out with the guys."

"Where are they?"

"Abel had to go home with his family, and Cade and Zack are hanging out with girls."

Tommy's voice sounded so disparaging that Jay had to chuckle. "You didn't want to hang out with the girls too?"

"Nah. I'm not ready for that."

"You aren't?"

"No way. Guess what they're making Cade and Zack do?"

"No idea."

"Pet the baby animals." He grunted. "Like Zack don't have a ton of them on his own farm."

"Sorry, but I'm afraid that kind of thing goes with the territory. Girls like baby animals. Most folks do, come to think of it. A baby piglet is cute."

"Whatev. Cade's only doing all that because he thinks Mary might kiss him."

"Whoa."

"Right?"

"How old is Cade?"

"Thirteen, but he has three older brothers." He lowered his voice. "He knows things."

Good grief. "Ah. That explains it."

"I guess." He kicked a bottle cap that someone had tossed on the ground.

Since they were near a trash can, Jay picked it up and tossed it in the can. "Don't be too hard on your buddies. You'll be hanging out with girls before you know it."

"Maybe not."

"What does that mean?"

"It means that maybe I'll be like you."

"Still not following, Tom."

"It means that I know you don't chase anyone."

"I am a little old to be chasing women, kid. Besides, it's not good manners. Ladies don't take kindly to being chased."

"You know what I mean." He waved a hand. "Mamm said you're a slow bloomer."

His feet stopped moving. "Our mother said what?"

Tom lifted his chin. "Don't get mad at me. I'm just repeating her words."

"She shouldn't have said that."

"Why?" He tilted his head to one side. "Is it a lie?"

"Mamm doesn't lie."

Tom wrinkled his nose. "So you are a slow bloomer?"

"No." Inside, he was mortified. He couldn't believe their mother was telling his brother that. And who knew who else.

"Something can't be true and false at the same time, Jay."

"It can." How did he even get involved in this conversation?

"I don't understand why you're acting upset anyway. Mamm wasn't being mean. And it's not like you've ever had a girlfriend," Tom added, like he was an expert on such stuff.

"What is that supposed to mean?"

"Pretty much what it sounded like." Tommy folded his arms over his chest. "Or have you? Was it a secret?" Looking intrigued, he added, "Do you have a secret love life that no one knows about?"

"Where do you think such things up?"

"You still haven't answered me, Bruder."

"I don't intend to. My personal life is none of your business."

"I guess not. But it sure don't seem like it's anyone else's either." He chuckled at his own joke before moving away.

Luckily, it was also before Jay could admit that Tommy might be right.

One of these days, he was going to find a way to get Beth-anne to finally trust him. He didn't know how and he didn't know when, but he was going to do it.

And when that happened, everything in his life would be good. No. Fantastic.

Wunderbaar.

Dear Reader,

Thank you for picking up Unforgiven. I hope you enjoyed reading this first novel in my new series set in Crittenden County, Kentucky.

The inspiration for Unforgiven comes from a variety of places. The first is the Rumors in Ross County series. I wrote this set of novels about a group of ex-cons helping each other adjust to their first few years out of prison. When that series ended, I still had Seth's story to write. Try as I might, I couldn't let him go. That is how Seth Zimmerman ended up in this novel.

When I was brainstorming ideas for Seth's book, I kept wondering who a former-Amish, hardened hero might develop a soft spot for—and that's when Tabitha's character was born. She's damaged but stronger than she realizes. Just like Seth and several other characters in the novel.

Finally, I wanted to touch a little bit on God's grace in this book. Almost every character in the pages struggles a bit with this concept. After all, it's so tempting to be hard on oneself, to maybe even believe that an action or deed in one's past could be unforgivable. When my characters embrace God's grace, they can move forward in their lives.

One final note, this novel is a work of fiction. Even though I've portrayed the area as a rather dark and foreboding place, nothing could be further from the *truth. I've been to Crittenden County many times and enjoyed myself tremendously. Everyone in both the Amish community and the towns was cordial and welcoming. If you get a chance to visit, take a turn around Main Street, have lunch at the café, go for a walk in the woods. Maybe even visit the Amish-run greenhouses in the heat of summer and pick up some tomatoes. They're as delicious as they look! Crittenden County is a lovely place, and I'm always grateful to return there in person . . . or when my imagination takes flight.*

Wishing you many blessings,
Shelley Shepard Gray

Shelley Shepard Gray is the *New York Times* and *USA Today* bestselling author of more than one hundred books, including *Her Heart's Desire* and *Her Only Wish*. Two-time winner of the HOLT Medallion and a Carol Award finalist, Gray lives in Ohio, where she writes full-time, bakes too much, and can often be found walking her dogs on her town's bike trail. Learn more at ShelleyShepardGray.com.

TRAVEL TO PINECRAFT FOR FRIENDSHIP AND NEW BEGINNINGS WITH SHELLEY SHEPARD GRAY

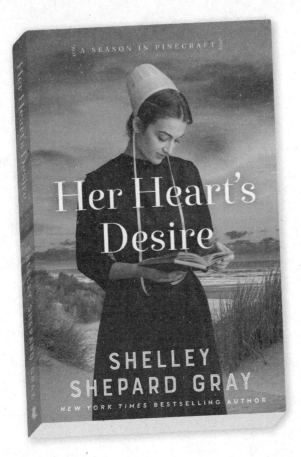

"*Her Heart's Desire* is a tender journey that explores friendship, heartbreak, second chances, forgiveness, and finding true love. Shelley Shepard Gray highlights that God's grace and mercy is with us even when we're certain we're alone and don't fit in with our community."

—AMY CLIPSTON, bestselling author of *Building a Future*

R Revell
a division of Baker Publishing Group
RevellBooks.com

Find more sweet romance in the rest of the

A SEASON IN
PINECRAFT SERIES

IF YOU LOVED THIS READ, TRY THESE AMISH STORIES NEXT!

Meet Shelley

AND ON SOCIAL MEDIA AT

 ShelleyShepardGray    ShelleySGray    Shelley.S.Gray